NO ONE HERE IS LONELY

ALSO BY SARAH EVERETT

Everyone We've Been

NO ONE HERE IS LONELY

Sarah Everett

ALFRED A. KNOPF
NEW YORK

THIS IS A BORZOI BOOK PUBLISHED BY ALFRED A. KNOPF

Visit us on the Web! GetUnderlined.com

Educators and librarians, for a variety of teaching tools, visit us at RHTeachersLibrarians.com

Library of Congress Cataloging-in-Publication Data
Name: Everett, Sarah, author.
Title: No one here is lonely / Sarah Everett.
Description: First edition. | New York : Alfred A. Knopf, 2019. |
Summary: Just as Eden's relationships with her best friend and family are falling apart, she discovers a means of communicating with Will, whom she had a crush on until his death two weeks before their graduation.
Identifiers: LCCN 2017055793 | ISBN 978-0-553-53868-7 (trade) |
ISBN 978-0-553-53869-4 (lib. bdg.) | ISBN 978-0-553-53870-0 (ebook)
Subjects: | CYAC: Death—Fiction. | Best friends—Fiction. |
Friendship—Fiction. | Dating (Social customs)—Fiction. |
Family problems—Fiction.
Classification: LCC PZ7.1.E96 No 2019 | DDC [Fic]—dc23

The text of this book is set in 10.5-point Mercury Text.

Printed in the United States of America
January 2019
10 9 8 7 6 5 4 3 2 1

First Edition

To Reg,
for everything

"I'M WILL," the voice on the other end of the line says.

I know, I think.

I hesitate.

"Hi, I'm . . ."

"Eden," he finishes for me. I can hear a smile in his voice, that lengthening of words that accompanies curving lips. "I know."

It shouldn't surprise me, how familiar he sounds, the way I can picture his easy grin across all the space between us.

But it does.

I clutch my phone tighter as the silence lingers, trying to think of what to say, of how to make this anything resembling normal.

"So tell me something, Eden," he says. And I can picture him now, long legs stretched out lazily, crossed at the ankles.

I rack my brain unsuccessfully for words, a not-abnormal occurrence in Will's presence. Except he's not in front of me now, waiting, and still my words form a tangled web in my mind.

I settle on something innocuous, casual. Maybe I'll mention the weather or what I ate for lunch or something about our past.

But my words rush out in front of me and suddenly I'm speaking and what comes out is the truth.

"You don't sound like a ghost."

1

I'VE CRIED MORE in the last week than I have in my entire life.

Today the waterworks start when I wake up to a last-day-of-school text from my best friend, Lacey. All it says is **WE MADE IT!!!!!** with an overabundance of exclamation points, but it's really all she needs to say.

Four years.

Countless hours of interminable lectures.

A hundred scandals.

Two boyfriends.

One broken heart.

There's a long green robe that goes all the way to my shins hanging in my closet. A short navy blue dress beside it that I'll wear underneath the robe. A pair of black pumps for the fifteen most important steps of my life so far, and I only hope I can stay upright in them.

We're graduating today.

FINALLY, I write back in all caps, and I mean that it feels like I've lived four different lives in the space of high school, that so many days felt unending, eternal—like hell. But I also mean that it's really over and they wouldn't let us go back even if we wanted to.

We made it, she says, but it's not totally true.

We didn't all make it. Some of us were short a few credits or failed a class or got knocked up.

Some of us were driving too fast around a bend two Friday nights ago.

One of us will never graduate high school.

I think of Will the whole time I'm getting ready. Curling my hair, getting dressed, doing my nails. When I drive to Lacey's and our moms stand shoulder to shoulder, wiping their eyes as they force us to take picture after picture in our graduation robes.

"Oh my God, not you too!" Lacey exclaims when she sees me tearing up beside her as my dad yells for us to say *pumpernickel.*

"It's sad," I sniff, defensive. I turn so Lacey and I are back to back, making finger guns to re-create the first-day-of-high-school pictures my dad took.

It's cheesy as hell, yes, but I can't wrap my head around Lacey's composure, her total indifference to the fact that everything is about to change forever.

"I can't believe Oliver got out of this," she sighs as we change positions at Dad's direction. Her twin brother, who is graduating with us and thus should be subject to all the parental weeping and reminiscing and photographing, left already to meet up with his friends before graduation.

After we're done taking pictures, we pile into our cars to drive to McKillop High. Lacey rides with me, and as soon as we get into the car, she turns the music up high and starts to belt along with the radio. We're driving past Avery Park when I get the sudden urge to pull over. Will used to live close by, but that's not why I'm stopping.

"What the hell?" Lacey says, turning down the music, when she sees where we've stopped.

"Let's go in the tunnel!" I say, already climbing out of the car.

"Are you serious? What are you, five?" she asks, correctly identifying the average age of the kids who are playing in the park right now.

"Oh, come on, Lace!" I insist. "For old times' sake."

Lacey has been edgy all day, and instead of letting loose with me, like I hope she will, she digs her heels in.

"We're going to be late! And we're going to mess up our gowns," she says. Normally, this is the kind of thing I'd be worried about, but not today.

Today there is this strange force pushing against my chest, a closed fist tight around my sternum. I wish I could burst into a run, outsprint the feeling. I wish I could leave it behind in this park Lace and I used to play in as kids.

I make my way to the start of the tunnel, a winding, cylindrical slide that used to terrify us when we were little. Lacey follows.

"Really?" she says, one last attempt to shame me into changing my mind, but it doesn't work. I climb the small stairs leading to the top of the slide, then, with one last look around to make sure I'm not endangering any kids, I push off down the slide. The tunnel is just as dark and winding as when we were little, but a lot shorter than I remember it.

When I climb out of the other end, I can't catch my breath from laughing.

"Dude," Lacey says. "Your robe."

I grab her hand and pull her toward the front end of the tunnel. "What, do they not give diplomas to people with rumpled robes?"

"Does it still make you want to shit your pants?" she asks, peeking into the tunnel.

"More now than ever," I say.

Apparently, those are the magic words, because after I go through again, she follows me, letting out a loud whoop that I hear from outside as she spirals down the tunnel.

When she climbs out, she is laughing, and I convince her to go back one more time before we leave.

As we start toward the car, I catch a bunch of parents side-eyeing us in our too-big graduation gowns. A chubby-cheeked kid suddenly bolts in our direction, nearly taking Lacey down in the process, as he runs for the mouth of the tunnel.

"Nicholas, you come back here!" A flustered-looking woman hurries after him, but he doesn't stop. I turn around to watch, silently rooting the kid on. I want to crouch down beside him and tell him to use the tunnel, to keep flying through the dark while he's still allowed.

"When's the last time we did that?" I ask Lacey when we reach my car, and she shrugs.

Then I'm starting the car and tears prick the backs of my eyes and I hate that so many Lasts happen when you aren't paying attention.

There would have been a day, just like any other day, when kid Lacey and Oliver and I would have raced to reach the tunnel first. We would have gone through it, whooping like Lacey did, like we always did, except that when we climbed off that day, it was the last time and we didn't know it.

"You know, our campers probably won't be too much older than those kids at the park," I tell Lacey as we pull into McKillop and circle the parking lot, looking for an empty spot.

"I'm hoping we get more like eleven- or twelve-year-olds," she says, typing something on her phone in the passenger seat.

When I start to climb out of the car, Lacey stops me.

"Do you think Will Mason's mom will be here?"

I look at her, surprised.

"I don't know. Why?"

She clutches her backpack. "I want to return the jacket."

After Megan Tomey found it the day after the accident, Will's jacket ended up with Lauren Herbert, who passed it on to Alex Reynolds, who passed it on to Lacey. The strangest kind of hot potato.

"No one wants to be the one to give it to his mother," Lacey says. Then she adds, "Maybe you could? If you see her?"

"Why can't you do it?"

"Because," she says. "Old people scare me."

I roll my eyes. "His mom is, like, forty."

"Fine. Older people scare me," she amends. "You know you're way better with parents than I am."

It's true: parents tend to love me. I'm not sure what this says about me.

"Anyway, I bet it would mean a lot to his mom to have it," Lacey says, looking down. "I just don't want to say the wrong thing. I . . ."

It's a strange role reversal, Lacey being the one who's afraid to do something, but I understand why she's nervous to speak to Will's mother, why Megan and Lauren and Alex were too. What do you say to someone who has just lost her son?

I also probably knew Will better than any of the other girls did.

"Okay," I say. "If she's here."

On our walk to the football field, I think about the last time Will walked across this field. The last time he spoke to his friends, a cluster of tall, broad-shouldered guys also on the lacrosse team who look sadder than you should on your last day of school, and I wonder if he told them anything important. Anything that mattered.

We're surrounded by our classmates, all in their graduation robes.

"I'm going to find Libby," Lacey says, disappearing before I have the chance to offer to go with her. I stare after her, wondering what is up with her today.

I find my parents already seated next to Lacey's mom, a few rows from the end of the stage. My mom stands up to give me a hug again, like we didn't just see each other a few minutes ago. Her eyes travel over my robe, in slightly worse condition than she last saw it, but she doesn't say anything. On any other day, she'd say something, but not today.

I bury my head in the crook of her neck and somehow I know that even if Will were here, today would still feel like losing something. There's something about happy moments, happy days, that feels a little bit sad. It's probably why people always say crap like how you can't have joy unless you experience sorrow, that the two go hand in hand. But really I think the sadness of happy moments is just the awareness of time passing. You always know the good thing won't last forever, and sadness is the acknowledgment of one second ending and the next beginning, then ending again.

I won't ever walk through McKillop's halls, late for class, late for anything.

I won't always know all the people I know now.

I won't ever fly through the tunnel without feeling slightly self-conscious, too big for it.

I won't always remember the first boy I ever loved.

2

I SHUFFLE FROM side to side, waiting as I hear movement on the other side of the door. I tug at my graduation dress, glance back behind me at my car. Lacey gives me a thumbs-up and I'm giving her one back when the door opens.

Immediately, I wish Lacey and I could trade places.

I wish I'd never agreed to do this. Or that we'd found Mrs. Mason at graduation so we didn't have to come all the way to her house.

One Last flashes lightning-quick through my mind: Will's last day at school, two Fridays ago.

He is leaning against his locker, talking to one of his friends, when he catches my eye. He walks over and throws an arm around my shoulder.

"You coming tonight?" He's asking about Brendan Colbert's infamous post-game rager.

"I can't."

"Can't or won't?" Will asks, seeing straight through my lie. "Come on, Paulsen. It will be fun."

"Yeah, pretty sure our ideas of fun are different. *Mason.*"

Will's voice drops. "They can't be *that* different." I shiver as his words tickle my ears. I never know how to take half of what Will says. Is he flirting? Just being friendly? Should I go tonight and find out?

"I can't," I say again, because there's what I hope the party will be like (dancing, laughing, easy conversation, hanging out with Will) and what I know from experience the party will be like (awkward conversation, Lacey getting drunk, Will hanging out with his lacrosse friends, someone puking on my shoes). Will sighs, letting his arm fall from my shoulder. He heads back to his locker, looking over-the-top devastated, and I laugh.

"It's okay," he calls after a moment. "I still love you."

It's hard to get that image out of my mind. Him grinning, saying *those words* to me.

Now I'm standing in front of a mirror image of him.

Will's mother has the same light brown skin as her son, but her eyes are ringed with red, grief etched into her skin like a carving. She blinks at me, waiting, so I step forward and introduce myself.

"I just wanted to give this to you. It was Will's." His name sticks to the roof of my mouth as I hold out his brown leather jacket to his mother. It smells exactly like him, a light, citrusy scent.

"Oh," she says, hesitating before reaching for it. It's like taking it means accepting more than just a jacket, like it's physical proof that he's gone.

"Thank you," she says at last. I feel the absence of the jacket in my arms the second it's in hers. I nod and start to back away, but she stops me.

"Do you want to come in?"

This time it's my turn to hesitate. I start to say no, but there's a desperate sound to her voice, a pleading in her eyes. I wonder if she's alone at home, if after the memorial two days ago she came back to a house that echoed with emptiness.

I know that Will was an only child, and that his father passed away when we were in middle school.

I have no idea why she's inviting me inside, but I hear myself agreeing before I think better of it. I shoot a helpless look in the direction of my car before I follow Will's mother inside.

She leads me into the living room, where all the curtains are drawn. The house is muggy, like the windows need to be opened. It's only the second time I've ever been in Will's house and I feel a pang of guilt. I'm a stranger eavesdropping on his mother's grief, gawking like it's on display. I wish more than anything that Lacey had just done this with me. After all, she was the one who took his jacket from Alex.

"Can I get you anything to drink?" Mrs. Mason asks, and I shake my head, follow her to the edge of a couch where she sits on the end opposite from me.

"So how do you know Will?"

"I'm his lab partner. Was. I . . ." My voice trails off and I wait for her expression to change, for her to call me on being an impostor. To say I didn't know her son in any way that matters.

But she keeps looking at me as if waiting for me to add something. I shift in my seat.

"Were you at the memorial?" she asks. More than half of McKillop High was there.

Were you at graduation?

I can't ask her that, can't bring up the fact that I just finished high school today. That this whole week has been about the start of the rest of my life, while for her it's been about learning to live without her son.

"Yes. It was beautiful," I say, because that seems like the kind of thing you're supposed to say. The service *was* nice, as nice as anything celebrating the end of the life of an eighteen-year-old boy can be. Even though his uncle's eulogy was peppered with jokes about Will being a rascal, about all the mischievous things he got up to when he was a kid, the air was thick with absurdity, the complete unfairness that Will Mason was really gone.

My heart pinches at the thought now. He'll never grin at me in the hallways again, never call me Eve like he used to because he liked to keep it "biblical," as he said. Before the party he invited me to—before the night he died—we were the kind of friends who hung out at parties and pep rallies, who partnered up whenever we were in the same classes, with the kind of de facto friendship that comes from having known each other since the fifth grade. It was completely uncomplicated.

"He was wearing this the night of the accident?" she asks, still cradling the jacket in her arms.

"Yes," I say. "He forgot it at the party."

I don't mention that I wasn't the one who found it.

I can't gauge the expression on his mother's face as she appraises me. It's like she's reading something on my face.

I shift on the couch.

"I should get going," I say. I almost add that my friend is waiting outside for me, but I don't.

She nods and stands with me.

I feel like I can't go without saying something more, without letting her know that we were thinking of him today, so I add, "We missed Will today. . . . I missed Will."

Her eyes fill with tears, but she blinks them away.

"Thank you. And thank you for bringing this by, Eden," she

says, but before I go, she stops me again. She goes to a drawer in the kitchen and comes back with a pen and paper. She scribbles something down before handing the paper to me.

"Here," she says softly. When I look, she's simply written *Will* and a series of numbers. I stare at her, confused.

"I thought you might like to say goodbye." Her voice is soft again, meaningful, like she's telling me more than she's saying. She's still holding the jacket and she's giving me a strange look and it's then that I finally understand.

She thinks Will and I were together.

That that's why I have his jacket.

That that's why my first stop after graduation was his house.

"I don't think . . . I mean, Will and I . . ." The words don't come. She's giving me an unreadable expression, almost sympathetic. I glance at the piece of paper, then back at her. I can't let her think something was happening between me and Will.

We were just friends.

Nothing ever happened between us.

I don't need to say goodbye, I start to say.

But then I realize that none of those things are true.

Will was more than my friend.

Something did happen between us.

I do want to say goodbye.

Whatever is happening on my face, she's watching, riveted.

It's only a phone number, I realize, looking down at the paper she's just handed me. It's not like she's given me nuclear codes or something.

"Will was, um, a good friend," I say at last, because the silence has gone on long enough and because it's true. Will was a good friend.

She nods. "Thank you," she says again, before I go.

I hurry out of her house, down her driveway and into my car, clutching the number in my palm.

"What happened?" Lacey asks, turning to watch me as I enter the car.

I shake my head and give her a quick rundown as I drive toward her house. "And then she gave me this."

She takes it from me, stares at the number.

"I think it's his phone number."

"No, it's a different area code," Lacey says, and when I look at the paper, she's right. It has an area code different from any in Erinville, different from Will's that I have saved in my phone.

"Maybe he had another phone," she says.

"Or it's some kind of message bank his mother set up for people to call and give their condolences."

"That makes sense," Lacey says as we reach her house. "See you in a bit?"

I tell her I'll be back soon, then I drive home to change out of my graduation clothes and pick up my stuff for tonight.

As soon as I enter the house, I am accosted by my parents.

"There she is!" Dad cries. "Our high school graduate."

He turns to my mom, who is sitting on the other side of the couch from him, her feet on his lap while he caresses them. "Can you believe we have *two* high school graduates? One more to go!"

Dad holds his hand up for a high five, and when Mom's palm touches his, he clasps his hand around hers.

"Ugh, don't make me cry again," Mom says.

"Because you never thought this day would come?" I ask, dropping my grad cap on the dining table.

"No," Mom says. "Because we're *ancient*."

Dad throws his head back as he laughs. "Speak for yourself. I personally don't feel a day over thirty."

Mom snorts, but it's a relief hearing him say those words. It's been just over two months since Dad's TIA, since the night my little sister screamed for Mom because Dad was suddenly slurring his words. The doctors called it a ministroke, a precursor to the real thing. A huge number of people who have transient ischemic attacks have severe strokes within a year. We've lived in a kind of terror ever since. As soon as we got home from the hospital, my mother spent the rest of the night purging the house of anything remotely unhealthy and, incidentally, of anything remotely edible.

"Delusion is a powerful thing," Mom says.

"Oh, is that an official diagnosis?" Dad asks with a laugh.

I don't hear Mom's response, but while they are busy flirting and arguing over who feels younger, I sneak upstairs.

Alone in my room, I let my mind drift back to what happened in Mrs. Mason's house, and I'm feeling conflicted and guilty and confused all over again. Did I give her the wrong impression about how I knew Will?

It doesn't matter what she thinks we were, I tell myself.

I pull out the piece of paper.

It's just a phone number. It's not like she gave me something precious, something that shouldn't belong to me.

I thought you might like to say goodbye, she had said.

And I realize I do.

I would like to say goodbye to Will. Maybe even more than goodbye.

I want to tell him everything I wasn't brave enough to when he was alive.

I want to tell him about the day I first noticed him, really noticed him. We were playing volleyball in seventh-grade gym class. Thanks to a particularly overzealous setter, I got hit in the face and blood came gushing out of my nose. Mr. Peters sent me off to the infirmary and Lacey wasn't in that class and suddenly Will put up his hand and asked if he could walk me to the nurse's office.

It was the most light-headed, dizzying walk of my life. And not just because I'd taken a volleyball to the face.

I want to tell him that it mattered to me that he was kind and funny and always in a good mood. That I always noticed.

It's stupid and it's too late for it to mean anything, but once I get the idea, I can't let go of it.

So, sitting on my bed, I dial the number Mrs. Mason gave me. As the phone rings, I start to compose my thoughts, figure out the right words to say what he will never hear.

I'm expecting to hear Will's voice.

A please-leave-a-message kind of spiel.

And I do hear his voice.

But it's not a voice-mail message.

"Hi, and welcome to In Good Company," his voice says. "I'm Will and you can reach me whenever your heart desires. Press one to register for an account with me."

My head is spinning as Will goes through a whole list of options, like some sort of automated machine.

The whole time he's talking, my heart does a series of flips in my chest, because it's him. He's *here*.

His mother didn't give me some extra phone number of his. And it's not a message bank for condolences.

She gave me a way to reach him, even now that he's gone.

3

"**HOLY SHIT,**" Lacey says later as I hold my phone between our heads. We're in her room and she's sitting on her bed with her legs folded. Between us, the recording I heard a few hours ago plays and Will asks us to register to speak to him anytime. I hang up the phone and stick it in my back pocket.

"Why would his mom give you this?"

I shrug, and the guilt comes back again. "Maybe she didn't believe me when I said I found his jacket. Like, she thought I had it for another reason."

Lacey leans over me to retrieve her laptop and googles In Good Company. Right away, we're on a page about the history of In Good Company. *So you'll always have a friend,* it says in big, bold letters under the title. We skim-read about how it was founded five years ago, how anyone can call in to receive a Companion.

"What's this?" I ask, and Lacey opens up a page about Cognitive Donors.

A heading precedes the opening paragraph: *Never leave your loved ones.*

Lacey and I take turns reading pieces of the information out loud.

"... *a compilation of voice recordings, personality tests and additional information is used to create a database of a Cognitive Donor. In the event of a Donor's passing, the individual joins our wide range of Companions, and his or her likeness can be reached at any time by family, friends and strangers alike."*

"So Will signed up to be a Cognitive Donor," Lacey says, her voice a whisper.

"*Customers are randomly paired with Companions, unless one has the contact number of a specific Companion. Following the death of a Cognitive Donor, his or her contact number is made available only to next of kin."*

"Holy shit," Lacey says again. "I mean, I've heard of stuff like this, but I've never known anyone who has done it."

"I can't believe *Will* did it."

Why would he do something like this?

When, after a minute, Lacey says, "Well, we're obviously not signing up," I deflate. I realize for the first time that I did plan to register. That I want to know more about this thing, this extension of Will that is somehow existing somewhere in the world.

"Why not?" I ask.

"Because it's creepy. Jesus, Eden," she says, like she can't believe she even has to point that out. She shakes her head. "God, and Mrs. Mason seemed so normal to me. Like, at the memorial."

"Kind of harsh, Lace," I say.

"What, you think it's normal to talk to your dead son? To go around inviting people to talk to him too?"

"If this Cognitive Donor thing is true, though, then *Will* chose to do this. He had to have signed up for it when he was alive."

When he was alive sticks to my skin like moisture.

I can't believe we're talking about Will in the past tense.

I can't believe we heard his voice.

"Still creepy," Lacey says, getting off her bed. She yawns as she stretches. "Let's figure out what we're wearing tonight."

And just like that, the conversation is dismissed, the idea of Will out of her mind. I know the lack of movement in my relationship with Will has always frustrated Lacey, but I'm surprised at her nonchalance.

"I kissed him," I blurt out now, and she freezes.

"What?"

"The night he died, the night of the party," I say, and it's two weeks too late. I should have told her the same night. I *would* have told her the same night, but four hours after, Will was dead.

"Oh my God," Lacey says, whispering, and she opens her mouth to say something else but it doesn't come out.

I laugh at her speechlessness.

"Is it that much of a shock to you? Am I that much of a lost cause?"

"Yes," she says, still looking flustered. "Yes. Why didn't you tell me earlier?"

"I couldn't," I say, and she nods like she understands. Pretty much since he died, Lacey and I haven't been able to even talk about Will without breaking down, which means we haven't really talked about him at all.

"So . . . what . . . how?" she asks, collapsing on her bed. I flop down beside her and give her the short version.

Sitting on the sidewalk outside Brendan Colbert's house, music spilling out to reach us, our legs touching under the umbrella of the streetlights.

Will leaning in.

Me freezing. Afraid. Always afraid.

"And then I just went for it. I kissed him."

"Holy shit cakes," Lacey says. "So what does that mean? Does that make you his . . . ?"

"Girlfriend? Oh God, no," I say. "It was one kiss. It might not have meant anything."

Lacey is staring at me, still, with something I can't read in her eyes. Something like awe.

"*What?*" I shriek, covering my face with my hands.

"Just," she says after a moment, "I mean . . . look at *you*!"

I start laughing at her reaction and she keeps staring at me, gobsmacked, frozen, until my laughter dissolves into hiccups, which turn into tears. And then I'm laughing and I'm crying, because I loved a boy for five years and the night something finally happened, he died.

"Tell me I'm not cursed," I say.

Lacey is silent for a minute, probably shocked at my display, but then she's in motion, folding me into her arms and rocking me. "You're not cursed," she says, but her voice is breaking. I'm not sure she believes what she's saying.

We stay like that for a few minutes, then Lacey stands up and forbids any more talk of curses and death and Will tonight.

"We're going to have a good night. No *but*s about it," she says, cutting me off before I can even start.

"We still have our—"

"*Zeeep!*" she says, using her fingers to clasp my lips together.

"Buhht ahh—" I mumble, trying to force out sound.

Lacey simply shakes her head. "Not happening."

I've brought a bunch of application forms for the camp we're both planning to work at this summer, the camp we grew up going to, and if I can't talk about Will, I'd rather we filled those out instead. But Lacey isn't in the mood to think about work or anything other than tonight's party.

I join her in rifling through her closet and looking for something to wear to the bonfire. As we do so, she complains about her brother, the fact that he's decided to come with us to the party. I make appropriately sympathetic sounds, but mostly my mind is still stuck on In Good Company.

Lacey settles on a pair of barely-there denim shorts and a sleeveless black shirt with the name of some band I will pretend to recognize for her benefit. I go with a short summer dress that belongs to Lacey, rendered even shorter by the fact that I have a good two inches on her.

"Stop yanking at it," she says, swatting my hand. "All you're doing is telling everyone you're uncomfortable."

"I'd rather tell them that than what color underwear I'm wearing," I say, and she laughs. Lace goes downstairs and returns with leftover pad thai. We scarf it down while putting the finishing touches on our makeup.

It's just after eight when we arrive at the Erinville river bottom, where the bonfire without fire is happening. Because of Will's accident, we are on thin ice, and any signs of a party would be asking for cops. Still, there is no way we wouldn't do something to celebrate graduating.

The air is cool tonight and the sun is just starting to dim in the sky. It's the perfect night to celebrate the start of summer.

My eyes roam across the splattering of McKillop kids forming clusters on the riverbank. I don't even know I'm doing it—looking for Will—until Lacey gently nudges me.

I know, her eyes say.

Will never missed a party. It was an unspoken routine of ours to enter any gathering and immediately scout out his whereabouts. His signature 'fro, big and thick, noticeable from anywhere: like a beacon of light, guiding you to wherever he was.

Incoming. Five o'clock, Lacey would cough, if she spotted him first.

What the hell is five o'clock? Just say right *or* left! I'd hiss back, casually running a hand through my hair.

Now his absence is the first thing we notice. The strange thing, though, is how indistinguishable this party is from any of the others we've been to in the past year. The same people are here, the same music is playing from a speaker behind us and I would bet good money that people are having the same conversations they have had all year. Who is dating who, who got wasted at the last party, who is going where for college, what everyone is doing over the summer. If you didn't know that one of us was missing—that one of us had died two weeks ago—you wouldn't be able to tell. The wrongness of it floats through the air, and I wonder how many of us are sensing it.

People talk about him, of course, about his memorial and memories they have of him. No one talks about the accident; it's like a tender bruise, impossible to ignore but too raw and painful to touch. Maybe it would make more sense if he'd been drinking, if he'd gotten behind the wheel after knocking back too many at Brendan's party. Maybe we could convince ourselves he even deserved it. But the way it actually happened—a little rain and a curve and Will hitting the gas too hard—it feels devastating.

It feels senseless.

I spot a few of his friends around. Just like at graduation, guys like Kyle Bennett, Brendan Colbert and Tommy Rodriguez form a forlorn cluster under a swatch of drooping trees. I wonder whether they know about In Good Company, that Will signed up to be a Cognitive Donor before he died. Is that the kind of thing they talked about?

Our first order of business is to procure cans of beer from the massive cooler that is the centerpiece of this party. Then we're weaving our way from group to group, like we often do at parties and even at school. Lacey and I are chronic blenders. The kind of kids who can slip into pretty much any group. At some point, though, I end up losing her, and then I'm caught in a conversation with Lauren Herbert about some new cleanse she's trying. Lacey and I refer to her as New Age Lauren—forever on the hunt for the ideal meditation spot or juicing regimen.

"It's, like, the perfect regimen," she gushes.

I feel an odd sense of fondness for Lauren tonight. For everyone here. It's more than just Will's death. It's that last-day-of-camp feeling, when all sins are forgiven and you're scrambling to get everyone's numbers because the summer is ending and you don't know when you'll see each other again. I want to throw my arms around Lauren and tell her what I wrote in her yearbook, make her promise not to change.

"That sounds really cool," I say instead. When I finally find Lacey again, she's planted herself in a little cluster on the beach with Hail and Libby and Vance, and they are passing what I hope is a cigarette between the four of them.

"Hey," I say, flopping down beside her. Lacey shifts closer to Hail to make room for me. I try to catch her eye, to make her answer the question in my mind, but she is too busy laughing at something Hail has just said. Either Hail has turned into a comedian overnight or Lacey has already had more to drink than I have.

"So what are we doing?" I ask pointedly, but with a decidedly nonjudgmental air. Lacey claims that I have a stick up my ass when it comes to the friends she made in shop class last semester, and I'm trying to show her that is not at all the case.

At least, it wouldn't be, if the smell of weed didn't follow them around like a shadow.

Lacey, intentionally or unintentionally missing my point, nudges Hail. "Tell her about the carnival," she says, already cracking up again.

I turn to Hail and try to follow a convoluted story about a bad pot brownie and a roller coaster and a girl with hair teased to high heaven. Hail has, it turns out, not blossomed into a comedian overnight, but I laugh politely and try to seem like my ass is completely free of foreign objects.

As Hail starts to tell Lacey another story, I turn and watch other groups milling around. A horde of people are having a stone-skipping contest behind us and I'm tempted to join them, but I don't want to leave Lacey.

This is one of our Lasts, and knowing it is like watching color fade into black and white, like watching day fade into the sunken grays of nighttime.

After a while, though, Lacey decides it's not a bonfire without camp songs, and so she coaxes a whole bunch of people to join our group, then runs back to the car she and Oliver inherited from their mom to retrieve the guitar she always conveniently just happens to have with her. She slings it across her body, and along with her loose curls and the way she's dressed, it has the effect of making her look like some tiny musical hippie vagabond. It's an aesthetic that works on her, though.

Speaking of things only Lacey can get away with: getting people to gather in a misshapen circle to sing camp songs while she strums on her guitar. Anyone else would be self-conscious, worried about being the person who always has to get up and perform at every party, but not Lacey.

Not even when the first few chords start out sloppy, her words slurring like her tongue is slightly heavy in her mouth.

She's definitely had a couple of beers.

Still, she closes her eyes and her voice rings out clear and earnest, louder than everyone else's. A tear slides out of the corner of her eye, and she keeps singing, doesn't wipe it away. I have the urge to reach out and brush it off her cheek, but I don't.

It's the first time she seems to have noticed the vibration of sadness in the air.

She doesn't seem to notice, though, that everyone else singing is doing so with a hokey sense of irony and irreverence. Or if she does, she doesn't care.

I've always envied that about Lacey, the permission she gives herself to feel things, no matter who is watching.

Even though she's drunk, she's still good, her raspy voice soothing. A gentle breeze makes the hair on my skin rise. It feels like a song in the dark, like a ghost in an abandoned house.

For the second time today, it feels like Will is here.

4

THINGS DETERIORATE QUICKLY.

First there's the skinny-dipping.

I know it's Lacey's idea, because it's number three on the list of things we plan to do this summer, things we plan to do before we head to college.

"I thought it would be, you know, private," I tell Lacey, unable to take my eyes off the kids around us in varying states of undress. For number three—*go skinny-dipping*—I'd seen us sneaking into the community pool near Lacey's house late at night, or the lake at Camp Rowan, not this.

Lace, who is now in her bra and underwear, rolls her eyes. She's set her guitar against a giant oak tree behind us.

"It's more fun this way." She tugs on my arm. "Come on, Eden!"

"Yeah, come on, Eden!" Marcus Tyme echoes from the edge of another group.

But I shake my head and stand in the shadows, holding her clothes. It's like sliding through the Avery Park tunnel and then visiting Will's mom put me over the limit of brave things I'm capable of handling in one day.

With a sigh, Lacey moves to the front of the pack. Hail leads the countdown, and on three, they all burst into a run and plunge themselves into the river.

As soon as it's done, when they all amble out, laughing, spitting out water, I feel a pang of regret. Frustration at myself.

Why couldn't I let go for just a second, for just long enough to join them? It *was* on our list.

The other half of my brain argues back about the reality of baring my ass in front of more than half my graduating class. No matter how daring and fun it sounds to throw yourself into a river on a night like this, reality is always messier, colder, more embarrassing, disappointing, and I don't know that I can take it tonight.

I'm bracing myself for Lacey's teasing, an epic display of disappointment at my chickening out. It's pretty common for us, Lacey reprimanding me for not doing something and me feeling sheepish, realizing it probably wouldn't have been so bad. But she is silent now as she takes her clothes from me, as she pulls them on.

There's a moment when she looks like she *might* say something, but then she changes her mind, and there's something about the look she gives me. She looks at me not like she doesn't recognize me, but like she doesn't want to.

Like she's exhausted in some way.

I tell myself it's from plunging into the river.

"I'm going with Hail to grab something from his car," she says, and there's a good chance that's a euphemism for something.

"Want me to come with?" I ask anyway.

It's the wrong move, because she snaps, "Jesus, I'll be gone for five minutes, not five years!" Then she laughs, but there's an unmistakable edge to her voice. I want to call her on it, to ask her why she's this pissed off about me not skinny-dipping, but I decide to let it slide.

"Okay," I say, watching her head off in Hail's direction.

It feels like there's something else bothering her, and I wonder if it's because of what I told her at her house, if it's because I kissed Will and waited two weeks to tell her.

I don't see her again for over an hour.

And when I do, I nearly have a conniption.

Lacey can barely stand without assistance.

"I'm fiiiiine," she slurs, sounding anything but. Drinking makes Lace even more headstrong than she normally is. It takes minutes before I manage to coax the half-empty can of beer from her hands. She keeps her guitar against her chest, a shield against the night.

"Stay here," I tell her sternly before leaving in search of Oliver, our designated driver. I haven't seen him since we got here. He didn't drift over when the camp songs started, like most other people, and he didn't join in the skinny-dipping. He's not among the little groups scattered around the riverbank and he's not by the car.

Where are you? I text, but after a couple of minutes, he still hasn't responded. I follow the sound of voices like a trail of crumbs into the edge of the woods. As I walk, I try to swallow the feeling of resentment, regret at coming out tonight.

I knew Lacey was going to get drunk.

It's a party and that's what happens at parties. More than that, we're celebrating being done with school. I can't judge her for having a good time.

Still, this is the exact reason I tend to avoid parties. In movies and in my head, high school parties are these fun, exciting affairs, opportunities to make memories you'll cherish forever. In real life, they are sloppy and loud and we all act like the worst versions of ourselves.

It feels exhausting and predictable, watching Lacey drink herself into oblivion. It used to be that we looked down on kids who did that, pitied people who had to be wasted to have any fun. We used to be able to make our own fun, people-watching or reciting our favorite movie lines or doing the most dorky and unpredictable thing we could at any given moment.

I miss the simplicity of that time, miss who we used to be.

It's why I'm so excited to spend the summer at camp. No drinking, no parties, no pot. Just me, my best friend and three wide-open months of adventures, new friends, new boys and the memories of all the years we spent at Camp Rowan when we were kids.

It's the one thing I'm allowing myself to feel hopeful about.

I keep walking until I make out two figures, a couple resting against the trunk of a tree. The girl lets out a sharp trill of laughter, and the sound of it is loud in the night, carefree. The boy leans forward to whisper something in her ear, his hands on her lower back. In the sliver of light that falls through the canopy of trees, I recognize Lacey's brother.

Oliver is exactly the kind of boy who would make a girl fall in love with him in the dark.

For some reason, I can't make myself step forward and interrupt them. Their laughter rings behind me as I turn around and head back to Lacey.

I'm hurrying back through the trees when something creaks behind me.

I jump when I hear my name.

Turn back, and Oliver is jogging toward me.

"Eden, hey," he says, catching up to me. His hair is sticking up in all directions, and he runs his hand self-consciously through it. I try not to stare at his rumpled shirt. "Is everything okay?"

"Lacey's wasted. I think we should head home. . . . I mean, if you're ready to."

"Uh, yeah," he says, pulling out his phone. "Shit. I'm just see-ing your text. Yeah, I'm ready if you are."

He follows me over to where Lacey is. In the short time I've been gone, she appears to have become surgically attached to Hail. She is sitting on his lap, a newly acquired bottle of beer in hand. I see Oliver's jaw tighten when he spots his sister. His re-action makes me feel validated in my assessment of Hail and Co.

Oliver crouches so he's at eye level with Lacey.

"We're going," he says, voice low.

"Going where?" Lacey asks, too loud, taking a swig from the bottle.

"Home."

She swallows with a gulp. "Who's *we*?"

"You, me and Eden," Oliver says.

Lacey leans closer to Hail. "Are *you* coming home with us?"

"Lace." I cringe, filled with embarrassment for her.

"Do you want me to?" Hail has the audacity to smirk back.

At that, Oliver reaches for his sister's wrist and pulls her up, completely ignoring Hail.

"You're *bad*," Lacey giggles, nearly falling over herself when she's upright. Luckily, her brother is supporting her. I plant my-self on her other side, and between the two of us we are able to keep her from face-planting.

"Do you have my guitar? I need my guitar," she whines.

"I've got it," Oliver says, pulling it across his own chest.

"Why are we going? We just got here." She keeps complaining all the way to the car, where we buckle her into the back seat. I climb in beside her, and not long after the car starts moving, she groans and rests her head in my lap.

"I'm so tired," she whispers to me. "I think I'm gonna hurl."

"Did she just say she was going to hurl?" Oliver's stern eyes meet mine in the rearview mirror. "Because she better not have said she was going to hurl in my fucking car."

"Nope," I lie, despite my annoyance with her. "In fact, she said she was hungry."

He harrumphs, disbelieving.

Lacey giggles. "It's *our* fucking car!" she shouts suddenly, a delayed response.

"Not tonight, it isn't," Oliver says.

"You're such a turd," Lacey slurs.

He bursts into laughter, then glances over his shoulder at us. "I'm a *turd*?" He looks at me. "Wanna filter that one for her?"

"She said you're a stud. Her favorite brother," I supply.

Oliver rolls his eyes. Soon we're pulling into their driveway, and then we're helping Lacey navigate the stairs as quietly as possible, so as not to wake up their mom.

"Shh," Oliver warns when Lacey's elbow hits the wall outside her room.

"*You* shhh," she spits back.

"Shut up, Lace," Oliver and I say at the same time.

In her room, Lacey immediately collapses onto her bed. I help her yank off her socks, and then Oliver and I get her under the covers.

I'm out of breath by the time we're done.

"Thanks," Oliver says, heading toward the door. He hesitates once he reaches it, and I get the sense that he's still embarrassed about the girl in the woods. Like Lacey, this Oliver is not the same person I grew up with, but it's different because he's not my best friend.

"Good night, turd," I say, to lighten the mood.

He laughs, raises one hand and then shuts the door.

I change into my pajamas, turn off the lights and then climb into the other side of Lacey's bed. She rouses as soon as I slide under the covers.

"Edie?" she mumbles into the dark, using one of her numerous nicknames for me.

"Yeah?"

"I love you, okay?" she says.

I smile into the darkness, my frustration with her dissipating. "Love you too." Before I've even finished speaking, I hear her soft breaths in the night, the rhythm of sleep.

A sliver of moonlight works its way into the room and I focus on it while I wait for sleep to come, focus on the sharp-angled shadows it creates against the walls. Instead of drifting to sleep, though, I seem to become even more alert.

I can hear the scratching of leaves outside Lacey's window, the creaking of the house, arthritic and slow.

Several minutes pass, then several more minutes, and I'm still awake. My mother always says that the hardest time to hide from your thoughts is in that space between late night and early morning. That it's when distraction falls asleep, when ghosts come out of hiding.

This feels like the exact crevice between late night and early morning.

I think back to earlier tonight, how I didn't get into the water and the way Lacey looked at me after. It reminds me of two Fridays ago, the party Will invited me to and how disappointed he seemed when I said no.

I ended up going, and I'm glad I did.

But what if the only reason I ever do anything brave is because someone makes me?

My mind drifts further back. To the memorial for Will, his absence at graduation, his house and his jacket, his voice.

The number I have for him.

I glance over at Lacey, and she's sound asleep.

Before I think better of it, I'm climbing out of bed, grabbing my phone and heading into the bathroom down the hall. I sit on the edge of the bathtub and go to my redial list. The last number I called was his. Will's, when I played the sound of his voice for Lacey.

When I hear it again tonight, a familiar shiver travels down my spine.

But something else too.

Curiosity.

A longing for something I can't name.

So I do it.

I use the credit card my sisters and I share for emergencies, and I sign up to talk to Will.

Whenever your heart desires, as he said.

I answer a series of questions during the sign-up. My name, my age, my interests, likes and dislikes.

And then finally, when it seems like this will go on forever, there is a click. The sound of an ending and the beginning of something.

"I'm Will," the voice on the other end of the line says.

I know, I think.

My heart is racing in my chest, my palms sweating.

What am I doing?

Lacey was right that we shouldn't sign up. That this wasn't for us. For me.

"Hi, I'm . . ."

"Eden," he finishes for me.

When I tell him he doesn't sound like a ghost, he laughs.

A full, hearty laugh that makes me picture him with his head thrown back, maybe clutching his side as well.

This is Will, I suddenly realize.

Will laughing.

Will existing somewhere, never gone.

"What exactly does a ghost sound like?" Will asks. "I'll do my best impression."

He proceeds to make a bunch of windy *whoo* sounds, and I can't help it. I burst out laughing.

"With all due respect, can I ask *why* you thought I'd sound like a ghost?"

"Because," I start, but I can't make the rest of the words come out.

Because you're dead.

Almost as if the words passed from my lips, he answers, and his voice is a whisper. "I'm right here."

5

I NUDGE LACEY awake in between scrambling for my shoes and triple-checking the résumé in my manila folder.

"Smsshrifma." Lacey mutters something inaudible before yanking the sheets back over her head.

"Lace, seriously," I say. "You can't be late. This is the last day of interviews."

"Mshpski," she responds.

I shake her awake again, determined to get a response out of her before I leave. "Promise me you won't be late!"

Finally she strings together sounds I can convince myself sound like "I promise."

I double-check my outfit in Lacey's full-length mirror, then grab my bag and slip out of the room.

"Eden! I thought I heard you come in with them last night," Lacey's mom says, emerging from the kitchen with a container of yogurt in her hand. She's dressed for work, in slacks and a silk blouse, even though today is Saturday.

"Hey, Mrs. M," I say, heading over to give her a hug. I breathe in her vanilla scent. When she's good—when she's healthy—she is the warmest person I know. When she hugs you, she doesn't let go until you do. "I hope we didn't wake you."

I'm feeling her out, trying to figure out just how much of Lacey's commotion she heard last night and whether we are in any kind of trouble, but she doesn't seem upset with us.

"You look ready to take on the world," she says when she releases me. "What's the occasion?"

"We have our Camp Rowan interviews today," I tell her. "Lacey's is this afternoon."

"She didn't tell me that was today!" she says.

We chat for a couple more minutes, mostly her assuring me that I'll do great, and then I hurry out of the house and get into my car, which has been parked in their driveway since I came over yesterday afternoon. Lacey and Oliver's car is gone, so Oliver is probably already at work.

I drive over to the Y, mentally rehearsing my answers to possible interview questions. I arrive five minutes early and am ushered into a cluttered office where a curly-haired middle-aged woman sits across from me.

The interview itself is quick and painless. I answer questions about why I love working with kids, or rather, I present the impression that I love working with kids. I tell her about my years going to Camp Rowan as a camper, how they were some of the happiest summers of my life and how I can't wait to go back as a counselor—things that are actually all true. Then the interview turns to logistics: my Social Security number, my bank account details. I pull everything out of the manila folder, and twenty minutes later, I have a job.

I call Lacey immediately and get her voice mail.

It's eleven-thirty and her interview isn't until two, so I decide not to get on her case for still being asleep. Given how drunk she was last night, she is probably battling a wicked hangover.

"Hey, it's me," I say after the beep. "So you were right, it was totally straightforward and I had nothing to worry about. Kim was really nice and it's pretty much a done deal. We're going to camp!" I give a little squeal. "Anyway, good luck with your interview! Not that you'll need it. Call me when you get this!"

After I hang up, I feel like doing a little jig. I can't remember the last time I felt this light, this excited. Definitely before Will's death.

Lacey and I went to Camp Rowan every summer, starting in third grade all the way till we were fourteen. It was my idea for us to go back this summer before we go off to college, before everything changes.

I picture late nights around a campfire, decidedly unlike the one yesterday. Toasted marshmallows instead of booze, songs sung through laughter and not through tears. Adventures and new memories, a welcome escape from Erinville, where the weight of Will's death hangs over everything like a dark cloud.

I know it's optimistic, imagining camp being the same as it was years ago, but I'm deciding to believe that, for once, reality can live up to my expectations.

When I arrive at home, my entire house smells like finger foods, like mini-pies and crab cakes and deviled eggs—and then there's the stuff we are actually allowed to eat. A bunch of vegan, gluten-free, low-fat options. When my mother started on our new health kick, she made it clear that it wasn't just Dad's new life—it was ours.

Now my mother is scrambling around like a crazy person. She gives me a look of disapproval the minute she sees me.

"Please tell me you're not wearing that," she says, appraising the pants and blouse I thought passed for professional.

"I'm not wearing that," I say, but she is in no mood for my jokes. Yesterday's version of my mother—sentimental and soft—is gone, and in her stead is the to-the-point, no-nonsense Mom I know.

"Eden, I'm serious. Go upstairs and change." She herself is in a knee-length black-and-white dress, with a tasteful string of pearls. "I thought you'd be here hours ago."

"I had my interview, remember?"

"Interview . . ." Mom gives me a blank look, then scans the living room for anything that is out of place.

"For camp? I told you about it yesterday morning before graduation?"

This does not appear to jog her memory. Instead of beating a dead horse, I turn the conversation to the only topic her attention is capable of handling right now.

"How is everything coming along?"

Mom sighs and is about to launch into a long spiel about everything that is going wrong with the preparations for the party she's throwing when my older sister appears at the top of the stairs.

"Mia?" I choke. Really it's a cry of excitement, but it comes out as a question.

We meet at the bottom of the stairs and exchange a quick hug.

"Holy . . . wow," I say. Unlike me, she is already in a dark green cocktail dress, the clean-cut image a sharp contrast to the rows of dreads on her head. I would have paid money to see Mom's reaction when Mia got off that plane. She looks beautiful, but my mother believes dreadlocks are what you get when you've given up. She believes in buns and ponytails, in clean, neat braids if you want something different. She has this belief that as one of the few black families in Erinville, it's our job to *exude* something that impresses people, something that feels a lot like perfection.

I haven't seen Mia since Christmas, and it's like she's become an entirely different person since then. Her face is rounder, her eyes twinkle in a way that makes me wonder what she's seen.

"Sorry I couldn't make it home for yesterday," she says, and I shake my head, still mesmerized by how different she looks, how much older.

Will college transform me the same way too?

I can't decide whether I want it to or not.

"It's okay," I say.

"You're not wearing that, are you?" Mia asks, and from the way she echoes Mom, I realize she might not have changed that much after all.

I sigh. "No, I'm going upstairs now."

I trudge up the stairs and into my room. I grab a shower, then get dressed for the party. Between Will's memorial and graduation and now this, I am basically out of semiformal dresses.

I decide on a maroon dress I haven't worn since last summer.

In the space of time I spend getting ready, my mind drifts back to last night, to hearing Will's voice and the way he had sounded the same as always. All boy and no robot.

All boy and no ghost.

I feel a sudden need to tell Lacey about it. I know she'll have something to say about the fact that I signed up, but it's already done. All she can do is call with me, experience the same sense of being transported elsewhere that I did when I heard his voice.

By the time I'm ready, the party has already started.

As I descend the stairs, I hear laughter, the clinking of glasses being set down on glistening silver trays, my mother seamlessly slipping in tidbits about her new teaching series while my father, her biggest fan, tries to hand-sell copies of her new book, *Happy Starts With You*, or even some of her backlist. People are eating it up too, because my parents are the kind of people you don't want to disappoint. People pack school gymnasiums and seminar rooms to hear my mother speak about getting what you want in life, and there's a three-month waiting list to get into my dad's dental practice.

Everyone has hopes and dreams, but my parents live theirs. Save the one hiccup with my dad's health, it's like life itself is afraid to disappoint them.

"It's all about putting out there what you want." This is Mom's standard response whenever she is asked how exactly she ended up with the perfect life. The husband, the career, the house, the girls. *The girls.*

"The Paulsen girls! Look at them! Just darling." Almost as soon as I get downstairs, I find myself sandwiched between my sisters while Mrs. Flynne, one of Dad's patients, coos over the three of us.

My sisters and I are somehow positioned in our birth order. Mia first, me next, then Samara. I think sometimes that we're like birds flying south for winter, innately forming a V shape wherever we go even though it's been months since we've all been together. Hundreds of dinner parties and awards nights and dance competitions will do that to people. It's easiest to understand our places relative to each other.

Mrs. Flynne pats all our hands affectionately and then I am gently extricated from the middle while she prods Mia for details about college and the youth UN summit she's attending in DC over the summer, then grills Sam on the short dance scores in her last competition. On the spectrum between normal and enchanted, my sisters' lives fall on the same end as Mom's and Dad's. It's just the way things are.

Later, I'm standing with my parents, talking with Dad's colleague Dr. Jensen and trying not to stare too hard at his miraculously restored hairline.

"So, Eden," he says. "I hear you're all done with school. Now what?"

"I'm working this summer, then going to State in the fall."

"What do you plan to study?"

"She's still mulling over her options," Mom cuts in, before I can embarrass them by saying I have no idea what I want to do with my life. In her mind, she's only helping me field the question, but there's a reason Mia gets to answer that question on her own and I don't. I'd be lying if I didn't say at least thirty percent of the appeal of going to camp is being surrounded by kids who don't give a crap what my plans are or what I want to study in college, whose foreheads don't immediately furrow at my lack of direction.

There's this moment around junior year when you stop being a person and you become the sum of everything you hope to achieve, your value determined by your future earning potential, whether you're going into the arts or doing something sensible and levelheaded, something sustainable.

My parents have never cared one way or the other what we do, as long as we excel at it. Mom has a chapter in one of her books called "What's the Point of Doing Something If You Don't Plan to Be the Best At It?" I know this because I've received many abbreviated lectures on the subject. It's not just a black thing (being twice as good, etc.); it's a Paulsen thing.

The conversation switches to something about overheads and Dad's practice, so I swivel away from them and head to the snack table. I covertly pull out and check my phone, but there's nothing from Lacey about her interview. She's probably getting ready for her performance tonight.

I shoot her a couple of texts.

How did it go????

Ready for your set yet? Wish you were here!

I've just put my phone back when it vibrates in my dress pocket. But it's a text from Sam, not Lacey.

OMG Dad just pinched Mom's butt. Can Mom do Closing Remarks yet???

Mia responds before I do. **Crap's sake. Eden, tell Mom it's Closing Remarks time!**

You tell her, I text back.

It's past four and I'm hopeful that things are wrapping up, that I'll soon get to duck out and go and meet Lacey. Lacey, the one person who is consistently on the same wavelength as me.

Across the room, though, my parents are still laughing in a group with a bunch of their friends and Sergiy, Sam's ice dance coach. Sam is standing with them, while Mia is still chatting Mrs. Flynne's ear off about all the fantastic things she's achieved and done this year, things even I don't know about yet.

With the rest of my family engaged in conversations that I am not part of, I spend the rest of the afternoon drifting from group to group, practiced grin in place.

At one point, it's like I come outside myself. I'm floating above, listening to myself give lifeless answers about graduation and what I'm doing for college and working at Camp Rowan for the summer. I don't know what it is about Mom's functions, about nights like these, but they turn me into a cardboard cutout of myself. It's like the room is so full of Paulsen excellence, I have no choice but to preemptively bore people with how completely ordinary I am.

When we were younger, people used to have trouble telling Mia and me apart, with our rich brown skin and black hair. Sam has the same full lips, our big, expressive eyes. These days, it's easier to tell the three of us apart, and not just because Sam is so much younger or because Mia suddenly has dreads. It's as if time has differentiated us, like particles sifting out of solution or atoms splitting apart; suddenly all the ways we're different are so obvious, the ways I am not enough of Mia or enough of Sam.

I wish sometimes we were still indistinguishable from each other. There are not particularly many people here tonight—thirty or forty, at most—but the room feels so crowded that only the smallest version of myself will fit.

6

"THIS SONG IS about feeling homesick for a place you haven't been yet."

I walk into Kiely's Coffeehouse a few minutes after six, just as Lacey is introducing the second song in her set. I'm overdressed, still in the dress and heels from my mom's party, but I'm just relieved to be out of the house.

Lacey's eyes are closed as she strums on her guitar, so she doesn't see me come in. The lyrics to "Someday Maybe" are soulful, melancholy, like the rest of her music.

I order an iced coffee and start toward my favorite corner in the café, but it's Saturday night and busy, so it's already occupied. I find the only empty table, then pull out my phone and record the next couple of songs. No matter how well her performance goes, Lacey likes to watch footage after and critique herself.

For the next thirty minutes, Lacey performs a mix of songs she's written and acoustic versions of popular mid-tempo songs.

"That's it for me tonight. Thank y'all for listening," she says. When people start to applaud, she curtsies, then packs up her guitar and water bottle. As Lacey makes her way from the front of the café, I'm preparing to ask about her newfound Southern accent. Except instead of walking in my direction, she turns and walks to her right, across the room from me.

I'm confused until I see whose table she's headed to.

Hail, Libby and Vance are here.

Vance half stands from his seat to give her a high five, Libby follows suit and Hail stands up to give her a hug. Lacey gives a little squeal as her feet leave the floor. Then the four of them are laughing and talking over one another.

I hesitate before walking toward them. Of all the things I hoped I'd be doing tonight, making small talk with Hail and Co. was not high on the list. Still, I can't just leave. I told Lacey I'd be here.

I'm halfway across the café when Lace suddenly turns around and waves at me. Vance must have seen me and told her I was walking over.

Before I reach their table, Lacey meets me, cradling a mug.

"Hi!" she says, giddy the way she always is when she's just gotten off the stage. "I didn't know you were coming."

"I told you I was," I say, then give her a hug. As I lean in, I catch a whiff of something sweet in her mug. Something that is definitely not coffee. I drop my voice to a whisper. "Are you drinking? Kiely will kill you."

Lacey laughs. "That rhymes." I start to wonder whether her post-performance giddiness has anything to do with endorphins.

"I'm serious," I say.

"It's fine. How will she know?"

My face remains disapproving until Lacey says, "Oh my God.

If I'd known you'd be like this, I'd have asked you to stay home."
She bumps me with her shoulder to show that she's joking.

I oblige her with a retaliatory bump and an unamused "Ha ha," but her comment hurts the slightest bit anyway. Would she have preferred I stayed home while she hung out with Hail, Libby and Vance instead?

We walk back toward her table.

"Oh! How was your interview?" I ask, turning to look at her.

All of a sudden, Lacey won't meet my eye.

"Lace?"

"Okay, don't freak out," she says, ensuring that I do just that. "I missed it."

"You did *what*?" I say, voice so shrill that Vance actually pretends to jump. We've reached their table now, and I grab an empty chair from a neighboring table but don't sit down.

"You did *what*?" I repeat, only slightly less shrill and loud.

"I overslept," Lacey says sheepishly.

I gape at her. "Today was the last day of interviews."

"I know," she says, decidedly less frantic than I am.

"Camp training starts next week."

"*I know.*"

"Okay," I say. "Okay. Here's what we're going to do. You're going to call Kim and tell her you're really sorry but you were super sick this morning and you'll make up the interview. Make sure you tell her how much camp means to you, how much you are looking forward to this summer and also—"

"Eden!" Lacey interrupts. "I've been thinking . . ."

I stare at her, waiting for her to go on.

"I'm not sure I want to go to camp this summer."

I know I'm looking at her as if she's just sprouted spare limbs, but I can't help it.

"We've been planning this for months."

"Yeah, I know," she says, sounding apologetic, and I suddenly wish we were having this conversation without an audience, away from Hail and Co. "But it's our last summer before college. I don't want to spend it all at some camp."

"It's not *some camp*," I repeat, feeling blood rush to my face. I grab Lacey's arm and pull her into a corner where only half the coffee shop can hear us instead of all of it. "It's Camp Rowan. I mean, it's all set up. The paperwork is filled out. We're getting assigned cabins in a couple of days. It's *literally all ready to go.*"

"For you," Lacey says, taking a sip from her mug. She makes a face as she swallows, doing a poor job of acting like it's only coffee in her cup. "It's all set up for *you*. And you can still go. You don't have to not go just because of me."

"Are you serious?"

"Yeah. Why *shouldn't* you go? You've been super excited about it."

"*We've* been super excited about it," I correct. But then I think of the number of times I reminded Lacey just to email and set up the interview, the number of times I had to remind her about the interview itself. And she's right.

Maybe I've been the only one excited about it.

"Why didn't you tell me you didn't want to go?" I ask, unable to hide my dismay.

"It's not that I don't *want* to go. It's just . . . I want to do other stuff. Like, Libby's uncle is looking for a receptionist at the country club. I'm thinking of applying."

"Oh," I say.

"Don't be mad," Lacey says, poking my arm.

"I'm not," I lie, but really I'm transported back to last night and the exhausted expression on Lacey's face. I'm wondering how long she has been planning this. How long she's been making plans for a summer without campfire songs and late-night adventures and years' worth of memories.

A summer without me.

7

BEFORE LAST YEAR, Lacey and I had spent every summer together since we were four. From ages four to eight, it was day camps and playdates, running barefoot through the sprinklers at her house or mine. From nine to fourteen, it was Camp Rowan. It was three hours northeast of Erinville, and our parents would take turns carpooling us there. On the drive over, we'd sing along to the radio and bop excitedly in our seats. Then we'd arrive at camp, where we always requested to be put in the same cabin. There were late-night campfires and groggy morning camp songs and sugary midnight snacks, contraband passed from cabinmate to cabinmate while our teenage counselor pretended not to notice. There were dual crushes, on the same boy or wildly different boys. Lacey would like the edgy camper whose hair was a color not existing in nature, the boy whose lip rings were confiscated at the start of camp and returned to him on the last day. My crushes tended to run the full spectrum of boys—class clown, jock, nerd— I had tried it all, but I was partial to nice boys who could make me laugh. Boys like Will.

Camp Rowan was where Lacey first got her period. Where I lost my first kiss. *Lost,* because Malcolm Denison had a vaguely reptilian tongue that tended to retract and protrude in turns. By the end of the longest fifteen seconds of my life, I had decided I wanted a do-over on my first kiss, but when I confessed to the girls in my cabin, they insisted that it had to count. The tongue made it irreversible.

The year we turned fifteen and got too old for camp, we spent the summer lazing about by the local pool, eyeing lifeguards but being too intimidated to talk to them. The summer after that was more of the same.

For as long as I could remember, summer had been synonymous with scouting out adventures with Lacey.

But last summer, the summer after junior year, was different.

From the day after the Fourth of July to just a couple of days before school started, Lacey had been with her dad in Los Angeles. She'd gone alone, because Oliver hadn't wanted to leave their mother after her latest bad episode.

It had been a lonely summer. I'd spent it working at my dad's practice, filing paperwork and answering calls, missing Lacey like a temporarily bandaged limb. I knew she was coming back, but in her absence, everything felt awkward and off balance, like I was compensating for the limb I couldn't use.

As strange as those two months were, things got stranger when Lacey returned.

Right away, looking at her was like one of those spot-the-difference games, a before-and-after side-by-side.

There was the tan, so strong that her arms and legs were dark deep into the fall. But she'd spent the summer on the beach, so that was to be expected.

There was the purple streak. It feels too easy to single out that one element, a change in her appearance, and cast it as the defining moment, the first-ever moment in our friendship when it seemed like our paths might be diverging.

But it was the first thing I noticed when she stepped off the Greyhound that had brought her from Beddingfield Airport. I had driven over with her mom and Oliver that evening, not caring whether they wanted it to be a family-only reunion. Or perhaps I was emboldened by the thought. If Lacey and I weren't each other's family, then what were we?

She stepped off, wearing distressed denim cutoffs almost identical to the ones that I was wearing. The same sunglasses we'd picked out for her at the mall a few weeks before she left, and the black-and-white Converse we both lived in.

Presumably, her mother and Oliver had already seen the streak when they had video-chatted earlier, because, save a tightening of the lips, Mrs. Murdoch did not react. Lacey and I had video-chatted a couple of times too, but not for the last three weeks—I hadn't even seen pictures—so I was the only one who exclaimed.

"Lace! Your hair! Your one beauty," I gasped as I hugged her, paraphrasing one of our favorite *Little Women* movie quotes. I said it quietly enough that her mother couldn't hear, because if I knew anything about Lacey and her mom, it was that they never really saw eye to eye.

Lacey was stepping back in almost the same motion that she returned my embrace. "It's on *my* head. You don't have to like it," she said with a tight smile. And then Oliver was taking her bag and her mom was giving her a stiff-backed hug and Lacey and I were sliding into the back seat of her mom's car.

"I was kidding," I said, even though I shouldn't have had to.

Though I had sounded a little alarmed and maybe even judgmental, I had only said what we always did to acknowledge any physical change in each other's lives. When, for instance, my mom had bought me a new winter jacket at the start of the year, Lacey had said, "Eden! Your coat! Your one beauty." And when she'd changed the layout of her room just before she left for her dad's, I'd walked in and gone, "Lacey! Your room! Your one beauty."

It was our thing. One of many.

"I know," she said, smiling more sincerely at me, but then she turned and faced the window, barely answering her mom's and brother's questions about LA and the plane and bus rides.

She was insufferable for the entire next week, even after school started. So much so that I let Mom drag me to Sam's skating lessons because Lacey never wanted to hang out, or if she did, she spent the entire time sulking or complaining about her mother. I mean, I got it. My mother is Maura Paulsen, PhD. She owns a company called Happy and You Own It. But there is only so much shit talking a person can take. And I especially felt guilty because I *loved* Lacey's mom; Mrs. Murdoch and I had always gotten along.

Exactly a week after the Saturday she got home, Lace's bad mood from hell ended. When she showed up at my house, the streak in her hair less vibrant than when I'd first seen it, she hugged my mom and then me, apologizing for PMSing, and I accepted her apology.

We sat in my room, going through the increasingly unsatisfactory collection of movies I had on my computer, and then she started to tell me why she'd been so angry.

"She lied to me," Lacey said, legs outstretched and back resting on the door of my room as a precaution in case my younger sister tried to come in. Sam, as a rule, exhibited no interest what-soever in my life unless Lacey was around, and then she tagged along nonstop, trying to listen in on our conversations. For what purpose, God alone knew.

"When I was gone, we had this long, like, heart-to-heart phone call in July and Mom was all *I'll talk to your dad* and she promised to at least think about letting me stay. Come to find out, she was never going to. The whole—"

"Wait," I said, stopping her. "Stay where?"

Lacey looked at me as if I was stupid, or like I hadn't been listening to anything she'd said. "In Los Angeles. My dad's there. Plus, LA is way better for my career. How do you do music in a shit hole like Erinville?" She kept talking, unable to feel that the air in the room had shifted, that I was gaping at her and that all I could think was *what*.

I interrupted her again, this time truly not having been listen-ing. "But . . ."

She stared at me, waited for me to go on.

What about senior year? And prom and driving aimlessly around Erinville, wasting gas and time and energy, because we have enough of all of them?

"What about Oliver?" I asked.

It was a good enough question. The twins had been insepa-rable when they were little. Round-faced, long-limbed kids who did everything together. According to their mom, they had cried together and yo-yoed laughter back at each other from across rooms as infants. When we'd met as four-year-olds, they'd taken me in together, almost a collective decision between them. The first time they were ever really separated was in first grade, when Miss McGurdle had called their parents in to say she was worried about their—*Lacey's*—emotional health. Lacey followed her brother everywhere, and the sooner they learned to differentiate themselves—the sooner they found separate identities—the better. Oliver was moved from our classroom to 1B across the hall, which, from what I can remember, was actual hell at the time—if hell is your best friend's high-pitched shrieking for hours and hours, days on end. Finally, though, Lace settled down, and it turned out Miss McGurdle had been right. LaceyandOliver and OliverandLacey and OliverandLace and LaceandOliver became two separate people. Their parents requested every year from then on that they be put in different classes, and when they could choose for themselves, they still preferred being in separate classes.

Still, up until, like, age ten, they continued to be The Twins at home. Their parents divorced when they were nine, and their dad moved to Los Angeles to pursue a new career as a production assistant. Apparently there was a second when their parents considered Parent Trapping the twins (their mom taking one and their dad the other), but no one could imagine tearing them apart.

Now there was no real danger in doing that anymore—they were so different from each other.

But Lacey paused a moment to think about my question before shrugging.

"I guess he'll visit," she said. "Though he and Dad aren't getting along. And then there's Christmas. No way she won't make me come and spend Christmas with her." Lacey wrinkled her nose as if the mere mention of her mother filled her with distaste. "Whatever. That's clearly not happening now. Might as well get used to being back here."

"Oh," I said, because it felt selfish to say she should stay here with me, if she missed her dad that much. Plus, she was right: she couldn't leave now. School had started. She couldn't move in the middle of the school year—in the middle of *senior year,* at that. The relief covered up any sense of guilt I felt at being glad her mother hadn't let her stay in Los Angeles.

Secretly, I also wondered how Lacey could be so selfish. It had been only a few months since her mom's last really bad spell, one of those stretches of weeks when Mrs. Murdoch didn't get out of bed. Would Lace really leave Oliver to take care of her on his own? As distant as I sometimes felt from my mom, I would never just abandon her. Sure, Oliver and Lacey would soon have to leave for college, but Lacey leaving before she absolutely had to—leaving to be with her *dad,* no less—would devastate Mrs. Murdoch.

A braver person would have called Lacey on this, but I didn't.

The conversation moved on to other things, and from then on, Lacey really did seem to have made her peace with being back.

So much so that when I got a text from Oliver a couple of days later, I was actually surprised.

Hey, Eden. Does Lace seem weird to you lately?

I hesitated as I thought about it. She'd explained her moodiness. She was sad at leaving her dad, which wasn't weird at all. It felt disloyal to tell her brother what she'd told me in confidence, especially since it involved the fact that she'd been ready to leave him and their mom and move to the other side of the country. We never talked about Lacey behind her back. For the past few years, we hadn't talked very much at all.

No, I wrote back. **Why?**

Oliver's response only said, **Thanks. Thought you would know best.**

He never asked me in person and I never brought it up either.

After that, the school year continued as normal, except that there was suddenly Hail and Libby and Vance. There were parties, and bottles of vodka hidden in the back of Lacey's closet or in the trunk of her car.

When I objected, Lacey would laugh and say, "There she is. *There's* Old Edith," poking me in the cheek with her index finger. Sometimes I stood my ground, accepting the nickname (which was only clever, by the way, because it started with the same two letters as *Eden*). Other times I gave in, and we'd sit in her room drinking and binge-watching bad TV while her mother was at work. Going to parties was a bigger ask. Sure, Will would be there, and occasionally they could be tolerable, but most of the time they were just so damn exhausting. And disappointing. Maybe that was the worst part—that I had this idea of what I wanted them to be. I wanted them to be fun, to make me forget myself, to make me feel brave and seen and like I belonged among all these people I'd grown up with—but reality was always so much worse.

The only times I ever truly felt brave or like I belonged were with Lacey.

So mostly I opted out of parties. Because we were us, though, I didn't mind Lacey going to them alone or even with her new friends. I knew that somehow, in the end, she'd always come back to me, just like she had when she'd gone to LA. It may not have been her choice to come back that time, but we always found our way back to each other.

It was just the way we were.

8

GOING TO CAMP Rowan alone is not an option.

It defeats the entire purpose, which was to have an awesome throwback summer with my best friend, our one last hurrah before we head off to State in the fall. Not to drive three hours by myself and have to look after a gaggle of preteens alone, to not know anyone at the camp.

When I get home from Kiely's, I email Kim, tell her something has come up and apologize profusely that I won't be able to make it this summer.

On Monday morning, two days later, I find myself trudging to work with my dad for the second summer in a row. I make photocopies, I leave voice mails to remind people about appointments, I make coffee and answer the phone.

The week—the first of the summer before college—flies by, repetitive and quiet. It feels like a letdown after all those months of looking forward to going back to Camp Rowan.

I keep wondering at what point Lacey changed her mind about going.

I tell her as much on Friday, when we're sitting on her roof late at night, watching the stars twinkle in the sky like we've done countless times through the years.

Lacey digs a spoon into a jar of Nutella, and sighs appreciatively when it enters her mouth. She'll eat Nutella with anything.

We're supposed to be making plans, figuring out our precollege to-do list, but I'm afraid to make more plans when I don't know why they changed in the first place.

"I wish you'd have just told me," I say. "Before I went for my interview and all that stuff."

Lacey sighs again, leans down so she's lying on her back against the tiles on the roof. "I don't know," she says. "You were so excited about going. God knows why—but I swear I didn't mean to miss the interview. I really did plan on doing it."

She offers me the Nutella, but I shake my head. I lie on my back now too, cross my legs at the ankles.

"You don't know why I was so excited?"

I'm incredulous.

I feel her shoulder lift against mine, a shrug.

"When's the last time you felt, I don't know, free?" I ask. "The last time everything was simple, and you could be whatever and whoever you wanted to be." The last time everything was possible.

For me, it's the last full day we spent at camp. Me, Lacey and this girl named Kelli who completed our trio that summer. We were the oldest group of campers that year, it being our last year, and we walked around like we owned every inch of Camp Rowan. We rolled up the sleeves of our camp T-shirts so they folded at our shoulders. A group of younger campers followed us around everywhere while we did mandatory junior counselor duties. In the dining hall, we sat with a bunch of other kids our age, the only co-ed group in the whole cafeteria. Lace and I always sat together, and on either side of us there'd be boys with hair that fell into their eyes, whose unending fart jokes we pretended to be repulsed by. Kelli was dating one of them, and they held hands under the table, since dating was strictly forbidden at Camp Rowan. There was a loosely enforced thirty-centimeter rule that had turned into a running joke—partly because it was *centimeters*, thanks to the camp directors being British, but also because there was never really any consequence for crossing this arbitrary boundary. Whenever two people were spotted walking together or sitting close together, particularly a boy and a girl, somebody would teasingly call out, "THIRTY-CENTIMETER RULE!" and wedge between the couple.

As a secular camp, Camp Rowan rejected the more popular "leave room for the Holy Spirit" phrase, but the sentiment was the same. And, presumably, thirty centimeters was more than enough for the Holy Spirit.

I know it's pathetic for the best time of my life to have happened when I was fourteen—and really, it's not like I don't have hundreds of other good memories—but there's something different about the time I spent at Camp Rowan, something pure and timeless, a freedom that I haven't experienced since. I know it would have been different going back as a counselor, but even just for nostalgia's sake, just for the proximity to all those memories before we left it all behind for good, it would have been worth it.

"The last time I felt free?" Lacey repeats. "Last summer, in LA."

Her answer doesn't surprise me, but it is a little disappointing.

"You're such a weirdo," she says, nudging me with her shoulder. "You act like everything good that will ever happen has already happened."

"It feels that way sometimes," I admit.

"No way," she says. "Like, we're *free* for real now. We can get tattoos." She waves her phone, with our list on it, and wriggles her eyebrows at me. It's number two on the list: *get a tattoo.*

"I can go back to LA whenever I want. I can go and start working on my music and my mom can't do a thing to stop me."

"Aren't you forgetting a little thing called college?" Lacey has a deal with her mom that after she gets a degree, she can do whatever she wants, devote her life to music like she's always wanted to do.

Lacey doesn't answer for a moment, then she says, "Speaking of college, what did you say happened to Mia?"

"Oh my God," I say. "She's like a totally different person. She got dreads. She wears makeup. *Makeup.* I swear, she even does her eyebrows."

"Oh, well, if she does her *eyebrows,*" Lacey quips.

I laugh. "No, I'm serious. I wouldn't be surprised if she does something other than study twenty-four/seven. She might even *sleep.*"

"My God," Lacey gasps, clutching her chest. "Not our Mia."

"Right? Mom has been too busy with the party and then with getting ready for that presentation, but it's only a matter of time till the s-h hits the fan."

We are quiet for a moment and then I say, "If one year in college can change *Mia,* I wonder what will happen to us in a year." I wonder if we'll be sitting here on Lacey's roof in a year's time, home for the summer with new stories and adventures, new lives under our belts.

Lace is more concerned about this summer, the one she seems to feel is spooling out too quickly around us.

"I can't believe you chickened out," she says. "What am I supposed to do, skinny-dip *twice*? Or just watch you skinny-dip?"

"We could just cross it off the list and consider it done. Say you took one for the team."

Lacey harrumphs. "Yeah, that's not happening. You're not getting out of this. There are only five things on the list. Five. We *both* have to do everything on it."

"I thought that meant doing it together." From the moment she got the idea for it a few months ago, the list has always intimidated me. The one comfort—the one thing that made it okay—was that we'd be doing it all together.

"It would have been together, if you'd joined in," she retorts.

"Well, if we'd gone to Camp Rowan, we'd have gotten the road trip out of the way," I shoot back, and then we are both silent, a standoff.

"We'll take another road trip," Lacey says. "Maybe the drive to State."

"Maybe," I say, though hell would probably freeze over before my parents passed on personally escorting me to college.

We are quiet then, and my thoughts trail off until they wind up where they've kept drifting to for the past three weeks.

"I can't believe Will is never going to college." He's never going to play lacrosse for the Bruins on the scholarship he worked so hard for.

"Maybe he's playing somewhere better," Lacey says, reading my thoughts, and I turn to her, surprised.

"Better than at State?"

"Maybe," she says.

"Lace," I say, voice shaking. "He's *dead*. How can you say that?"

"I just mean," she begins, "we don't know where he is. Maybe it's someplace better than here. *Hopefully* it's someplace better than here. We have to believe that, right?"

"Right," I say, but something still feels wrong about what she's said. He's dead. He's not coming back.

No matter where he is, he's no longer with his family, with his friends. Will didn't want someplace better than here; he wanted to play lacrosse in college.

I can't get over the unfairness of the fact that he will never get his wish.

With the conversation turned to Will, I remember In Good Company for the first time. Signing up in Lacey's bathroom while she slept, a week ago. I still haven't told her what I did.

I start to say something, but Lacey is speaking over me.

"So who kissed who?" she asks. "That night. Who made the first move?"

My mind flashes back to the night he died, to Brendan's party, to Will's lips millimeters from mine.

Lacey could never stand the way things went with me and Will, the silent pining, the quiet wanting, the waiting for him to notice me. She thought I should have done something, should have *made* him notice me. Should have told him straight out that I was in love with him.

"I did," I say. Lace keeps watching me, waiting for more, but I'm not really in the mood to talk about it. What does it matter who kissed who?

I'm never going to see Will again. I had five years to make something happen with him, and I wasted them being afraid— that I wouldn't say the right thing, that I wasn't good enough, that

I wasn't the type of girl he went for, that he wouldn't like me back, that he *would*. All of that no longer matters.

Everything we could have been died that night along with him.

Lacey shifts beside me, but neither of us speaks.

In the silence that follows, I have my chance to tell her about calling Will, the way it felt to hear his voice again, but for some reason, I can't make the words come out.

9

EVEN IN THE summer, I never have enough layers for the ice rink. After all these years, you'd think I would have developed a system, but I'm still always at least one layer short. Today, as soon as Sam peels off her sweater to go out onto the ice, I steal it and pull it on, even though it's about three sizes too small.

It's Saturday, so the rink is open to the public, which means it is teeming with families and couples. A few people are on the bleachers, spectating like Mia and I are, but most of them are here enjoying the coolest place in Erinville today.

If anyone had asked, I would have given a hard pass to the notion of spending my first day off all week watching Samara's practice. And I'm sure Mia would have too. But no one did ask, and my mother did "suggest" we all come, and so we are here. Sam and her dance partner, Ty, are practicing a new routine with Sergiy while my parents and Ty's mom lean over the wall and try to watch them through the mess of people on the ice. From this far away, I can hear Ty, ever the diva, complaining about bumping into people when he spins out of his twizzles, and my mother keeps holding out Sam's bottle every few minutes to remind her to hydrate. It's not an official practice—those are normally three days a week after school, and a little more sporadic in the summer—but they apparently had to practice today because they are behind on some new choreography. If it was an official practice, parents would not be allowed to lean over the walls. I once saw Sergiy yelling at a mom for trying to get on the ice to fix a bow on her daughter's costume during a lesson. "This," he said, drawing an invisible circle around the rink with his finger, "is my classroom." He pointed toward the bleachers. "That is your space."

In his defense, she was a complete stage mom.

But if Sergiy hadn't won an Olympic medal for Ukraine, like, twenty years ago, and if he wasn't the only decent ice dance coach in the vicinity of Erinville, parents might pull their kids out. Granted, for every parent who considers Sergiy a tyrant, there's one who thinks he hung the moon and stars and calls him "Buns and Thighs" behind his . . . well, buns and thighs.

It is one of the grossest things in the world, sitting through a practice or an ice show where people my parents' age are drooling over their kids' teacher. Serg is not completely innocent in this, though. He is definitely aware of his best features, frequently playing them up in tight black pants and tight shirts that show off his biceps. He's probably just as obsessively dedicated to pumping iron in the gym as he is to flawless lifts and perfect synchronicity in his students.

"Why did you decide to move here, Serg?" Mom asks every few lessons, thanking her lucky stars. "Don't get me wrong, we're grateful. *So* grateful. But why Erinville? Of all places!"

I think it's because he has family nearby or something like that.

"For a long time, we were worried we might have to let go of the sport, or move, if Sam was going to continue," Mom had said in a low voice at the last lesson I came to.

"If I hadn't come, you better have moved," Sergiy had responded, pointing at the award-winning duo of Paulsen-Wolfe. "It would have been a waste. A big shame."

If they hadn't been doing so well, I'd have said Serg's words were proof that Mom's kissing up was paying off, but the past three years that Ty and Sam have been dancing together have proven that he is right.

Future Olympians, competition judges have told us.

Born performers.

Gifted beyond their years.

Sergiy's goal—and Mom's and Ty's and Sam's—is to make Paulsen-Wolfe a household name someday, and they are well on their way.

Right now, my parents are talking with their heads close together, laughing as they watch the kids perform. I wonder if they are tempted to rent a couple of skates and glide out onto the ice themselves, disappear into the crowd like the lovesick teenagers they sometimes act like. My parents have always been PDA-prone, but they've taken it to a new level since Dad's TIA. It's as if realizing what almost happened has made them hold on to each other that much tighter.

Beside me, Mia gives a big sigh and shifts in her seat. "I could have been prepping for the summit right now," she says. And it reminds me that she's only here for a couple more weeks. Soon, she'll be gone for the rest of the summer. My sisters and I have never been the closest, but up until Mia went to college, we at least always knew about each other's lives.

I don't know whether she's made friends or whether she likes her classes or why she suddenly looks so different. She doesn't know that the boy whose picture has been splattered all over the news for weeks is the same boy I've been in love with since I was thirteen. She doesn't know that I heard his voice again a week ago or that I'm thinking about him almost every time I'm silent.

And now she's leaving again.

"Are you excited?" I ask, knowing what her answer will be. Spending the entire summer in DC, going to Congress and doing whatever else she'll be doing, has been one of Mia's dreams since she was a kid.

To my surprise, she only shrugs. "I don't know," she says. "It feels like it's so soon."

The unexpectedness of her response reminds me again of how different she seems, how different she looks, and I have to ask her about it.

"So what's Stanford like, Mee? Yah," I add when she turns to glare at me.

Mee-yah. She's always hated any and all nicknames.

"Big," she says, giving nothing away.

"I can't believe out of all of us, you ended up in California," I say. Mia, who refused to go to Camp Rowan and spent all her summers at science day camps, both because she loved science and because she could never deal with sleepaway camp. She missed home too much, missed *Mom* too much.

"What's that supposed to mean?" she asks, offended.

"I just mean . . . Lacey's, like, obsessed with LA."

"She's going to State, though, isn't she?" Mia asks, and I nod.

That's the one thing that makes the thought of college less daunting. The fact that I'll be with Lacey, that I already have a roommate, a partner for class assignments, someone to brave the cafeteria with.

When I say this to Mia, she says, "You talk about it like it's high school. It's so . . . different."

"How?" I ask.

"I don't know. But nobody gives a shit what you do. It's like for the first time in your life, you get to make your own choices, your own mistakes. And you have absolutely no one to hide behind."

I stare at her as she speaks, at the way her face is rounder, the sleek gloss on her lips. "That sounds lonely," I say, because that's all I can think. Is that how Mia has felt all this time, being away at college?

She shrugs.

"Maybe it's different when you go in knowing people," I say gently.

"Maybe," she says.

"Has Mom said anything about your hair?" I ask now, because I have to know.

"Nope. She's very deliberately *not* saying anything about it," Mia says with a smirk, and it surprises me, the fact that she's not terrified of pushing Mom's buttons. That she seems to genuinely not care what Mom thinks of her dreads.

Mia pulls out her phone to check something.

I glance up and notice that Sam is off the ice, taking a swig from the water bottle Mom was holding before. She's still wearing her skates as she wobbles over to us.

"Can I borrow someone's phone?" she asks, a strain of panic in her voice. Mia throws her phone down to Sam, whose eyes immediately become fixed to the small screen in front of her.

"Oh my God," she says dramatically, dropping onto the nearest bleacher.

Mia and I exchange a look. "What's wrong?" I ask.

"Ty had the stomach flu three days ago. He spent all day throwing up and he only *just* told me. I'm going to die."

"Are you feeling sick?" Mia asks.

"Not yet," Sam says, "but obviously it's only a matter of time."

"He's probably no longer contagious."

"You're contagious for three days after." Sam waves the phone impatiently. "We're *right at* three days. How could he be so selfish? What if I throw up?"

"Pretty sure throwing up is not fatal," I say, which is exactly the wrong thing to say, because Sam narrows her eyes at me.

As far as my younger sister has ever been concerned, throwing up is terminal.

"Did I say you could wear my sweater?" she spits at me. "Your arms are stretching it out!" She is not incorrect, but I don't see any reason to admit that.

"You're not even using it," I point out.

"Right. Because you are wearing it," she says, holding out her hand for it.

Seriously?

I roll my eyes and peel off the sweater, throw it down to her.

She slips it on before heading back onto the ice. Probably just to keep me from using it. Sam is as famously unaffected by the cold as Ty is incapacitated by it.

When she gets on the ice, she keeps her distance from Ty, until we hear Serg scolding them because you can't exactly dance with a good five feet in between you.

Mia snorts a laugh. Then she says the most unexpected thing she's said all day. "God, I've missed you guys."

10

ON MONDAY MORNING, my father perches on the edge of the desk I share with his secretary and leans close so only I can hear. "Eden, I have some very important business for you. A top-secret mission," he says.

He hands me a white, card-size envelope.

"What's this?"

"Ah, well, it wouldn't be *secret* if I told you, now, would it?"

It's only nine a.m. and there's not enough coffee in my bloodstream to handle my father's sense of humor this early.

"So what am I doing with it?"

"I need you to deliver it to a top-secret address."

"Is the address too top-secret for me to know what it is?"

"It's on the front of the envelope," he tells me with a wink before disappearing into his office.

I turn the envelope over before answering the ringing phone beside me and roll my eyes when I see it's addressed to Dr. Maura Paulsen.

Official business, my ass.

It would be just like my parents to write raunchy letters to each other and then to have their *child* deliver them.

After I finish on the phone, I stop in at my dad's office to give him a piece of my mind, but he's already elbows-deep in somebody's mouth in the exam room. I stand watching him for a moment, not to be a total creep, but because of how happy he sounds, chatting to his dental assistant as he works. The only person happier at work than my mom is my dad. He jokes that life after the TIA is like living in California, waiting for the Big One, the hypothetical earthquake to end all earthquakes. You know there's a good chance it's coming; you just don't know when. I know the possibility of another stroke, a bigger one with permanent damage, terrifies him because he could end up losing the fine motor skills he needs as a dentist. What would he do if he can't fix people's teeth? Who would he be?

I return to the reception area and explain to Bethany, Dad's perpetually pregnant secretary, that I'm heading out on an errand for him.

"Oh, you get to go out into the sunshine?" she muses. "No fair."

"I know," I say. "Nepotism at its finest."

She laughs. "Grab me a Diet Coke on your way back?"

"Okay," I tell her, then head out of the office.

My parents' offices are across town from each other, a setup probably designed to prevent them from passing love notes to each other throughout the day, but one that they seem to pay little mind to.

I pull up in front of the professional building my mom works in. It is gray, dusty-looking in the way many old buildings are. Mom rarely sees patients these days; most of her time is spent writing, working on her latest book or whatever presentation she's giving next.

I don't come here very often, so I never remember the code I need to get inside the building. I pull out my phone and call Mom. It rings and rings, then goes to voice mail.

I'm typing out a text to her when I see it.

When I see her.

Far across the parking lot, at the side of the building, which is reserved for emergency exits, Mom is holding the glass door open while Sergiy backs out.

Sergiy.

My sister's coach.

My mind is already searching for an explanation. He's there to talk about Sam's routine or maybe Mom forgot to pay him or maybe he needs an advance on his next check or maybe he's going back to Ukraine? What if he's going back to Ukraine and Sam and Ty won't have a coach and he wanted to break it to my mother gently?

But he does not seem to be breaking any bad news to her, and she does not seem to be pushing him away when he wraps his arm around her lower back and pulls her in close.

No.

Sergiy takes over holding the door open with one hand while the other arm encases my mother. They obviously don't want the door to close, or Mom will be locked out and have to go around the front, the way she gets in in the morning. The way I get in. The way my dad gets in when he comes to visit her.

No no no.

No.

She's resting her head against his chest, and then after what feels like years he kisses her on the forehead, saying something, which causes her to nod. And then he's reluctantly backing away from her and walking toward his car somewhere in this parking lot, and Mom goes inside and finally lets the door close, with her on the right side of it.

And this is how I watch everything I've ever known collapse.

Against the backdrop of a building that is gray and dusty in the way old buildings often are.

I stay frozen as Sergiy enters his car on the other side of the parking lot and drives off.

Then I lean my head against the steering wheel and try to remember how to breathe. Tears feel like acid stinging the backs of my eyes, and no matter how hard I blink them away, they carve a trail down my cheeks.

I stay there for ten minutes, struggling for air, struggling to figure out what to do next.

I reach into my bag and pull out the envelope that Dad sent me here with.

There's no way I'm going in after her, no way I'm giving this to her now.

Before I can stop myself, I rip open the envelope.

All that's inside is a printed piece of paper—a flight itinerary for September 14, the weekend my mom is supposed to be presenting at a conference in Montana. It's ages away, but my mom hates flying and he wants her to know that she doesn't have to go alone. He's planning to go with her.

He's planning to go with her, and for all I know there's no conference. It's just some elaborate ploy for her to meet with Sergiy and continue to screw Dad over.

I crumple the piece of paper in my hand and toss it into the back seat.

I want to scream at her.

I want to march inside my mother's office and shout until my voice is hoarse. I want to tell her what I saw, make her explain herself to me.

Maybe I'm wrong.

Maybe there's some kind of explanation for what I saw.

Except that there isn't.

There's nothing she can say that will make the way Sergiy was looking at her, the way he touched her—the way she touched *him* back—okay.

My phone vibrates then.

A text from Dad.

Is it handled? he says, still keeping up his covert-business spy persona, and my heart breaks a little more because this is Dad. Dad, who has loved my mother since they were nineteen, who would do anything for her.

Two months ago, he could have been dead.

My throat feels tight, like all my breath is trapped inside.

I stare at my phone, fingers poised to type, but I can't make them move.

I can't tell him what I saw.

How am I supposed to go back to work and face him after this?

I could call Mia, but I can't imagine myself saying the words.

Mom is cheating on Dad.

Mom is cheating on Dad with Sergiy.

There's only one person I can imagine telling.

I send a text to Lace.

Call me ASAP.

11

I WAIT HALF an hour in my car in front of Mom's office building, but Lacey still hasn't responded.

My phone vibrates with another text from Dad.

Everything OK?

Before he tries to call me, I text him back. I don't trust my voice right now. Don't trust the words that would come out of my mouth.

Yep. On my way back, I write.

Even as I send those words, a sick feeling swirls in my stomach. I can't imagine anything being okay ever again.

I drive back to Dad's office and pull into the parking lot, but I can't bring myself to leave the car yet. I kill time trying to fix my tearstained face, trying to wipe the tracks of mascara from underneath my eyes.

When there's nothing left to do, I take a deep breath and climb out of the car.

"Oh, there you are! I thought we'd lost you to the sunshine," Beth says when I enter the office.

"Sorry. It took longer than I expected," I mumble, willing myself to look her in the eye, to act normal.

"Did you get my drink?" she asks, rubbing her swollen belly.

"Oh, shit," I say. "I mean, shoot," I amend as a frown etches itself into her forehead. "I'm so sorry. I can go back and get it."

"No, that's okay," she says, waving her hand.

"Are you sure? I can go back. It won't take long."

"No, no," she says. "What I need more than anything right now is for you to man the phones while I go pee for the hundredth time today."

"Sure," I say, and watch her disappear down the hallway to the bathroom.

Right on cue, the phone starts ringing. I reach for it as I pull up the booking page on my computer.

The woman on the line wants to see Dad to get her broken tooth looked at. She launches into a story about how she was eating popcorn and then heard a crunch and I try to follow what she's saying but I feel disoriented, like I've been spun in a circle several times.

I hang up with her and am busy booking another patient when Dad comes out of his office. He is grinning, pleased with himself, as he approaches me.

"Did you get it done?"

Shit.

"Um, yeah," I lie.

"What did she say?"

"She didn't read it yet," I say. It's all I can think of off the top of my head. Dad frowns and I stare hard at the computer screen.

I hope to God he doesn't text or call her and find out I never delivered it.

"Well, thanks for doing that," he says.

I nod, feeling panicked in the silence that follows. I'm afraid if he looks too long, he'll see the truth scribbled on my face. Thankfully, Bethany chooses that moment to reappear and then she and Dad are chatting about some paperwork. Once he goes in to see his next patient, I feel the tension leave my body.

"Did you just book in Mallory Hemsworth?" Beth asks me.

"Yeah," I say.

"You have her in for three *a.m.* next Wednesday."

"Oh God. Sorry."

"Here, I'll fix it. And Tom Bailey? You have him in for September fifteenth, but your dad is away that day."

September 15. The weekend Dad booked off so he could go to the conference with my mother.

The thing I just don't get is *why*.

Why would she do something like this, when they are the happiest people I know? What is worth ruining our entire family, destroying my father, over?

"Maybe you could do some photocopying," Bethany suggests gently.

I spend the rest of the afternoon photocopying hundreds of new-patient forms, until I somehow manage to jam the printer. After several minutes of trying to fix it myself, followed by more failed attempts by Bethany, I am demoted to organizing and filing patient folders.

At the end of the day, I breathe a massive sigh of relief and am packing up my stuff when Dad sticks his head into the break room.

"Can't wait to get out of here, huh?" he asks.

"It's just—I have to meet Lacey. We're hanging out," I lie.

"Ah," he says. Then, after a moment, "Are you sure you're okay? You've seemed distracted all day."

"I'm good," I say, unable to meet his eyes. "I have to go. I'm running late."

"Okay," he says. "See you at home."

I nod. He gives me a kiss on the forehead and then I slip past him and out of the clinic.

In my car, a tidal wave of emotion threatens to overtake me, but I do everything I can to push it down.

I pull out my cell phone.

Still nothing from Lacey.

It's just after five.

Mom will be home by now.

I feel sick at the thought of facing her. Watching her pretend, lie to our faces.

I could beat my dad home and confront her. Make her explain everything, when it started, how, where, why.

Why.

How long has she been lying to us? To my dad?

What if it's worse than I can imagine?

What if she's in love with Serg?

I'm too afraid to hear what she'll say.

I can't go home.

Right now, it feels like I can never go home again.

I drive to the only place I can think of.

12

I KNOCK ONCE on Lacey's front door and wait.

Knock again and there's no answer, no movement on the other side of the door.

Suddenly everything I've been suppressing is rising up in my chest and tears are streaming down my face.

I pound on the door, not even caring whether my mascara is ruined or if Mrs. Murdoch is home and thinks I'm a lunatic. But there's no answer.

I suddenly feel too heavy to move, like I've dunked myself in a swimming pool fully clothed. I lean back against the side of the house, defeated.

There's no one home.

Lace, I need you. I text it, then send it out again telepathically, with a bat signal or anything that will reach her.

Put out there what I want, like my fucking hypocrite of a mother would say, but nothing happens. Lacey doesn't write back.

Pushing myself up from the wall, I start slowly down the porch steps. I'm almost at my car when the front door creaks open behind me. I whirl around, but it's Oliver, not Lacey.

He's quickly slipping a dark blue polo over his head. It has the words MORE FOR LESS in big, bold letters.

"Hey, Ed—" He stops short when he catches a glimpse of my face, bloated and puffy-eyed, and then he steps out the door, barefoot, toward me. "Shit. Are you okay?"

I take some quick swipes at my face, then fold my arms across my chest. Embarrassment makes me defensive. "I was looking for Lacey," I say.

Oliver doesn't take any more steps toward me, but he watches me carefully. "She's not home yet, but she finished at five, so I'm guessing she'll be here soon," he says.

"Do you think I could wait?" I ask. "Till she gets here?"

"Yeah, sure," Oliver says, pushing his hand through his hair. He throws a quick look over his shoulder and into the house.

I follow him back inside, and the reason for his hesitation immediately becomes clear.

A tall girl with blond ringlets of hair framing her face is standing in the living room.

"Eden, this is Beckah," Oliver says, shutting the front door and coming to join us in the living room. "Beckah, Eden."

She gives me a little wave and smiles at me. There's a tiny gap between her two front teeth, but somehow it only adds to the brilliance of her smile. She's *gorgeous*.

"Nice to meet you," I say, suddenly feeling like a total idiot for coming here looking the way I do. Sure, I couldn't have sprouted an extra twelve inches between Dad's work and Lacey's house, but I wish I'd at least taken the time to fix my smudged makeup before pounding on the door like a freaking moron. Or I could have just waited in my car. My voice still has that after-an-ugly-cry nasal quality.

"Beckah runs for Dale Heights," Oliver says, then turns to her. "Or I guess *ran*, right?" He rubs the back of his neck.

She laughs, a throaty, warm laugh. "*I'm* not going back. I don't know about you," she teases. I can't tell whether she's the same girl from the last-day-of-school bonfire. Probably not.

I force out a laugh, hoping it sounds authentic. It's doubtful that I manage this, judging by the way Oliver is looking at me.

Before things get even more awkward, I decide to excuse myself. "I'm going to go upstairs and wait for Lacey," I tell Oliver, and he nods, a concerned look on his face.

"Nice meeting you," Beckah says as I turn to go.

I hurry upstairs to Lacey's room. The inside is typically messy, clothes strewn everywhere, books and magazines spilling from her shelves onto the floor. There's nowhere to sit on her bed and I don't think she's seen the surface of her desk in years. I pull open her window and climb onto the roof.

Once I'm there, I let out a long breath and close my eyes.

Lacey still hasn't texted me back. She's probably driving home from work.

I spend the next few minutes looking down at the street, trying to wash the image of Sergiy and Mom from my mind. I feel like I need to sterilize my brain to get the sight of his hand on her waist out, to get the look she gave him, intimate and knowing, off my mind.

I'm looking down at the ground below when I see Beckah striding across the street to a light blue Volvo. From this far away, the only thing I can see is that she is about seventy-five percent legs. No wonder she caught Oliver's attention.

"Mind if I join you?" Oliver asks, and I jump at the sound of his voice. "Sorry," he says.

"It's okay," I say. He flops down next to me, leaning back on his palms.

"Beckah seems nice," I say, because it's something to say.

"Yeah, she is." He rubs the back of his neck. "You okay?" he asks, looking over at me.

I play with a loose string on the bottom of my shirt. "I'm fine."

Oliver nods, but there's a flicker of something in his face, something that looks a little like hurt. There was a time when there was no difference between Oliver and Lacey for me, when they were both the people I knew best in the world. But time changes everything, and it's been years since Oliver and I have hung out, since we've talked about anything that matters.

"Can I do anything?" he asks. "I know I'm not Lacey, but . . . maybe I could help."

The kindness in his voice makes me feel like crying all over again.

I consider doing it, just coming out and spewing the words, but I can't string any sentences together. I can't imagine hearing those words out in the open without Lace's calmness, her ability to take charge and fix things, coaxing them out.

"I don't think so," I say, after several moments have passed. "Thanks, though."

Oliver keeps watching me, tugs on one of the springy curls at the back of his head.

Silence spools out like a ball of yarn between us, and I feel a pang of regret at rejecting his offer. It's true that there's nothing he can do, but maybe I'd feel better not being the only one holding this gigantic secret.

"*More for Less*," I say, pointing at the blue polo Oliver is wearing. "You're working there all summer?"

Oliver nods. "They're hiring, if you're interested," he says. "I know you and Lace were supposed to go to Rowan."

"I'm working at my dad's for the summer," I say.

We both turn to look out onto the street again. This time, the silence is softer, less tense.

"You should stay for dinner," he says. "I'm making this turkey chili."

"You cook?"

Oliver pretends to be wounded by the surprise in my voice. "Your tone is very hurtful," he says, but almost immediately he's grinning at me. "Of course I cook. Not *well*, necessarily. Just . . . you know, I do it to help Mom out sometimes."

He plays with a feather resting against the tiling on the roof.

All of a sudden, my mind flashes years back, to the days soon after Lacey and Oliver's father left. Lacey and I spent every waking moment at my house, because their house was bleak and Mrs. Murdoch was prone to bursting into tears at any given moment. Later, she wouldn't get out of bed at all. I remember how their house seemed to have tilted, like one half of it was on level ground and the other had sunk into sadness. We liked being at my house better because it was still upright. My parents were still laughing at each other's jokes and checking out each other's butts and the one thing I never had to worry about was them, because they were solid and because of that *we* were solid.

I was solid.

For all the time we spent avoiding their house, Oliver never did, preferring to stay close to Mrs. Murdoch, to make sure nothing happened to her.

He still hasn't changed very much.

"So, dinner?" Oliver asks, cutting into my thoughts.

Before I can answer, though, a gray car turns onto their street.

"She's here," I say, and Oliver glances up to confirm this, which means we both see what happens next. Lacey's car pulls only halfway into the driveway before it stops, then begins to back up onto the road.

"Where's she going?" I ask as her car pulls back out onto the street, then disappears from view. I can see my car from here, parked by the curb next to her house, and she has to have seen it, so why would she leave without saying anything if she knows I'm inside?

The pieces rearrange in slow motion in my head, and suddenly everything from the last few weeks—the unanswered texts, the way she blew off her Camp Rowan interview, how much time she's been spending with Hail and Co.—it all makes sense.

But just in case it didn't, a phone vibrates between us. Oliver reaches into his pocket and pulls it out. I can see the exact moment he regrets doing so. There's a split-second frown on his face and then he looks up at me, but I already understand.

"That's Lacey, isn't it?"

She saw my car.

She's seen my texts.

She's asking him for a favor—to get rid of me, or lie for her, or tell her when the coast is clear—and even as everything inside me seems to explode, everything is finally making sense.

"Eden—" Oliver says, trying to explain, even though he can see in my expression that it's too late.

I know what's going on.

"Listen, she's being weird. I don't know what—"

"It's okay," I say, cutting him off, and I'm already standing, moving around him to climb back into Lacey's room.

My body is warm with humiliation.

Lacey is avoiding me.

"I'm going to go," I say, a calm I don't feel taking over my voice, even as the refrain from earlier, in Mom's parking lot, overtakes my mind. *No. No no no.*

I climb back into Lacey's room, and a second later, Oliver is back inside too.

"Could you do me a favor?" I ask, anger superseding every other emotion.

Oliver is still trying to defend her, to make me feel better. "She's being weird with everyone, Eden."

"Tell Lacey," I say, the edge in my voice making me feel powerful. "Tell your sister to go and fuck herself."

I think my voice cracks on the last word, but it doesn't matter. I'm already racing out of their house, and if Oliver says anything else, I don't hear.

By the time I reach my car, hot tears are starting to blur my vision, but I force them back.

I get into my car and drive to the last place I want to be.

I drive home.

13

THEY'RE IN THE middle of dinner when I get inside. Sitting around the dining table, talking and laughing just like normal.

So she's really doing it.

She's really going to pretend she hasn't just fucked over my dad.

"Eden!" Dad says. "Your mom just tried calling you. She said you didn't mention you were meeting Lacey?"

I'm storming past them, head fixed straight forward, because I can't see her face. I think I would actually explode if I had to look at her.

"Where are you going?" Mom asks me.

I don't answer, just keep moving forward, my messenger bag slapping at my thigh with every aggressive step.

"Eden?" Mom calls again.

The sound of cutlery clanging against plates grows irregular, my sisters probably slowing their eating to gape at me.

"I'm not hungry," I snap, still not stopping to look at her.

"Eden, come on, that's disrespectful. Your mom is having a

conversation with you," I hear Dad say, standing, as I reach the stairs and start to take them two at a time. It makes my stomach roil to hear him defending her.

I've just reached my bedroom and slammed the door shut behind me when there's a knock on the other side of it.

Dad pokes his head in, and he's frowning.

"What was all that about?" he asks, sounding disappointed.

I look away from him, move some stuff around on my desk so I don't have to make eye contact. There's nothing worse than Dad's disappointment. It is all big, sorrowful eyes and a gentle voice, meant to make you feel like absolute crap if you didn't already.

"I ate at Lacey's," I lie.

"Then you should have let us know you were doing that. And the way you acted down there just now? Unacceptable. You owe your mother an apology."

He never once raises his voice as he speaks, and it takes everything I have not to tell him that I never intend on speaking to her again. Not if I can help it.

"Your mother didn't get the envelope you delivered. You didn't tell me you didn't see her," he says.

I think fast. "I slipped it under her door. Maybe someone took it or something." The lies are just spilling out of me tonight.

Then I remember that no matter how many lies I tell, I can't be as bad as Mom, and that makes me feel the slightest bit better.

"Oh," Dad says. "Are you sure everything is okay?"

I nod.

"Sorry about the letter," I say.

"That's fine," he says, coming over and giving me a hug. "Apparently I just need a more reliable courier service next time."

I force a laugh, wait until the door has shut behind him to have my full meltdown.

How can she sit there and eat with them?

How can she let my dad hold her hand and brag on her in front of his friends and pinch her butt at dinner parties, and the whole time she's just playing a stupid game?

She's just . . . I can't even wrap my head around it.

That my mom, who writes books and speeches and stands on stages around the country, telling people they can have the perfect life she has, is doing the one thing she can do to fuck it up.

How long has she been doing it?

How damn *stupid* are we, the four of us, worshipping at her feet and believing that she is something she is not? What about everything she says about how all our actions reflect on our family?

There is something that feels so patently unfair about the timing of all this. The fact that it's happening just after Dad's TIA. The fact that I'm heading to college in a couple of months and everything is changing and the one thing that isn't supposed to change is my family, my home.

How could she *do* this?

My parents got the fairy tale, the happily ever after. They're not supposed to be broken and fucked up like everyone else is.

I get into bed fully clothed, pull the covers over my head.

I stay curled up that way for what feels like hours and then there is a knock on my door. I hear it swing open before I even have the chance to answer.

"Honey, is everything okay?" Her voice betrays nothing that would suggest she knows that she's why I'm not okay. With the sheets still covering me, she can't see my face, so it's easier to talk to her, to lie to her.

"Upset stomach," I say, because it's the only thing I can think of.

She takes a few steps into my room and then I can feel the weight of her knee pressed into my mattress while she places her hand on my body. The urge to jerk from her touch makes me realize that I've said exactly the wrong thing.

"Do you want to try some Pepto? What did you have for dinner?"

"I'm fine. I think I just need to sleep it off."

I feel her hesitation, but, thankfully, she doesn't argue with me. "Okay. But I don't think I have to tell you that no matter how you're feeling, taking it out on us is not the way to deal with things. You were really rude tonight."

I'm not apologizing.

There is no way in hell I'm going to apologize to her, when what she has done is so much worse. I stay frozen, burritoed in my sheets. She thinks she can wait me out. One, two, three minutes, but I can wait forever.

Finally she says, "Did you . . . When you came by today, was it before or after lunch?"

I immediately understand what she's asking: Was I there when Serg was? Could I have seen anything suspicious?

"After," I lie. I swear I hear her exhale in relief. "Why?"

I'm daring her to tell me the truth.

She won't.

Of course she won't.

But I give her the chance anyway.

"I stepped out before lunch," she says. "I just wondered if you came by when I was out."

I didn't know how much her answer, her honesty, would mean until she lied.

"So you came by in the afternoon?" she asks again, double-checking, reassuring herself that she's safe. It's such weak re-assurance. She could easily find out the truth by asking Dad when I left for her office, but she won't. It's easier to believe what she wants, to believe what I'm telling her.

"Yep," I say. It's all I can manage without my voice breaking.

"You're sure you're okay?" she asks. "You don't want something for your stomach?"

I don't answer. I refuse to give her anything by crying in her presence.

After a couple of minutes, she sighs, rises and heads out of my room. Hopefully she thinks I've fallen asleep.

I lie there, replaying everything over and over again, seething at Mom, at Lacey, mostly at Mom. In some ways, they are exactly the same, breaking something solid for no apparent reason. Lacey is Mom, abandoning the person who trusts her the most. Mom is Lacey, proving how little I matter, how little Dad matters.

My mother is a liar.

I think what hurts the most is that what I saw makes every-thing invalid. The way she rallied around Dad when he was sick, eyes swollen, face free of makeup. Every word she's ever said about how to conduct yourself, live your life, find your happiness. Everything she says about her family being the thing she most values.

She doesn't give a fuck about us. She cares about selling some picture of perfection, fooling us into playing the correct roles without us knowing we're doing it.

The urge to scream and throw something is gone now, and all that's left is this burning need to talk to someone. To tell someone what I saw.

I consider crossing the hall and going to Mia, but if there's one person it would devastate almost as much as Dad, it's Mia.

She thinks the world of Mom.

I have to figure out what to do, how to handle this on my own.

I reach for my phone, and of course there are no messages or calls from Lacey.

Of their own accord, my fingers start to dial her number, and then it's ringing and I'm listening to her tell me to leave a message and I've never wanted to talk to my best friend more in my life.

And she doesn't want to talk to me.

I feel a physical pain in my chest, like something breaking.

I sit there for a long time, desperate to hear a voice I recognize, someone I can trust. I'm mentally going through the names of people I know.

New Age Lauren.

Megan Tomey.

Alex Reynolds.

But the truth is, I don't know them nearly well enough for a conversation like this. The fact that Lacey and I floated from group to group in high school has come back to haunt me. It means I know a little bit about a lot of people, but not a lot about any of them.

Lacey used to feel like enough.

And then it hits me.

Will.

He's dead, the voice in my head tells me.

I remember standing at his mother's door, handing her his jacket like a peace offering. The number she gave me in return.

He's dead.

But that doesn't mean I can't talk to him.

14

"**EDEN!**" He says my name the way you say an old friend's, a familiarity and warmth in his voice that make me instantly feel a little better. And he sounds so much like himself, so much like the Will I knew, that it makes me want to cry. "I hoped you'd call again. How have you been?"

The first word that comes to mind is *horrible,* but I don't want to start the conversation off on a bad note, so I make a noncommittal noise.

I scoot backward on my bed till I'm leaning against the wall, then I bring my knees up to my chest.

"Tell me something good," I whisper, desperate to flush every bad thing today has brought out of my mind. My mother, Serg, Lacey.

"Let's see," Will says, sounding like he is actually thinking about it. "Oh! The Bruins beat the Cavs last night. Last game of the season."

A smile starts to stretch across my face, because he *definitely* still sounds like himself. He still sounds like the boy I loved for all of high school.

But almost immediately, the warm feeling of recognition is replaced by something else.

"How do you know that?" I ask, voice low.

"I have my ways," he says, and I can hear the smile in his voice.

"No, seriously. How do you know that?"

"The same way anybody knows anything," Will quips. "The internet."

"You can get on the internet?" I ask, my mind spinning at the thought. It occurs to me that I know practically nothing about how this whole Companion thing works. It's a computer program, right? Full of information about the Cognitive Donor—about Will. So it makes sense that it would be interested in lacrosse.

"I get updates," he says. "It all gets uploaded to the old memory."

"Oh," I say, and a strange sense overtakes me. Like maybe calling Will tonight—or ever—wasn't a good idea. Like maybe I'm in over my head.

I mean, I'm talking to a *program*. A program designed to be exactly like Will, but a program all the same.

He gets *updates*.

How fucked up is that?

Neither of us is speaking, so I pull up the internet on my phone and check the results of the game the Bruins played against the Cavs.

"So what was the score?" I hear myself asking. It's not that I don't believe him, exactly. I just need to hear it from him for some reason, to feel like we are existing in the same universe, not some parallel world in which Will is still alive.

"Seventeen to ten," he says without missing a beat. Then, almost like he can see me, can sense my disbelief, he adds, "Hilson scored twice in the last quarter, and Jerry had an unbelievable save in the third or the Cavs would have gone up on us. Any further questions?"

I don't know if any of what he's said is true, but he's right about the score and, therefore, probably everything else too.

"Um, no," I say. "No further questions."

He laughs. That deep, full laugh that always sent tingles down my spine.

"So you're fine with it?" I ask. "Following the Bruins, despite . . ." I hesitate. "Everything."

Despite being dead.

Despite never getting to play for them, like he always wanted to.

I swear I can feel him shrug through the phone. "I don't know, Eden," he says. "I have to be, right?"

And of all the things that have caught me off guard since the first time I spoke to Will on the phone, it is this that shocks me the most.

He sounds . . . *wistful*. Like there are things he misses about being alive, things he remembers, things he wants.

And yet he's a program. A series of zeros and ones on a computer somewhere.

"Do you remember me?" I ask now, my voice small, and I hold my breath for his answer. Him remembering me would mean that I meant something to him, that all our interactions were more than just flirting and joking around, that what happened between us on the night he died mattered.

"Not specifically," he says, after a beat. "I don't remember *anyone* specifically. But it doesn't mean I don't know you."

"Right," I say, swallowing the surge of disappointment.

"All it means," he says, cheerful, "is that you have to remind me who you are. How did we know each other?" I hesitate.

He wasn't my boyfriend. I don't want to lie to him.

"We were friends," I say.

There's a breath of silence before he says, "Okay. So tell me something, friend."

"Something good?" I ask, echoing the start of our conversation.

"Anything," he says.

I rack my brain for the next few seconds, wondering what I should tell him. Just like the first day we spoke, I think about saying something neutral, something innocuous. I could tell him how I broke the photocopier at work today. I could tell him something true, like the fact that I am secretly more terrified than excited about college, that the thought of everything and everyone I know changing terrifies me. It makes me think of plates shifting, the ground quivering underneath me while I try to find something strong enough to hold on to.

I could tell him how much I miss him.

"I found out my mom is cheating on my dad," I breathe into the phone.

I hadn't even realized it was in the running for what to say to Will, but somehow it explodes out of me and there's nothing I can do to stuff the words back inside. I feel sick hearing the truth out loud, then paranoid, because what if somebody else has access to these conversations? What if the words I say to Will aren't just between the two of us?

And now I'm starting to sweat because the only person I trust with the truth—the person I really wanted to be telling this to—is Lacey. I want to hear her reassuring voice, want to cry on her shoulder and let her promise me everything is going to be okay, even if she doesn't know that it will be.

I want my best friend.

"Holy crap," Will says. "I'm sorry, Eden."

Somehow his voice manages to sound kind and sympathetic, like he really is sorry, and I'm busy wondering how that's possible—how a computer can possibly feel sorry for me—when I remember about Will's family. How he lost his father when he was thirteen, so clearly he must have known that feeling of something precious splintering, and I realize that maybe it is possible that he understands exactly how I feel.

"Thanks," I say.

"How did you find out?" he asks.

I'm caught off guard again. I don't know what I thought would happen after my confession—that we'd move on to other things and never speak of it again, that Will might bring the conversation back to something good, something happy and carefree, just like he used to be.

But instead, he's asking me about it, letting me talk more about it.

Still, I hesitate. What if this conversation really isn't private, what if it's one of those things other people listen to for quality assurance purposes or whatever? What if he feels like he has to ask but doesn't really want to hear about it?

"It's a long story," I say.

"I have time," he says with a chuckle, and it hits me that he does have time. He's not going anywhere.

And even if he doesn't really want to hear about it, I don't have to worry about boring him or oversharing or saying the wrong thing.

He's not a person.

And yet he's Will.

I can trust him.

So I take a deep breath and start at the beginning, start at this morning at work with my dad, and end at tonight and getting back from Lacey's.

I tell him everything that happened, leaving nothing out, and he does exactly what I'd hoped he would do.

He listens.

15

WILL ALWAYS HAD a knack for making me feel better, from the day he walked me to the nurse's office to the occasions when he'd saved me from being the last person picked in gym class, but my favorite memory with him had happened on my birthday, in January.

It was the kind of morning that feels too early no matter how used to it you are. Missing the warmth of my bed, I trudged to chem class and slid into my seat on the lab bench I shared with Will, New Age Lauren and her lab partner, Megan Tomey. I was pulling out my books when Lauren jumped up to give me a hug. "Lacey told me it's your birthday! Happy birthday, girl!"

She was heading back to her seat when Will sauntered in, right as the late bell was going. He had a talent for doing that, cutting it so close that he was technically late but not late enough to get in trouble for it. I swear I saw Mrs. Phillips glare at him as he came in. He sat at his usual spot between Lauren and me, and immediately turned to me.

"Eve," he said. "It's your birthday?"

"Yeah," I said warily, because birthday attention had a distinctly embarrassing tinge to it, and because Mrs. Phillips was starting to lecture and I didn't want to get in trouble.

Will, naturally, was unconcerned about such things.

"Why didn't you tell me?" he asked.

"Shh," I said as Mrs. Phillips's eyes drifted in our direction.

Will lowered his voice but leaned in close. "Why didn't you tell me?" he repeated.

"Um, because it's not a big deal," I whispered back. "And you don't tell me when it's *your* birthday."

Which didn't mean that I didn't *know* when his birthday was. Of course I did. But it wasn't because he'd told me.

"March twenty-seventh," he said easily, and I pretended to take note of it.

I assumed that was the end of it, until later, in English class, I saw something move out of the corner of my eye. I'd been taking down notes on *Beowulf,* sitting three rows from the front and in the middle of the room. Neither Lacey nor Will was in this class with me, so I could be my truest, dorkiest self: a model student. A model student who still only managed to get B's, but that was neither here nor there.

That day, though, for whatever reason, I happened to glance in the direction of the open classroom door and saw Will gesturing wildly. At first I thought it was to one of his friends, Marcus Tyme or Brendan Colbert or someone else, but if that was the case, why was he looking right at me?

Did he want me to get someone's attention for him?

"*You,*" he mouthed, pointing right at me.

Foolishly, I pointed back at myself and mouthed, "*Me?*"

"*You,*" he said again, and when I stared at him, dumbfounded, he looked exasperated. He proceeded to do a series of complicated motions that looked suspiciously like thumb wrestling, and I could only gape at him.

"What?" I mouthed.

He started a new series of motions, and it took several seconds to realize he was making the gesture for *phone* with his hand.

Ohhhh.

He wanted me to check my phone.

But Mr. Mayer had the strictest no-phone policy in the school. How did Will expect me to pull my phone out of my backpack right in front of everyone?

Even Lacey knew not to text me during English.

Will was still waiting, though, looking frustrated.

"I can't," I mouthed, and shrugged helplessly.

He must have thought I still didn't understand him, because he started repeating the *you* and *phone* gestures.

I know, I can't! I wanted to shout back.

I glanced at Mayer, then back at Will, who was showing no signs of giving up.

Finally I took a deep breath, leaned down, opened my backpack and in one quick motion, slid my phone onto my lap.

I checked that no one had seen me pull it out, then discreetly ducked my head and opened up the last text message I'd received.

Can you get out of class? Will had written.

Um, *no.* I looked at him and shook my head.

In return, he vigorously nodded his head.

I forcefully shook mine.

He nodded so hard I was genuinely worried he'd hurt himself.

In a burst of courage, I raised my hand.

"Um, can I get a bathroom pass?" I blurted out when Mayer stopped mid-sentence.

"Fine. Hurry up," he said, and just like that, it was done. I had gotten out of class.

I hurried out of the room, phone hidden in my sweatshirt, and met Will, who had ducked out of view in case Mayer happened to glance at the doorway.

"You are the worst freaking charades player I've ever seen in my life," Will whispered.

"No, *you* are," I shot back.

"How did you not know this meant *phone*?" he asked, waving a fist with his thumb and pinky sticking up.

"I thought it was, like, surfing or something. Hang ten. I don't know," I said, and he burst out laughing.

"Like I'd be asking you to cut class to go surfing. Wait—actually, why *didn't* I think of that?" he said. "Apart from the fact that it's, like, twenty degrees out."

"Why *are* you asking me to cut class?" I asked.

"You'll see," he said, leading me to the cafeteria and then to a table at the far side of the hall, next to windows overlooking the front of the school.

Sitting in the middle of the table was a single piece of cheese-cake with two forks beside it.

"Sit," Will ordered. I hesitated, and glanced around to make sure no one would call me on cutting, but mostly it was just a bunch of other students there, hanging out in the cafeteria during their free periods.

"What's this?" I asked.

"Birthday cake," Will said, sitting down across from me. He picked up a fork and signaled for me to do the same.

"Seriously?" I said, my breath catching in my throat.

"Actually, no, but it's all the caf has for dessert today. I'm not a miracle worker." He grinned at me. "Happy birthday."

"Will," I said, struggling to find words. "This is, like . . ."

The nicest thing anyone has ever done for me.

"Dig in before I finish it all," he said, chewing vigorously.

I sat down and picked up the fork and took a bite.

It tasted a little plasticky and too sweet, but it was definitely the best piece of cake I'd ever had in my life.

"First rule of fight club," Will said, pointing his fork in my direction. "Birthdays are always a big deal. That's what my dad always said," he added, his voice growing softer. "I think because after he got sick, he knew that we wouldn't have that many together, so we always did something huge to celebrate."

"Like what?" I asked.

It was one of the few times I'd ever heard him talk about his dad.

"Like, we went to Galileo's one time and ate so much ice cream I threw up on the way home. Another time he let me stay up all night so I could celebrate all twenty-four hours of my birthday. Of course I only made it to, like, two a.m. Then he took us to Yosemite for my mom's birthday. Stuff like that."

"Your dad sounds awesome," I said.

"Thanks," he said quietly, and I could tell he didn't want to keep talking about him.

"Why did you do this?" I asked. "Seriously."

He shrugged. "It's not a big deal."

"It is, though," I said. "You got me cake. We're both cutting class."

"Actually, it's my free period," Will admitted. "But you're making me kind of sad for you, Paulsen. Don't you and Lacey do this kind of stuff all the time?"

Cut class and hang out in the cafeteria, right under the very noses of our captors (i.e., teachers)? I gave an unladylike snort. "Lacey *tries*." It went without saying that she was often less than successful; it also went without saying that these were the kinds of unnecessary risks that I normally didn't take.

Will laughed. "Lacey would. Anyway," he continued, "we're friends. This is what friends do."

I could have forced it, pushed him to explain why he'd really done this, why he was always so sweet to me. But it occurred to me that his answer could break my heart; it could break my fantasies about what we were and what we someday could be, and I didn't want to take the chance. What if he felt sorry for me? What if I was one of those popular-guy-befriends-a-less-popular-girl jokes? Okay, I was getting carried away; Will was way too genuine for that.

And he proved it by pulling me into a hug just before I went back to class. I hugged him back, breathing in his clean, orangey scent.

"Thanks, Will," I whispered.

16

I'M STILL TALKING to Will, telling him about my mom and Serg, when Lacey starts calling me. I cancel her call and keep speaking, but almost immediately another call comes through, then another one. After canceling the third call, I feel a pang of uncertainty.

Why is she calling so many times?

Is everything okay?

Is it her mom?

"Will, can I call you back?"

"Sure," he says. "Whenever your heart desires."

"Thanks. I'll call you right back," I say, then hang up.

I'm anticipating another call from Lacey, but she must know I've been screening her calls, because a quick succession of texts lands on my screen instead.

Pick up!

Sorry I missed you. O says you're pissed? I forgot something at work and had to go get it before closing.

I roll my eyes as I read her texts. I'm almost insulted by how lame an excuse she has. She forgot something at work so she hightailed it out of her driveway, even though she knew I was there waiting for her, and oh yeah, she also texted her brother to cover for her while I was standing right there?

Another text appears: **I'm in your driveway. Come down!**

Then another: **My mom's going to get on my case for being out so late. Hurry up.**

I lift a slat at the bottom of my blinds so I can see the driveway below. The old gray Toyota is there and I can vaguely see someone's figure behind the wheel. I throw on a hoodie over my pajamas, then open my bedroom door and check that my parents' lights down the hall are out. They are the definition of morning people, so they like to be in bed by ten p.m. Sam's and Mia's lights are both still on, but that doesn't matter.

I hurry down the stairs, open the front door and am hit with a wave of humid air. The temperature in our air-conditioned house fooled me into thinking it would be relatively cool outside. I walk down to the driveway and stand in front of Lacey's car, the headlights glaring at me.

It's too bright to tell who is who, but I can see that there are at least two people in the car.

An angry drumbeat leaks out of the car when she opens her door—the passenger door—and climbs out. When I squint really hard, I catch a glimpse of Hail's military-style buzz cut, his angular, almost square head behind the steering wheel. Oliver would kill Lacey if he knew she was letting Hail drive their car. Thankfully, Hail makes no move to get out of the car with her.

Lacey is wearing the cutoffs we both own, a thin-strapped tank top and a pair of round, dark sunglasses perched on the top of her head, though the sun set a good hour ago.

I fold my arms across my chest, a clear warning that she better have a good excuse for what she did. Lacey doesn't seem to catch this, though, because she's coming around to the front of the car, and instead of saying anything to me, she leans down to look at the front bumper and touches it.

"Shit. Guess it did scratch," she says. I look down and see that the paint has come off just above the right headlight, and there's a small dent there.

I'm not going to ask what happened to her car. I'm not going to ask where she's been, what she's doing out with Hail. I won't ask why she never answered my texts, never bothered to find out why I called so many times or why I came looking for her at her house.

"Why are you here?" I ask. Still frowning at the bumper, she looks up at me now and her expression changes.

"You *are* mad," she says. "Look, I know it seems shady, but I'd forgotten my water bottle at work and you know how I'm trying to hydrate this summer, so I had to go back for it. And I know it doesn't seem important, but if I hadn't gone back someone would have claimed it as their own by tomorrow morning. There's this guy I work with, I swear to God he's a total kleptomaniac."

I just look at her.

"What?" she asks after a minute.

"How stupid do you think I am?" I ask. "You knew I was waiting for you. You were purposely avoiding me."

"*Or,*" Lacey spits, "I have a life and can't always be waiting by my phone all day."

"I never asked you to!" I protest. What the hell is going on? I'm the one who's supposed to be angry; I'm the one she blew off.

"Well, then, what's your problem?" she asks. "Is this because I have other friends? Is that it?"

I can tell that she's confident in her theory. I inadvertently glance at Hail in the driver's seat, and I wonder how much of this he is hearing.

"I'm allowed to have other friends, Eden. And how many times have I asked you to come out with us and you don't?" Barely taking a breath, she continues, "And, like, I get that you think you're so much better than them—"

"I do *not* think that!" I argue, looking again toward the windshield, trying to see if Hail can hear. I hate that we have to hash this out here. That I can't even talk to her without some stranger overhearing everything we have to say to each other.

"You so do," she says with a humorless laugh. "You think you're better than them and you think you're better than me and it's, like, I get it. You have good grades, a perfect family, the perfect life. . . ."

"You don't even know what you're talking about. You have no clue," I say, a quiver traveling from my chest to my words. In fourteen years, Lacey and I have rarely fought. For the most part, there have just been passive-aggressive texts and the odd day or two of the cold shoulder. So these words—what she's saying—were always going to hurt. But today, after everything that's happened, it feels like she's dug a metal pole right into my chest.

"Oh right, I forgot. Your life *isn't* perfect. You get B's instead of A's. You're not some brainiac or an ice dancer," she says with an eye roll, but there's a little hint of a smile on her face, like she thinks we've gotten all our anger out of our systems. Like we can now go back to some semblance of normal. "Your poor parents."

You never expect the things you tell your best friend, the things you confide in her, to come back and haunt you. You never expect to hear them in her voice, taunting, unrecognizable.

But the final straw, the thing that really changes everything, is when I catch a whiff of Lacey's breath, a hint of cheap beer and God knows what else.

I feel like I'm about to burst into tears, and not for the first time today. But I refuse to do it in front of Hail, refuse to do it in front of her.

"Go home, Lacey," I tell her, tired.

"Wow," she says, disbelief in her voice, and she starts to back up. Like I'm being unreasonable. And maybe that's the *actual* final straw, the thing that makes me lose my last strand of patience.

"Why are you being such a bitch?" she spits.

"Why am *I* being such a bitch?" I repeat. "Because I needed you today, Lace. I really needed you and you weren't there for me."

"Because I have other things going on, Eden, okay? Because it's fucking summer and I have a job and I have a life and we're eighteen, not eight, and maybe, just maybe, we don't have to do every single thing together."

The words rush out of Lacey in one fell swoop, and as soon as they are out, I can tell that she regrets them.

"What did you say?" I ask, voice low.

She hesitates. "I just mean . . . like, I can't always drop everything to be there for you."

"I didn't fucking ask you to!" I spit. "And I never said we had to do everything together."

"Right, but you . . ." She fiddles with the sunglasses perched on top of her head.

"I what?" I ask.

"You're pissed at me because I didn't go to camp, and you have every right to be. I flaked, I get that," she says. "But then *you* should have gone, if you wanted to so badly. You didn't have to stay because of me."

I open and shut my mouth, unsure of what to say.

"And it's always like that. It's like we're not allowed to be two separate people."

I am silent for several seconds before I say, "I stayed because camp was *our* thing, together, and I didn't want to just leave you this summer."

"You wouldn't have been just leaving me!" Lacey says, exasperated. "It would have been fine. *I* would have been fine."

"I never, ever said we had to do everything together," I say, feeling my eyes start to water.

"Of course you didn't *say* it, but we both know it. I have to hold your hand for every single thing. That's the only way you ever *do* anything. The one time I didn't, you bailed on skinny-dipping."

"Oh my God!" I say, frustrated. "This is because I didn't go skinny-dipping with a bunch of creeps from school? I can do it, okay? That's what you want me to do? I'll do it."

"It's not just skinny-dipping. I get that you need me, but I can't . . . I won't always be here."

"What does that mean?" I ask, and my voice is shaking. "What?" I push.

"You'll freak out," she says, not looking at me.

Oh God.

"I won't," I say, feeling my stomach start to churn.

"You *will*," she insists.

"I won't," I say firmly, trying to assure myself as well as her.

"I don't think I'm going to State," she says after a moment. She watches me carefully after saying those words and I watch her back, inspecting every inch of her face for a smile, a crack, any sign that she's joking, but it doesn't come.

"What do you mean?" I ask, trying to keep my voice calm.

"I think I'm going to LA in the fall," she says, staring down at the ground.

"Lace," I say. "But you promised . . . your mom . . ."

"I'll deal with that," she says with a wave of her hands. "I've been talking to my dad about moving in with him at the end of the summer."

I suddenly feel light-headed, feel the urge to sit down. I lean back against the car, no longer caring about Hail watching our conversation.

"Are you okay?" she asks after a moment.

"Yeah, of course," I lie, because I can't admit that my plans for the next four years are unraveling before my very eyes, that I can't see myself roaming a college campus alone in just a couple of months, that my breath is feeling caught in my throat.

"Promise?" she asks, and I nod. Another lie.

"The sooner I go, the sooner I can get started trying to get signed and working on my own music and everything."

"Oh" is all I manage to say.

"I'm sorry. I know I should have said something earlier, but I wasn't sure and I didn't want to upset you."

"But now you are?" I ask. "Sure?"

She nods.

Hail taps once on the windshield, and Lacey glances toward him.

"I have to go," she says.

"Okay," I tell her.

She turns and reaches for the passenger door.

She raises her hand as she slides back into the car and I wave back and there's something different about how we say goodbye tonight, something final.

I turn around and go inside.

I don't hear them drive off.

17

I CAN'T MAKE myself get out of bed the next morning.

When Mia comes in to check on me, I make her tell Dad that I'm not feeling well and can't go to work today. Mom sticks her head in to check on me a few minutes later and I pretend to be asleep.

I stay in bed all morning, reeling from the last twenty-four hours.

Finding Mom in Sergiy's arms.

Lacey blowing me off, our fight.

Then the thing that stings the most after sleeping on it—the fact that Lacey isn't going to State with me.

The fact that when she bailed on camp, she was bailing on something altogether bigger, something that meant way more.

I'm going to college on my own.

I have no flotation device, no life vest, no partner for group projects, nobody to explore campus with.

Lacey is going to LA.

And even worse, even more painful than the words she did say, are the words she didn't.

She feels like I've been holding her back, like I'm a burden.

How long has she felt that way?

How long has she been plotting her escape?

I remember the day she got home from seeing her father, those tiny, almost imperceptible differences in the way she stood, the things she said, the things she did. Then the more glaring differences—her hair, the drinking, Hail and Libby and Vance.

She's been separating herself from me for the past year.

I've just been too stupid or too blind to notice.

Tears rise in my eyes but I blink them back.

I won't let myself cry.

I won't let myself do the thing I most want to and call Lacey.

Instead, I go with doing the thing I *least* want to.

I climb out of bed and drag myself downstairs to scrounge up some breakfast. I have to blink twice when I see Mia. She's sitting with her legs folded underneath her in the living room, watching TV. I don't think I've ever seen Mia this idle in eighteen years. Even when we were kids, she was always doing *something*, mixing potions or reading books or tagging along wherever Mom went.

Once I'm dressed, I find my keys, head outside and climb into my car.

I drive around aimlessly at first.

The world suddenly feels made up of places I need to avoid. Dad's work, Mom's work, Lacey's house.

I end up at Avery Park.

It's just before one p.m. and full of little kids and their parents, the kids dangling upside down on the monkey bars and running up and down the slides and teetering on the seesaw.

I make my way over to the tunnel and there's a little girl climbing to get to the mouth. I watch as she is swallowed by the dark, then spit out the other end. She is giggling when she comes out and immediately runs back to the start to go through again.

I wait until she's gone through one more time and then I climb on and slide through myself.

It is a relief shrinking down to fit through holes that once seemed big enough to swallow me, and I think of Lacey and Oliver, how we dared each other silly, spun around in giddy circles, how we were each other's constants.

Things are so different now, it makes me want to cry. It makes me want to crawl back inside the tunnel and hide away until the world resets itself, until we go back to being the versions of ourselves that I recognize.

But I can't do that, can't just wait for everything to become simple again.

I have no choice but to leave the tunnel.

I'm walking back to my car when I hear my name.

I turn around and Will's mother is a few feet behind me.

"Eden," she says. "I thought it was you."

"Hi, Mrs. Mason," I say. My smile falters when she's close enough for me to make out her face, to see how sunken her eyes are, to see the circles around them like they've been ringed in permanent marker.

"Oh, please call me Elyse," she says, and her voice is small. In fact, all of her makes me seem gigantic in comparison. Her collarbones stick out at sharp angles and she's drowning in a long knitted sweater even though it's more than eighty degrees out.

"It's good to see you again. Do you live around here?" she asks, and I remember for the first time today that she does. Will did.

"No. I drove here to . . . I just needed to think."

Her eyes grow unfocused while I'm answering her question.

"Do you mind . . . Could we sit?" She points out a bench not far from us.

She seems exhausted, as I follow her to the bench, and I'm hit with this overwhelming sense of guilt. Why didn't I go back to check on her after the first time? Has she been eating? Has she been sleeping?

Does she have anyone checking up on her?

"Will made me come outside." She blurts it out of nowhere, a statement meant for the middle of a conversation, not the start of one.

"What?" I say.

"Will told me to come outside. To take a walk," she says, and all I can do is stare at her.

Will.

"I just talked to him a few . . . a while ago," she says, like she can't place anything in time. The only word I can use to describe her is *dizzy.* She seems off balance and tired and sad, and I understand that it's because he's gone, that she's spinning with grief. But I don't know what to say to her, how to respond to what she's just said.

"You talked to him?" And then it hits me.

Will.

In Good Company Will.

And I feel both relieved that's what she meant and disappointed that's what she meant.

"Have you talked to him?" she asks.

I don't know why I do it, but I lie.

"No."

She nods, is quiet for a few seconds before she says, "I couldn't bring myself to for a long time, even after I gave you his number. It doesn't make any sense."

I don't know whether she means being able to talk to him or the fact that he's gone.

"It feels . . . ," she says, searching for the right word.

"Like him?" I offer, remembering what it felt like to talk to him last night. It felt easy and real, like I'd dialed my friend Will's number and talked to him about my best friend being a bitch. It felt like what might have happened a month ago.

"Like him," she confirms. She doesn't ask me how I know this if I didn't speak to him. Instead, she frowns, as if she's surprised to hear the words she's just said out loud. "Does that sound . . . Is it crazy?"

"No," I say, and I'm thinking of pouring out my heart to Will and feeling like he understood. Feeling like I had one friend in the world. "How did you find out about it?"

I think for a second that I'm going to have to explain my question, but she understands. "I got an email a week after the accident. I thought it was a scam," she says. "I was furious. But then I started researching it—In Good Company—and it wasn't at all what I thought." She shakes her head. "I thought it was something illicit."

"I'd never really heard of it," I tell her.

She nods. "There's another company that uses the same technology. They use a Cognitive Donor's information to create a Companion, but their Companions are programmed . . . differently. It's called Necromantech," she says, and I try not to react to what she's just said but I'm pretty sure I make a face. "I think that's why so many people have the wrong idea about In Good Company. That, and it just seems impossible, speaking to someone who's . . ." Her voice trails off.

Dead.

Speaking to someone who's dead.

It's like she can't force the word out.

"He doesn't remember anything," she says. "They say he's designed to have all Will's traits, to be *like* him but not a replica."

"It's a computer," I say, stating the obvious.

"I don't understand why," Elyse says suddenly. "Why would he sign up for it? He was *eighteen*. There's no way he could have known that he would . . ." She skips over the word. "Do you know? Did he tell you anything?"

Will's mother is looking at me, expectant, hopeful, and somehow she still thinks that I knew Will. That I was *with* Will.

I start to tell her that she's wrong, that I don't know why he would have signed up to be a Cognitive Donor, that I didn't know Will the way she thinks I did.

But at exactly that moment, a memory body-slams me and it's April again, the week after my dad's TIA, and I'm in the student parking lot at school.

I've just gotten out of my car when I hear someone calling my name. Of course I recognize his voice. I'd know it anywhere.

"Hey, Paulsen," he says when he's in front of me. He sticks one elbow onto my shoulder. "How are you doing?"

"I'm okay," I say, even though I'm tired and scared and sleep-deprived.

"And how's your dad?" Will asks.

I can't help my smile. It means the world that he cares enough to ask.

"Better," I say. I don't add the *for now* that seems to hang over everything, over my family, but I think Will can sense it.

He surprises me by bringing up his own dad, the first time he's done so since my birthday in January.

"He was sick for so long," he says. "And then when he died, he was just gone. It's like he vanished into thin air.

"It scares me. The thought that you can be here one day and then gone the next, and there's absolutely nothing left of you."

His voice breaks at the end of his sentence and he clears his throat.

"What I mean is—the important thing is that your dad is still here. There's a big difference between here and not, you know? You shouldn't waste the time while he's here worrying about when he won't be."

The image of Will against the backdrop of a dewy spring morning fades, and I'm back on a bench with his mother and I know why he signed up for In Good Company.

"He wanted to leave something behind," I say now, and I'm positive it's true. "Something of himself."

Elyse nods, her eyes filling as she watches me. "I wish we'd talked about things like that more while he was here," she says. "The last few years, after his father died, he felt so hard to reach, so distant."

"*Will?*" I say stupidly, because *distant* and *hard to reach* are words I would never use to describe Will Mason.

"He could be difficult. I'm sure you know," she says, offering me the closest thing to a smile she's given since we met. But she's wrong. I don't know. I'm having a hard time imagining a Will who was anything but easygoing and calm and sweet.

"It makes me feel better," she says. "Knowing that he had you. That he was happy before."

I swallow the lump in my throat, try to speak, but I can't take it from her. I can't tell her the truth. *Besides,* I tell myself, *who knows what would have happened if he was alive?*

Will wasn't my boyfriend, but maybe he would have been. The last night changed everything.

"I'm so glad I ran into you, Eden." She manages another smile, and it's only a shadow of Will's, but she looks so much like him that it reminds me of his anyway.

I'm sorry, Will.

I think he would understand me not telling her.

No, I *know* he would.

"Me too," I say.

Before she goes, she pulls me into a long hug, and I wonder about the last time she hugged anyone, the last time she talked to someone she can see.

She leaves and I watch her walk across the park, her figure growing smaller and smaller until she disappears.

18

INSIDE MY CAR, I pull out my phone and dial his number.

Will picks up on the first ring.

"Eden!" he says, and I think I could get used to the way he sounds whenever I call, like he's been there all along, waiting for me.

"Hi, Will," I say, then add, "I'm sorry. I know I promised to call back last night but everything got kind of crazy."

"It happens," Will says, as easygoing as I remember, and I feel a pinch in my chest. I've missed him.

I missed him at graduation, his fan of dark hair, his wide smile, how easy and comfortable he was to talk to. I missed him at the bonfire.

I've missed him every day since he's been gone.

And this, speaking to him even in this weird, complicated way, makes me feel like he's back. Like I'm talking to the real Will, just like Elyse said.

"I just ran into your mother," I tell him.

"How is she?"

"Not great," I answer honestly. "We all miss you. A lot."

Tears are building inside me, and without thinking, I spit, "Why were you going so fast that night? What could have been so important?"

"That's how I died?" Will asks, his voice breathy. What is it like for everyone but you to know how you died?

"Yes."

It's not fair, I think.

It's not fair that he died before we could become more than just friends. That he died before he could go to college. That he died at all.

"I'm glad you're still . . . I'm glad you're here, though," I say. "I think your mother is too."

He's silent a moment before he says, "What did you two talk about?"

"You."

"All good things, I hope."

"Half and half," I say, and he laughs his deep, full laugh.

"You're lucky I can't ask her about it," he says.

"What do you mean?"

"Well, I don't share data between users. So the version of me she talks to is completely independent of the version of me you talk to. You could pretty much say that I'm all yours."

I snort at his quip.

"So were you okay last night?" Will asks now. "You hung up in such a hurry."

The memory of last night comes flooding back to me.

"I got into this fight with my best friend. Lacey," I say.

"Man, that sucks," he says.

"Yeah," I say. "And she basically told me she needs a break

from me, and oh, by the way, our plan to go to college together? Completely out the window."

"Eden," Will says, sympathetic. "That freaking sucks."

"Thanks," I say with a sigh.

"So do I know Lacey?" Will asks. "Did I?"

"Everybody knows Lacey," I say. "She's the girl who randomly pulls out her guitar and plays at parties."

"Oh, *that* Lacey," he quips, and I laugh.

"You'd like her, though." I feel oddly protective of Lacey. Despite everything. "You *did* like her."

"I'll take your word for it," Will says. "But for the record, for this fight? I'm on your side."

I snort. "You don't even know what happened."

"I don't need to. I'm automatically on Team Eden." I laugh, but I hate the idea of being on opposing sides. Team Eden has always been Team Lacey.

"I've known her since we were four," I tell Will. "Fourteen years."

"Wow," Will says. "That's, like, our whole lives. That's three and a half presidential terms."

It's forever, I think. Long enough to forget what the world feels like when you have to face it alone.

"This is, like, the second fight we've ever had," I say. "And the first actually had to do with you."

"With me?" Will echoes.

I nod before realizing he can't see me. "Yes, but anyway, you and Lace were friends too. We went to school together for, like—"

"Whoa, whoa," he says, interrupting me. "You can't do that!"

"Do what?"

"Tell me you had a fight about me and then *not* tell me what happened."

"I can't tell you that," I say, suddenly regretting ever bringing this up. Who knew ghosts/computer programs/whatever this Will is were this nosy?

"Why?" he pushes.

"Because," I say. "It's embarrassing. And really, really stupid."

Will laughs and I find myself grinning while holding the phone to my face.

"What a coincidence," he says. "I like embarrassing and I like stupid."

"Okay," I say, "but you have to promise not to laugh at how lame it is."

"Promise."

I sigh, feeling all of thirteen as I launch into my story. "So eighth grade, you and I sat next to each other in math class, assigned seating and all that. So we got to know each other pretty well. You were always trying to copy off me."

Will snorts. "Yeah, right. Sure it wasn't the other way round?"

"It definitely wasn't the other way around!" I say. "No offense, but I would not copy off you in math. Not even if my life depended on it."

"Ouch," he says, sounding wounded, and I laugh.

"Anyway, Lacey kept pestering me to tell you that I liked you, and then—"

"Wait, wait, wait," Will interrupts. "Hold up. You liked me?"

Shit, why did I agree to tell this story?

Well.

It's out now, so I soldier on.

"I wouldn't listen to her because, like, who does that? You were popular and I was just, like, this dork you talked to while copying my math homework. I mean, before we became better friends and . . ."

"Eden," he says after a moment.

"Yeah?"

"You liked me?" he repeats.

My face floods with heat and I suddenly feel like a pimply pre-teen again. Or like Will is here in the flesh and he's asking me this, and I'm about to admit to him that I've had a crush on him forever.

"Did I not mention that?" I ask.

"No, you did not mention that," Will says, and I swear I can hear the smile in his voice. How can a computer program smile?

"This changes everything," he says mischievously.

"Why?" I ask warily.

"Because now I don't have to worry about impressing you. I know you already like me, so I can be a total d-bag and it won't matter."

I laugh, surprised, both at what he said and the way he said it. "D-bag," I echo. "Will?"

"Eden?" he parrots.

"Please tell me you don't still say *h-e-double hockey sticks*."

"H-e-double hockey sticks," he says.

"Say *shit*," I say.

"Shoot," he says.

"Say *damn*."

"Darn," he says.

"Holy fuck," I say. "You still don't swear."

"Are you freaking done yet?" Will asks in mock exasperation, and I burst out laughing. He is exactly the same as he has always been.

Will is a walking paradox.

A broad-chested jock's jock who also went to Mass on Sundays, didn't believe in taking the Lord's name in vain and never said a foul word.

That Will is dead.

But he's also here, talking to me, like nothing ever happened.

He left something behind.

"You didn't finish your story," he says now, and I swear I can hear him blushing, the flush of his face at my teasing. "You stopped at *you liked me*."

I roll my eyes even though he can't see me.

"Anyway, Lacey walked up to you one day in the cafeteria and just told you. She just blurted it out. *Eden is in love with you*.

"I was so humiliated I hid in the bathroom for all of lunchtime and then afterward I didn't speak to Lacey for the next three days. Until she went to you and took it back. She covered for me, saying it was actually her who liked you and she'd just made that up because she'd gotten nervous."

Will snorts. "And I bought it?"

"Um, you acted like it," I say. "I mean, things were weird for, like, a week but then it went back to normal."

"Yeah, no," Will says. "I totally knew."

"No, you didn't!" I cry, horrified. I used to wonder if *that* was why Will was nice to me, if he felt bad for me because of what Lacey had told him. But he never mentioned any of it, never seemed to even remember it, and why would he? It was so long ago. The whole thing was just a stupid, childish game.

"She did a take-back? That's the oldest trick in the book. There's no way I believed Lacey."

"Okay, stop it," I say, feeling a little sick at the thought. "You're freaking me out."

Will laughs. "Sorry."

We are silent for a while and then it all comes roaring back to me, the reality of the mess my life currently is. I don't know what to do about my mom. I can't look my dad in the eye.

I'm not sure I still have a best friend.

"I need a reset on this whole summer," I say now.

"A take-back?" Will offers, and I smile.

"Something like that." Then, "Actually, yes, exactly like that."

"So do it," he says.

"How?" I ask, but even as I'm doing so, the answer pops into my mind.

I can't go back to work for my dad. It's too late for me to go to camp and I still don't want to go without Lacey.

But there is somewhere else I can spend my summer.

More for Less is hiring.

When I hang up with Will, I call Oliver.

19

TWO DAYS LATER, I'm sitting in front of a tall bald guy whose desk is covered in piles and piles of papers. The man, who introduced himself as James, has a solemn face and a booming voice that seems to launch out of him.

"So why do you want to work at More for Less?" he asks.

"Um, well, it's a great local store that has served the community for years and has an excellent reputation and I'd be honored to be a part of the team."

He just looks at me, completely unimpressed.

I squirm in my seat.

"This your first job?" he asks after a minute.

"No, I worked for my dad last summer," I say. "Answering phones and booking patients and stuff."

Crap. Who says *and stuff* in an interview? Way to be specific.

"Your dad is Dr. Paulsen? Paulsen Dental?" James asks, looking up at me. "He fixed my crown a few months ago."

"Oh, cool," I say, because I'm not sure what else to say, and James does not seem keen on small talk.

"So you're looking for something easy for the summer, anything that pays and isn't with your dad, until you head off to college?"

"Uh, yeah," I say, feeling sheepish at his ability to see right through me. I really thought that my local-store-that-serves-the-community spiel would get him.

He scribbles something down on a notepad in front of him. "You're looking for full time? Part time?"

"Full time," I say.

"And when are you available to start?"

I blink at him. That's it? He's giving me the job just like that? "Right away."

"All right. Let me just grab some forms," he says, standing and going to a cabinet in the corner of his office.

I spend the next few minutes filling out paperwork.

"We're training a new set of hires starting next Monday," James tells me after I hand back all the forms. "Will you be able to make it at eight a.m.?"

"Absolutely." I thank him and then hurry out of his office.

Oliver is waiting near the supermarket exit doors. "How did it go?" he asks as I reach him.

"Eh," I say with a coy smile. "I guess I work here now."

Oliver grins at me. He raises his hand for a high five and I meet it.

"That's awesome. When do you start?"

"Monday."

"Great. So I guess we'll be seeing a lot more of each other," Oliver is saying, only to be interrupted by some guy behind us calling for him.

"Murdoch! Save it for after hours."

Oliver rolls his eyes and turns to me. "I should get back," he says. "See you next week?"

"See you next week," I say, and I'm still smiling when I head outside to my car.

I had been a little nervous about telling Dad I was coming for this interview, that I wanted a change for the summer, but it went better than I imagined. All he said was that More for Less had won Erinville's Local Business of the Year last year when Dad had conceded his nomination, after three consecutive wins.

"And they more or less deserved it," Dad had said, beaming at his own wit.

"Ugh, you did not just say that," I'd groaned, and he'd just laughed.

Now I send him a text, telling him I got the job.

Excitement makes me want to text Lacey too, to share the good news with her, but then I remember our fight and decide against it. I'm going to give her space.

Still, I feel the need to tell someone.

"Hi!" Will says brightly, answering on the first ring.

"Guess what?" I say. "I got a job."

"That's fantastic. Where?"

I tell him the details about More for Less, how Oliver had gotten me an interview for this morning.

"And then you went in there and killed it."

I laugh. "I definitely did not kill it," I say. "I think they're just desperate."

"I prefer *you killed it*," he says.

I enter my car and let out a long breath, put my phone on speaker and set it down next to me.

"It's so hot," I say, rolling down the window while I wait for the air conditioner to kick in.

"What's it feel like?" Will asks in a soft voice.

"Um, hot?" I repeat.

He chuckles. "I know that," he says. "I just mean . . . like . . . I don't know, what does it feel like?"

I take a minute to think about it, what he's asking.

I'm not really doing anything. Just sitting here.

But Will can't do that, will never be able to do that again.

Does he miss it?

Existing?

What *does* it feel like?

I close my eyes and try to focus on breathing. In and out.

In and out.

"The sun is warm against my skin," I tell him. "It's burning the back of my neck especially."

"Is it bright out?" he asks.

"It is. It's perfect weather. Barely any clouds in the sky and there's a tiny little breeze that has just started. It makes my skin tickle.

"The leather seat of the car is warm. This is probably TMI, but my thighs are sticking to the seat." He asked for it, so I'm giving him the full experience. I'd probably never have said that to the real Will, though.

"What else?" this Will asks, voice still soft.

"Um." I think about it. What else does being alive feel like? What does it feel like to be trapped in the skin of this moment, existing in this second?

"It feels like summer," I say at last.

"I love summer," Will says, and there's a smile in his voice, but this time I swear I can detect a hint of sadness, or maybe that's just from me.

20

THE ALARM ON my phone exists for one reason, and one reason alone: sabotage. My plan was to wake up at six-fifteen and then to spend the next hour slowly going through my morning routine, calmly preparing for my first day of work. Instead, I wake up at seven-fifteen on Monday morning and have to spend the forty-five minutes before my first-ever shift scrambling around like a crazy person and bargaining with Sam for shower time.

Afterward, I rush downstairs and my parents are in their usual spots, next to each other at our dining table.

"Look, Maura," Dad clucks. "Our little girl, ready for her first day in the workforce."

There's not much to look at. My work uniform is just a pair of jeans, the blue More for Less polo shirt and my Converse. Picking out my outfit was one thing, at least, that I did not have to worry about this morning.

I make a point of not looking at my mother as she says, "I'm sorry, why aren't we counting the summer she worked for you? That was the workforce."

I run into the kitchen to rustle up a container of low-fat yogurt and a gluten-free granola bar for breakfast. The kitchen is spotless, just the way Mom likes it.

"I thought you could pack some leftovers for your lunch, Eden," Mom calls from the other room.

"Don't have time," I huff, yogurt and granola bar in hand, as I re-enter the dining room. I throw my breakfast in my messenger bag, stick my phone in my back pocket and dig around for my keys in the glass bowl where keys go to die. It is the one area of disorganization in our house. It would be so easy to fix—just hang our keys like normal people—but it's like Mom's outlet or something. Her release of imperfection.

One of them, anyway, I think with a queasy stomach. I glance at Dad now, and he's chewing vigorously while reading on a tablet. It would destroy him, if he knew.

"What time do you need to get there? Eight?" Mom asks, interrupting my thoughts.

"You have exactly twelve minutes," Dad says. "You know, it's not too late to abandon your glamorous retail life and come help your poor old dad get his filing system under control."

"Eric Andrew!" Mom says, swatting his hand. "You let her go and find another job, so stop trying to get her to change her mind! I actually think it's wonderful that Eden has set her mind on something for this summer, even if it is a little different, and is sticking to it."

"Sticking to it? The girl is not even out the door," Dad points out, laughing.

One of my least favorite things in the world is when Mom case-studies us. Case in point: *I actually think it's wonderful that*

Eden has set her mind on something for this summer, even if it is a little different, and is sticking to it.

It was bad enough before, when I had no reason to read into everything she says and does, but now it grates on me even more.

I try to tell myself she doesn't do it on purpose; her job just bleeds into our lives. Or our lives bleed into her job. Either way, Mia had a meltdown a couple of years ago when she discovered that Mom had used a potty-training anecdote about her in one of her older books.

I guess Mom gets some points for trying to act supportive of my job. The problem is that when you have one daughter whose plans include rubbing elbows with senators all summer and another who is destined for the Olympics, it feels like a letdown to be like, *Oh, and that one is bagging groceries.*

I find and rescue my keys from the bowl and then run for the front door.

Mom protests as I leave that I didn't hug them goodbye.

"Sorry, I'm late," I say, which is true. The rest of the truth is that I don't want her to touch me.

I drive to More for Less and find the employee parking. I pull in, then start to back out to correct my parking, when I hear a sudden crunch.

Oh God.

I've hit another car.

I scramble out to face a tall girl with dirty-blond hair and a deeply impatient look on her face.

"*Shit,*" she cries as she inspects the front right corner of her car. There's a coin-size dent there, but mostly we've just exchanged paint.

"I'm so sorry," I say, even though I'm not totally sure whose fault this was. I glance at my phone screen and it's 8:01.

"Um, do you want my number? My insurance?"

The girl is quiet for a moment, then she releases an exasperated breath, blowing up her bangs. "No, whatever," she says, getting back into her car.

I stare after her for a second and then do the same. After I've parked, I hurry inside the building.

This is not how I saw my first day of work going.

Outside the staff room, a bunch of people are assembling. Thankfully, there is no sign of James yet. I look around to see if I recognize anyone. One of the new hires is a smiley woman in her twenties whose polo shirt is tucked into her jeans. She's talking to another newbie, a junior I recognize from school. I think her name is Shelby. As they are talking, the girl from the parking lot sidles up to them. She gesticulates wildly as she speaks, clearly reporting what happened. I have a feeling that in her version of the story, I rammed right into her, not bothering to check my back, when in actuality the coast *had* been clear—she'd just come out of nowhere.

I stay at the back of the group, not keen on having another run-in with her so soon.

The other two new hires are a tall, long-haired blond guy who looks about seventeen and a short black guy of the same age with dreadlocks. Contrary to my mother's theory, he does not look like someone who has given up. I wonder how much more she's been wrong about.

The two guys are discussing some video game I have never heard of.

Around us, six or seven workers are stocking shelves and

cleaning tills, and there is a lot of activity coming from the bakery section.

I look around, trying to spot Oliver.

I suddenly feel desperate for a friendly face, desperate to know even one person here.

The group chatters around me, people introducing themselves and making idle talk as we wait.

The woman in her twenties looks friendly, like the kind of person I could just slip next to and start a conversation with, but at just that moment, the girl from the parking lot, who is standing beside her, spots me and shoots me a dirty look. Her friend Shelby follows her gaze and then they whisper to each other.

Perfect.

Really mature of them.

It shouldn't bother me at all, but all of a sudden, a well of bitterness springs inside me and I find myself resenting Lacey.

This—working at a grocery store, alone—was in no way how my summer was supposed to go. She was supposed to be my right-hand man, my co-counselor, for the duration of camp. For more than just camp. We were supposed to conquer our precollege to-do list, and now she's off working at Libby's uncle's country club while I'm here. Alone.

Better get used to it, a tiny voice in my head says, and now all I can think of is weeks and weeks of this. Then months, then years. Wandering campus alone, struggling to find the friendliest face in the crowd so I have someone to talk to.

None of this was supposed to go this way.

My throat is tightening, tears forming in my eyes, but they would be disastrous right now so I push them back.

At exactly 8:05, the Employees Only door that we're all standing in front of swings open and James and his light-reflecting head appear. He's carrying a stack of what looks like files in his hands.

"I'm popular today. How is everybody?" he says in a deep-timbred voice that makes every word sound like a cross between a threat and the rumblings of someone who is falling asleep. *Sort of like Batman,* I think, making a mental note of how to describe it to Lacey later.

And then I remember that Lacey and I aren't exactly speaking.

There might not be a Later.

People mumble a smattering of *good*s in response to James's question.

"I have employee packets for everyone," James says. "Cate?" he calls. The smiley twenty-something woman steps forward with a grin.

"That's me," she says, taking her packet from James.

The girl from the parking lot steps forward next when James calls for a "Jenn." He doesn't call out everyone's names, just some—maybe people he doesn't remember from the interviews.

James is handing the guy with dreadlocks his packet when the automatic door not far from us opens. Relief fills me when I see that it's Oliver.

He's sticking a water bottle into an empty-looking backpack, running shoes hanging off it by the shoelaces. He makes a point to walk by and brush against my arm on his way into the staff room.

"Hey," he whispers.

"Hey," I say back, and I wonder if he can hear the relief, the grateful recognition, in my voice.

I know someone!

I snap back to attention just in time to notice James holding out a big brown envelope to me.

As Oliver passes into the staff room, I notice the broad smile Jenn gives him, and she gets an easy grin in return.

"Morning, James," Oliver calls.

James responds with a gruff rumble, presumably *hi,* and then he goes back to pointing out stuff on his copy of the papers he's just given us.

I turn back to him and try to listen, try to orient myself to what is going to be my life this summer.

21

WHAT JAMES SAID in my interview about this job turns out to be true: it's easy. Like in all stores with computerized registers, there is minimal math required. It's so straightforward there is barely a need for cashiers.

But James gives an impassioned lecture at the start of our orientation about why he employs people instead of using self-checkouts like virtually everybody else.

"For some people, when you give them their change, you are the only person who will touch their hands that day."

Every station has a sanitizer dispenser, so this is not as bad as he makes it sound.

"It's BS that when you say *community*, people think about some online forum and robots, virtual whatever. We try to be different here. Plus," he adds, "a few of our customers are elderly citizens."

Most. Or all. Everybody else shops at FastMart and other places where you can run in and check yourself out in minutes. But More for Less is famously a little bit geriatric in population.

Which is kind of ironic, because most of the people who work here are young. High school students, or college kids home for the summer.

After we're shown into the staff room, where there are several couches and a coffee maker, sink and microwave, we're all assigned lockers to dump our stuff into. It feels a little bit like the first day of school, being shown around and introduced to people who seem much older and wiser. At some point, we pass Oliver in Meats, where he is putting some fresh cuts on a tray below a display window. His head is covered in a blue surgical-looking cap, as is the head of the man beside him.

As we walk by, the man yells, "Hey! New kids!"

Oliver laughs and they both wave at our group. Apparently deciding that their friendliness outweighs the condescension in their action, a couple of people up front wave back. James completely ignores all of them.

Shelby and Cate, the smiley woman, are dropped off at the bakery when we circle back a second time, having been shown every nook and cranny in the store. We lose Longlocks, the tall one with the blond hair, to Meats, and then the rest of us—Dreadlocks, Jenn and me—are led to the front of the store to be introduced to our "mentors," who are just people who already work here.

"You guys apply to be cashiers or just get put here?" Dreadlocks asks me and Jenn as the three of us lag a few feet behind James.

"I applied. You?" Jenn says.

"Me too," I say.

"I told them to put me wherever," the guy says. A subtle look at his name tag tells me his name is Thomas.

"Okay," James says when we get to the front. He is looking at a clipboard to see who he's paired each of us with. "Mark, you take Jennifer. Helen, Thomas is with you. And Sheridan, you're with Kennie."

It takes me a couple of seconds to realize he is talking to me. *Sheridan.*

It's written on my employee packet—and on my name tag too when I pull it out of the brown envelope. I forgot to mention at my interview that I go by Eden. I could say it right now. Just casually, the way I have many times when a sub calls roll. *I prefer Eden,* but somehow the words don't come out.

"You're with Kennie," James repeats, pointing at someone about five aisles away from where we're standing.

"Oh, thanks," I mumble.

"Over here!" Kennie calls out, waving her arms as I start to walk over. "I'm hard to miss!"

She is.

Kennie towers above everyone else. She is curvy and bright-eyed, and as soon as I reach till 9, I'm nearly bowled over by the confidence she exudes. Her hair is in long black braids down her back, and she's made a little tie on the side of her boring polo shirt, which I realize instantly is the only way to avoid looking frumpy in our uniforms. I fight the urge to immediately do the same to my shirt.

"Hello!" she says warmly.

"Hello!" I echo, overcompensating for how flat I feel.

"Sheridan, right? I'm Kennie."

"Nice to meet you," I say.

"How old are you?" she asks, tilting her head to the side.

"Eighteen. You?"

"Twenty-four. You're a baby!" She says it playfully, but I immediately feel small, like how out of place and exposed I feel, being here alone, is obvious to everyone.

We don't have any customers at the moment, so Kennie runs through everything at our checkout station. Buttons to contact the bakery, Meats, the staff room. How to open the register. Where receipts come out.

Her phone has been making a series of tiny beeps the whole time she's been talking, and after a while, she pulls it out of her pocket to glance at it. James was adamant that we aren't allowed to use our phones during working hours, so mine is stowed away in my messenger bag, in my locker.

"It's nine-fifteen," Kennie says. "There's a sweet old couple—the Jeffersons—they come in every morning around nine-thirty for bread and milk. Like it's 1955. It's so cute. They try and come to me if they can. Hopefully they'll be your first customers."

Kennie gets her wish, and a few minutes later, I am passing change to a small elderly woman who keeps one hand on her husband's walker while she pays. "It's so nice to meet you, dear. Will you be here tomorrow?"

"Every day this week," I say, hoping I can make it to Friday.

"That's wonderful. We'll see you tomorrow!" she says.

"You train her good, Kennie. Be on your best behavior!" the husband says as they slowly start to leave.

"Aren't I always?" Kennie retorts, and then the three of them burst into rapturous laughter. I smile, pretending to get the joke, watching how Mrs. Jefferson keeps her hand on her husband's back while they walk, even as her own body hunches up at the top. I've always imagined my parents would look something like that when they're old.

"Cheeky." Kennie shakes her head, still smiling after they've left. Her phone beeps again and she pulls it out once more, appearing to fire off a few texts.

"What's the busiest time?" I ask, looking around at the mostly empty aisles, trying to make conversation.

"Hmm, really depends," Kennie says, still distracted by her phone. "Eleven till noon. Then again, after lunch can be pretty crazy too. I . . ." She trails off. "Oh no. Applebee's is off by that bridge, right? Close to the hospital?"

"Yeah, I think so."

Kennie groans and taps her temple. "Think, think, think."

"What's wrong?" I ask.

She sighs, lowers her phone for the first time in minutes and leans closer. "I double-booked myself for a date. You'd think I'd learn but . . ." She shakes her head while I watch her, amazed.

"You double-booked a date?"

"I'm supposed to meet one guy for dinner at seven-fifteen, but Drinks Guy is at eight. So I was thinking, maybe a quick dinner and then run off to drinks?"

My expertise in dating is so poor that all I can offer is a noncommittal sound, which I hope sounds like a byproduct of thinking and not, say, acid reflux.

"You okay?" she asks. "Do you need a drink?"

"Oh no, I'm fine."

"The fridge in the staff room always has waters, if you ever do," she says.

"Thanks," I mumble.

A second passes before she goes back to her date dilemma.

"I don't think I can make Drinks unless I leave, like, twenty minutes into dinner. And Dinner is actually promising."

"Oh, uh . . ." I don't think I've ever even managed to attract the attention of two guys at the same time, let alone book two simultaneous dates. Who is this person?

"You know what? I'm just going to text Drinks and see if he can meet next week. If he can, great. If not, it's not meant to be and I'm not going to stress. Each day has enough trouble of its own."

"That's true," I say, nodding sagely.

"I know, I'm kind of old-fashioned and I'm supposed to be part of the Hookup Generation—which, by the way, what even is that? Like, how far do you have to go for it to qualify as hooking up? Anyway," she continues, and I don't think I've ever heard someone interrupt herself so many times, "I believe in dates. I like dressing up and shaving my legs and making an effort, you know? Like the good old days." She says this last bit with a wistful sigh.

"Yeah," I say, and am relieved to see a man making his way over to us with a basket of groceries. After that, things pick up and we fall into a pattern of Kennie supervising while I scan people's groceries. She discreetly checks her phone in the increasingly small windows of time when no one comes to our aisle.

I don't feel much like speaking, and, thankfully, Kennie doesn't seem to mind.

I try to imagine myself doing this for a couple of months, till the end of summer, and find that I can.

I start to feel that thing that comes bubbling up right before things go terribly wrong. I think it's called hope. Trying to implement some of the positive thinking that Maura Paulsen, PhD, would suggest, I have been telling myself: *This isn't so bad. This is pretty easy. I haven't messed up that many times.*

And it's mostly true. But then, too quickly, Kennie is announcing that it's time to break for lunch. All of us new hires have lunch at the same time during this week of orientation, along with a few of the other workers. The other mentors who have supervised new cashiers stay at their tills, but Kennie pokes at a switch so our light goes off.

"Great job. You learn fast!" she says.

"Thanks."

She surprises me by giving me something between a hug and a shoulder squeeze as we start toward the staff room. I didn't think we had reached that stage in our relationship, but maybe she's just one of those super huggy people.

"What are you doing for lunch? I'd hang out but I'm off to pick out a dress. In thirty minutes." She laughs at her own ambition. "Wish me luck!"

"Good luck!" I say cheerfully.

"Thanks," she says, and then she works a combination for one of the higher-up lockers and breezes out of there. The staff room is filling up with this morning's group of new people, plus a few more I don't recognize. A microwave dings and the smell of mac and cheese circles the air, causing someone to inhale appreciatively.

"Someone's lunch is about to be awesome!"

I look around, trying to figure out where to sit, who looks the friendliest, where there actually is a free space. The newbies are mostly sitting together, but the only empty space by them is next to Jenn and I'm not so sure about that. Plus, I didn't bring a real lunch.

This is the part of the day that I did not anticipate, the one that makes me want to go running home. My rage at Lacey is rising again as is my embarrassment at standing too long, surveying seating options, because there's nothing that betrays friendlessness like looking around for somewhere to sit.

This is the start of my new life.

This is what college is going to be like.

I can't stay here.

On the third attempt, I manage to get my combination, and then I am hurrying out of the staff room, out of the store and toward my car in the parking lot.

My eyes are cloudy by the time I climb behind the wheel.

Sitting in your car fighting tears on the first day of work is the equivalent of sitting on a school toilet with your lunch tray on your lap and your legs folded under you so no one can see your feet beneath the door.

Pathetic.

I pull out my phone and call Lacey. It's the middle of the day so she's probably working, but I take the chance, hoping she picks up.

She doesn't.

My phone still out, I call the only other person I can imagine being free and willing to talk right now.

Whenever your heart desires, he said.

"Eden?"

"Hey, Will," I say, breathing out slowly into the phone.

"Is everything okay?" he asks.

"Yeah. It's just, you know, my first day of work," I say.

"How's it going?"

"Meh," I say. I tell him about backing into Jenn to start the day. Then finishing off the morning by skipping out of the staff room and coming to my car to have a bawling session.

"I just don't feel like I fit in here, you know?" I tell him. "Or anywhere."

It stings. My mind whirs back to school, to Camp Rowan, to the safety of having Lacey by my side. What if I never fit in anywhere again? What if Lacey was the piece of me that made it possible to jump between groups of people, my adapter?

"I wish I was there," Will says.

"Do you miss it?" I ask, voice soft. Being alive, being human, being *here*.

"That's not what I mean," he says, not answering my question. "I mean I wish I could be there. With you."

A small shiver runs down my back.

Maybe it's the thought of Will, real live Will with the big hair and wide, flashy grin, maybe it's the thought of him wanting to be with me, when he could be anywhere else in the world.

"Maybe you can be."

"I'm listening," Will says.

"What if you go back in with me? For the rest of my shift?" I ask, perking up at the thought. "I could just leave you on the whole time. We won't be able to talk, obviously, but you'd be there."

It's pathetic, but for some reason this thought is the most comforting one I've had all day. I don't have to go back into More for Less alone.

Will will be with me.

22

AFTER LUNCH, I follow Kennie's lead and bring my cell phone with me to the till. The whole time I'm working, bagging groceries, ringing up people's purchases, Will is on the line in the pocket of my jeans.

I'm self-conscious at first, imagining the real-life Will beside me, watching me flub my way through my first day of work. But before long, I relax.

I imagine he works here too, our elbows touching as we stand side by side, just the way they did in bio lab.

At the end of the day, I climb into my car, relieved to have survived.

"Will?" I say into the phone.

"That was impressive," he says. "You already have the hang of it."

I snort. "Yeah, right. I almost gave that woman twenty dollars in change instead of twenty cents."

"I didn't say you were *perfect*," he says, and we both laugh.

The rest of the week is more of the same. I keep Will on throughout the day, then talk to him in my car at lunch.

Kennie, who is still required to supervise me, and I fall into a routine of scanning and bagging groceries, switching out a few times a day. Whatever it is that made Kennie seem *above* everything the first day is clearly noticeable to everyone, because by our second shift, both Jenn and Shelby show up to work with their polo shirts knotted on the side like Kennie's. To my knowledge, Kennie never comments on it, but I get the sense not much escapes her notice.

Not only is Kennie beloved by all the other employees at the store, she is clearly unafraid of being caught breaking James's no-phone rule, because her phone is glued to her side or hand all day as she juggles appointment after appointment. It's like she's working two full-time jobs, running her social life and doing the cash register. Three jobs, if you count having to mentor me.

If she minds this, though, she never shows it, frequently complimenting me on my work or asking me to do some mental math for her so she knows what to schedule when.

"So, um, how many people are you dating?" I finally ask on Thursday morning, before lunch.

"A few," she says dismissively. "But these aren't *all* dates. This is the first time I've been home since the fall—I'm in grad school—so I'm catching up with people. If I don't write it down, I'll forget. And I don't want to hurt anybody's feelings, you know?"

"Oh, definitely," I say, as though I too am juggling an astronomical social calendar. In actuality, the last person who texted me was my dad, and I haven't heard from my best friend since our blowup a week and a half ago.

What *would* my life be like if it hadn't been just Lacey and me, us against the world, for so long? What if I'd spent high school making more friends, taking chances on people, people like Will?

I'm catapulted back to all the times Will would casually sling his arm over my shoulder, all the times he would touch me when it wasn't absolutely necessary.

He was here, within reach, and I never did anything about it. Not until the night he died.

How different would my life be if I had been braver?

A few minutes before lunch break, Kennie looks at me and asks, "Hey, what do you do for lunch, Sheridan?"

I shrug nonchalantly. "Usually I leave." For my car.

Every day.

"You should hang out sometime," she says, and I promise to, though I am actually getting pretty comfortable with the whole lunch-in-the-car arrangement. I usually sit in there and listen to music, eat my lunch and talk to Will, which is pretty good for passing the time.

As soon as my shift ends on Friday, a sense of relief washes over me. I survived the first week without any major catastrophes.

After retrieving it from my locker in the staff room, I pull my messenger bag across my body, return Cate's wave and weave around people as I make my way out. I squint at the sun as I step outside and dig around the bottom of my bag for my keys.

I pull out my phone from my pocket.

"God, how bored must you be? I must be the worst of everyone you talk to."

It's something I've thought a little about, Will talking to other people. I know what he told me before, about not sharing data between the people he talks to. I know he talks to his mother. But does he talk to any of his friends? And does my being on the line with him all the time prevent them from reaching him? I ask him about it.

"It doesn't work that way," he says. "It's like going on a website. Multiple people can be on at the same time."

"So are they?" I ask, intrigued. "Like, are you talking to someone else right now?"

"You know I can't tell you that," Will says, his voice gentle, and I feel a little scolded. "I *can* tell you, though, that I was riveted—listening to you count change? Fascinating."

"Oh, shut up," I say. I'm about to come up with a clever retort when I hear footsteps behind me. I turn to find Oliver walking toward me.

"I have to go, Will. I'll call you back, okay?" I say hurriedly. For the first time all day, I switch off my phone. I watch Oliver approach.

He's out of his work uniform and in a brown T-shirt and black running shorts. His shirt is emblazoned with some faded band logo I don't recognize, like he's owned it forever, and there are headphones around his neck.

"Hey," he says as he catches up to me. He's grinning at me, a sly smile. He has a whole collection of them, and having known him for so many years, I'm sort of an expert on them.

"Hey!" I say. For most of the week, I haven't really remembered we work in the same store.

"How's it going, *Sheridan*?"

There it is. The reason for the sly smile.

I cringe when I hear the name. I feel like I've been caught stealing someone else's identity.

Oliver's still smiling, though. "I don't think I've heard anybody call you that in, what, five years?" He scratches the back of his head, as if trying to remember something. "Thought you hated that name."

I shrug. *Things change.*

I try to push the memories back, of fighting with Lacey, of watching my mother and Serg, of Will's funeral.

One of the few things I've never told Lacey—because she would murder me—is that I understand the fuss over her brother. I'm obviously not one of those girls who uses terms like *bedroom eyes* in describing him, but I've definitely been privy to the Oliver Murdoch charm offensive. His dark brown hair is just the right amount of messy, his limbs all lean, strong from years doing track. His eyes are brown too, and he's been charming mothers and their daughters and granddaughters since kindergarten, without ever having to do a thing. In fact, I'm not sure he even knows this is the case.

He's leaning against my car now, hip against the glass of my passenger window.

Who am I kidding? He totally knows.

"Well, don't worry," he says. "Nobody's calling you that anyway. They're calling you the Ice Queen."

"What?" I shriek. "Why?"

"You keep to yourself. You're MIA at lunch. Chris said he hadn't heard you utter a full sentence."

Chris?

"Tall blond guy? He's one of the newbies."

Oh, he's Longlocks.

"And then you never hang out after work," Oliver says.

"I didn't know people were hanging out! It's only been five days!" Both my volume and my pitch are skyrocketing by the second.

Oliver laughs. "Relax. It's all good. But since I know you, I did get nominated to ask if you wanted to come out with us tonight. I think we're just doing Juno's?"

Juno's is a diner across town, with a proper jukebox and leather booths, that my family goes to once in a while to do breakfast for dinner.

As much as I like Juno's, I can think of nothing worse than heading to dinner with the group of strangers I trained with and have barely exchanged two sentences with.

I can't believe they think I'm an ice queen.

I can't believe they're nominating people to talk to me. Oh my God.

"Um, now?" I ask.

"Five-ish?" Oliver says. It's just after four.

I could take a chance and go, but all I foresee are awkward conversations, struggling to find anything in common with the people I work with, or, even worse, all of them ignoring me.

"I have to . . . I wish I could come but I have this . . . *thing* tonight," I say. I know he doesn't buy my excuse, but he just nods. Squints up at the sun.

"Next time, then. They'll be very disappointed."

"Sorry," I say.

Oliver taps on the hood of my car. "Well, I'll see you around," he says, starting to back up. He puts his headphones on and fiddles with his phone.

I can't believe they call me the Ice Queen, I think as I throw my bag in the passenger seat and start walking over to the driver's side.

Like he can read my thoughts, Oliver shouts over his shoulder, "I'll put in a good word for you."

I hope he means it, and that it works, because the idea of a group of people hating me makes my skin hurt like it's been stretched too far. I've never been able to handle conflict, never been one to ruffle feathers.

But now I wonder if that's just another way to be invisible, if all that means is that I never had any impact, never affected anyone or did anything worth doing.

Lacey's words from that night come back to me.

I have to hold your hand for every single thing. That's the only way you ever do *anything.*

I climb into my car, but I don't start it.

I dial Will's number instead.

"Howdy," he says.

"I need your help."

"I'm listening."

"Lace and I had a list, a bunch of stuff we wanted to do the summer before college."

"Like what?"

"Fun stuff," I say with a shrug, even though he can't see me. "Obviously they're not happening now. At least not with Lacey." I pause for a bit. "But I want to do them. And I want you to do them with me."

23

I DECIDE TO start easy, with the most doable thing on our list.

"So the first order of business," I tell Will, looking at the list on my phone. "Number four. *Do something dorky like sneaking into a movie.*"

"Hold on," Will says. "That's on your *list*? Sneaking into a movie?"

"Yeah. Why?"

"That's so . . . I mean, it's not exactly skydiving."

"What, you think it's boring?"

"I don't think. I know," Will says. "And you do too. You called it dorky."

"No, Lacey did," I admit. "We were coming up with things we wanted to add to our Before College list and every single one of them was her idea. So it was my turn to choose something and this was mine. I was going for wild and daring, but according to Lace, it ended up somewhere around dorky."

Will is laughing on his end and it makes me crack up too. It's

Friday evening and I'm sitting in the crowded parking lot outside the movie theater complex.

"I'm actually really nervous," I admit.

"Wait," he says. "You've never snuck into a movie before? Never?"

I feel a prick of annoyance at his incredulity. Is it some rite of passage in high school that I never heard of, was never invited to be part of?

"Nope," I say. I've always been a chronic rule follower, and proud of it. "You have?"

"Who hasn't?" Will snorts. "I mean, apart from you."

I make a face. "Wait a second, though," I say. "How do *you* know you have, if you don't remember anything?"

"Because," Will says, voice a little patronizing, "everyone has."

"Whatever," I say.

I climb out of my car, still holding Will in my palm, and walk inside. I stick in my wireless earphones so I can hear him without having my phone on speaker.

"I hope you have nine-one-one on speed dial," he says.

"What? Why?" I ask, alarmed.

"Just in case, you know, the thrill is more than you can take."

"Oh, shut up," I say, smiling. He's making it out to be completely lame, just like Lacey would have, but I'm pretty sure I could get in actual trouble if I'm caught.

I join the line for the box office, and Will and I are silent for a few moments, so I don't seem like a psychopath talking to myself.

When it's my turn, I ask for a ticket to *In a World Like Ours,* this indie film I've never heard of before.

"Hey, how is it sneaking in if you're *buying a ticket*?" Will asks in my ear, distracting me from what the ticket attendant is saying.

I ignore Will as I take my ticket from her. "Thank you," I say with a smile. If I get caught, at least maybe she'll vouch for me being a nice human being. Or something.

I walk over to the concession stand and join the shortest line for snacks.

"Eden," Will says, drawing out my name in my ear.

"Will," I mutter under my breath.

"What are you doing?" he asks.

"Getting some popcorn," I say. When it's my turn, I order an extra-large bucket of popcorn, an extra-large Coke and two packets of candy.

Will starts laughing in my ear, a wheezing, out-of-breath laugh that makes me have to stop and pretend to be getting an extra straw.

"Why are you laughing?" I hiss at him under my breath.

"Because I know what you're doing," he says.

"What am I doing?"

"You just bought the whole freaking concession stand because you feel guilty."

He does know what I'm doing.

"I just . . . At least I'm technically *giving* them the money, in a roundabout way."

"Mm-hmm," Will says, and I can still hear the smug smile in his voice.

"And I thought I'd pay to see *In a World Like Ours* but then sneak out and go see something else. Like *Invaders* or something."

"Ah, you're theater hopping."

"Exactly," I say. I want to pay for *In a World Like Ours* because it's an indie film and I can hear Lacey in my head, her familiar refrain about independent artists and supporting good art.

When I say this out loud, Will takes offense. "Hey, who says *Invaders* isn't good art? Just because it's, like, a blockbuster."

I'm in no mood to argue with him, so I join the line. The ticket taker tears my ticket and directs me to theater 9. Right across the hall is *Invaders*. I can totally do this.

I glance behind me, making sure no one is paying any attention to me, and then I hurry into theater 6.

"I did it," I whisper to Will as I shuffle along in the darkness, finding a seat at the very back of the theater.

"Way to go," he says, sounding like he's repressing a laugh. "Welcome to a life of debauchery."

I smile to myself.

It feels strange to sit alone in the dark, to have such a big bucket of popcorn and not be passing it to Lacey, whispering about which of the previews are for movies we want to see. To be honest, the whole thing feels a little anticlimactic. I thought it would be thrilling and fun to sneak into a movie, but Lacey was right. I should have picked something more daring for my contribution to the list.

Why don't I ever do anything brave?

"You're making me hungry," Will says, reminding me that I'm not totally alone.

"Oh, sorry. God, you should have told me I was chewing like a monster."

There's a grin in Will's voice when he says, "You don't chew like a monster. Maybe like a small marsupial."

"Ha," I say.

Soon the movie is starting, and as the first scene begins, a chase scene, I yawn. I guess I only thought about the sneaking-into-the-movie part and not the *seeing-the-movie* part. I kind of wish I was in theater 9 instead, about to watch a gripping low-budget story about star-crossed lovers and not the second film in the reboot of a superhero-versus-alien series.

"You're bored," Will says, like he can read my thoughts. "Sneaking into a movie didn't get your adrenaline going?"

"Not exactly," I admit.

"I am shocked," he says.

"Oh, shush," I whisper, and try to focus on the movie. A few minutes pass and I'm barely keeping track of the plot. I really wish I was somewhere else.

"Three, two, one, aaaaaand *spandex*," Will says out of nowhere.

I nearly choke on my popcorn. "What?"

"We're playing a game. To keep you awake. And *I'm* trying to predict when the first dude in tights is going to show up on-screen. Was I right?"

I snort. "Nope, try again."

It's on Will's fourth guess that the hero, an everyman who transforms into a caped renegade, appears on the screen.

Will keeps a running commentary going throughout the film, predicting what's going to happen and what *is* happening, and I laugh under my breath.

"New rule," he says. "You take a drink every time someone says something about saving the world. And not just baby sips either. Like, chug it."

"How many times do you . . ."

"The world is in danger, Mitch. It's up to us to do the right thing."

"Drink!" Will commands.

"They didn't exactly say . . . ," I start to argue.

"*You and me together. Saving the world.*"

"Drink!" Will yells.

Laughing, I take a gulp of my drink.

"*That's what you wear to save the world?*"

"Oh God," I say, reaching for my drink again. Someone a few rows ahead turns back to look at me, and I school my expression, keep it impassive as I stare straight ahead.

"DRINK!"

Stifling laughter, I reach for my cup again even though I didn't even hear what they said. I'll take Will's word for it.

"Okay, that is definitely some slo-mo action," Will says. "The love interest is walking toward him now, right? Wait, she's *strutting.*"

"She's more than the love interest! She's his partner," I argue under my breath.

"Right, but they're still giving her the slo-mo, wind-in-the-hair treatment. Tell me I'm wrong."

He's right.

It's a full-on Bond-girl-emerging-out-of-the-water moment.

"How the hell do you know that?"

Will snorts, clearly proud of himself. "How many of these movies do you think I've seen?"

"So, what, now it's just ingrained in your mind?"

He doesn't remember me or his family or how he died, but he remembers the formula for bad superhero/alien crossover movies.

"Absolutely," he says, not the slightest bit embarrassed by this.

The low timbre of his voice tickles the insides of my ears every time he speaks, and I imagine he is next to me, our arms touching on the armrest in between us. I shift when he shifts. Our eyes catch at select moments in the dim light reflecting off the movie screen, and we exchange shy smiles.

Is this what it would have been like if Will had lived? If I had taken a chance, made the first move earlier?

I know it's impossible, to feel his presence so acutely. And I would feel crazy, would feel like I was imagining the intimacy of this moment, if he didn't say, "So how am I doing so far?"

"What do you mean?" I ask.

"Well, I made you pay for your own ticket. You bought your own snacks, and I've been talking throughout the movie. Not exactly on track for a date two, huh?"

"A date two," I repeat quietly. "That would make this . . ."

"A date," he finishes for me. "What else do you call going to the movies on a Friday night with a pretty girl?"

I roll my eyes. "You don't even know what I look like."

"So tell me what you look like."

I hesitate. For some reason, this suddenly feels like we are sharing secrets in the dark. It feels like giving him something, the ability to identify me in a crowd, the ability to imagine me correctly.

"Well, I have black hair," I say. "Past my shoulders. I have dark brown skin. And big everything on my face—big lips, big eyes, big nose."

"So I was right," Will says.

"Right about what?"

"That you're gorgeous."

I feel my face heating up then, and I'm silent. Is Will *flirting* with me?

He can't be, right?

Except he just said we were on a date.

And he just called me gorgeous.

Is that what the real Will had thought? Is that why he said it?

I remind myself that he is just a computer program, that all he has inside him are traits that belonged to Will. He doesn't have his memories, his experiences, his truths.

The real Will was flirtatious, so this Will is being flirtatious.

Or is it more than that?

"I have to pee," I blurt out. It's true. All the drinking at save-the-world references has taken its toll. "I'll call you back," I say.

"Okay," Will says.

I know I've done it again when I hang up. I've freaked out at the slightest possibility of a thing, a chance, with Will.

Except it's not a chance, is it?

Will isn't here.

I sneak out of the theater and find the nearest bathroom. I'm washing my hands after when someone calls my name.

"Oh my God, Eden! I haven't seen you since the last day of school." It's New Age Lauren. We hug and then spend the next couple of minutes catching up. She's working at a tea shop this summer and going to fashion school in the fall. She's seeing *In a World Like Ours* with some friends she works with.

As our conversation lulls, she looks behind me. "Are you here all alone?" she asks.

I hesitate, feel my face flush, and then quickly say, "No, I'm not," before I even realize that it's true.

I'm not here alone.

"Oh, okay," she says. "I'd have said you should come join us. I bet no one would notice."

She's asking me to theater hop. I suppress a laugh at the irony.

"Well, say hi to Lace for me." Lauren gives a wave before flouncing out of the bathroom.

Of course she assumed I was here with Lacey.

The fact is that if we hadn't fought, I *would* have been here with Lacey.

She was my person, the one I did everything with.

And I was hers.

Or at least I thought I was.

Will could have been my person. Will could have been who I was here with tonight.

I hit redial after I leave the bathroom.

He picks up on the first ring, waiting, as always, for me to call.

"I don't want to go back inside," I tell him. "Let's do something that's actually daring. Something you would do."

I can hear the grin in his voice. "I thought you'd never ask."

24

IT'S THE SECOND weekend of summer and Lacey's leaving for her dad's in a week.

Consequently, she won't take no for an answer; we're going to Jenna Lloyd's party.

"To christen my trip," Lace insists, reaching around her guitar for her purse in the back seat.

"We could have christened it with a movie and Nutella chocolate chip cookies," I shoot back as we climb out of the car. Lace moans, salivating at just the thought of the recipe we tried out at her house two nights ago, but remains undeterred.

"Come on, it'll be fun!"

"That's the thing," I say. "It never really is."

She hip checks me, turns and starts toward the brightly lit house, which is already thumping like the start of a tension headache.

A few minutes later, we are stationed in the kitchen, making small talk with a bunch of kids from our art class, when there are rumblings around us, of people jumping off the roof.

"Like, to die?" Hallie Finn asks, alarmed.

"Into the pool," someone answers.

Lacey and I exchange a look and, by wordless agreement, follow the group of people heading into Jenna's backyard.

The pool is glistening and huge, and it makes the figure standing on the edge of the roof look minuscule in comparison. The distance to the pool looks dangerously long. Actually, everything about the fall looks dangerous, but the person standing up there calls down to his friends on the ground.

"Ready?"

I recognize his voice before his face, and my heart skips a beat. It's Will.

"Holy crap," Lacey says out loud, catching on at the same time.

Someone starts to count him down. "On five, four . . ."

On three, his eyes flicker to the ground and they catch on mine. His gaze lingers on me for a second and I wonder if he can tell my heart is in my throat, and I'm about to yell to him not to do it, don't do it, when his face breaks into the widest smile. And then it's time and he's still looking at me as he launches off the roof. He lands with a monstrous splash in the pool and then he's shaking his hair out, like a wet puppy dog, laughing with his head thrown back, talking to his friends, and it's only then I realize I've been holding my breath.

Jumping from a roof into a pool is something Will would do.

Thankfully, there are no pools in sight after I leave the theater, but that doesn't appear to present a problem.

He asks me to drive to the nearest gas station, so I pull out of the parking lot and drive toward the Gas 'N Go a couple of minutes away.

"Do you have a sweater or a bag or anything?"

"I have a hoodie in my back seat."

"Perfect," he says. "Put it on."

I do as he says, making a mental note to stick my hoodie in the wash when I get home. It smells like must and sweat and car.

"Let's go inside," Will says, and we walk through the glass doors into the small, fluorescently lit building.

"Hi." A sleepy-looking woman in her forties greets me as I enter.

"Hi," I say back. I still have my wireless earphones in, so she doesn't know I'm on my phone.

"What do you feel like getting?" Will says in my ear. "Pick out something. My treat."

"What do you mean, *your treat*?" I say with a laugh. And how exactly is this supposed to be daring?

"Exactly what I said. Take whatever you want."

"Um, okay. I'll take a Snickers bar," I say.

"Great. So reach for it with one hand, and then push it up the sleeve of your hoodie."

I'm frozen with shock. "What?"

"Stick it up your sleeve and . . ."

"No, I *heard* you. Why would I do that?"

"You said you wanted to do something daring."

"I didn't think that meant—" I lower my voice. "I didn't mean *stealing*."

"It's just a chocolate bar."

"Exactly. I could pay for it. It barely costs anything."

"But that would defeat the purpose."

"Which is what, exactly?" I hiss. "To wind up in jail?"

Will laughs, a hearty, full laugh. "We're not going to jail."

"We will if I get caught."

"So let's not get caught," he says, as if it's just that simple. As if all I have to do is decide not to get caught and I won't.

"Will," I say, turmoil stewing inside me. "I can't."

"You don't have to," he says. "But if you want better than sneaking into a movie, this is it."

I say nothing, trying to decide what to do.

"Okay, here's a compromise," Will says. "Put down a couple of dollars on the shelf, so you're technically giving them *something*, and then take the bar."

That does seem a little better. Less terrible. But only slightly less.

"My mother would kill me."

It's out before I register it, but it's true.

If she knew where I was right now, what I was debating doing, she would legitimately murder me. "Other people can do whatever they want to," she always says, but in her mind, the rules are different for us. Because we are black, because we are the Paulsens. Excellence courses through our veins.

Excellence is not shoplifting a candy bar from Gas 'N Go.

And yet I find myself doing exactly what Will said. Pulling two dollar bills out of the pocket of my jeans and placing them on the shelf. Then reaching for the chocolate, slipping it up the sleeve of my hoodie.

Because my mother isn't here.

Because Will is.

Because my mother is a fucking hypocrite.

"Now what?" I whisper to him.

"What else do you want?" he asks.

"Some gum?" I say, a question.

Will laughs. "Are you sure?"

I'm not, but before I can change my mind or think anything through, I reach for a rectangle of strawberry bubble gum and stick it up my sleeve.

Then add another pack.

And a grape one for effect.

"Whoa, whoa, whoa," Will says when I've been quiet for a beat too long. "Don't take the whole store!"

I laugh and the woman behind the counter glances up from her magazine, her eyes landing on me. I immediately want to confess everything, to apologize and tell her what I did and never, ever do anything like this again. But that would be the exact opposite of daring.

That would be doing what I always do: never taking a chance, never putting myself at risk for good or bad things.

I'm walking toward the door of the store and the woman, still watching me, says, "Have a good night!"

"Thanks," I say. I reach for the door and it happens so fast and all of a sudden one of the packs of gum is on the floor. I freeze, hoping to God that she didn't see it drop, that if I just ignore it, she won't notice.

"Is everything okay?" she asks.

"Yes, thanks," I answer. I kick the traitorous pack of gum to the side with one swipe of my foot and in the same motion I'm pushing the door open and starting toward my car. I start off walking briskly, but by the time I reach it, I'm running. I jump into the driver's seat, laughing and shaking and knowing that was the stupidest thing I've ever done, but the woman manning the store is not out here chasing after me.

"For all I know, she's calling the police," I tell Will.

"Over a pack of gum?" he asks, when I explain to him what happened. "Not going to happen."

"But she might know I took something else."

"Nah, I doubt she'll notice a couple of packs of gum and a

candy bar," Will says as I'm starting my car. "Plus, you did pay in—what did you call it at the movies?—a *roundabout* kind of way."

"You seem to have a lot of expertise on this," I point out.

"Let's just say it doesn't feel unfamiliar," he says with a grin in his voice, and it's weird because I'd never have put Will as the kind to steal. He always seemed so *good* and earnest.

"*Now* you can cross off the first thing on your list. Theater hopping was just not going to cut it."

I laugh as I drive home, and it's strange how I feel.

Elated and reckless and silly and a little bit sad. Part of me wants to call Lacey to tell her what I just did and why, to tell her Will was with me and that she was wrong about me needing her to make me do things. The other part of me just wants to hear her voice.

I push the thought out of my mind and remember Will's smile just before he jumped into Jenna's pool. I imagine he is with me, right now, giving me the same smile.

"If you weren't with me, do you know what every day would feel like?" I ask Will later that night. "Like freshman year."

"What happened freshman year?"

"Lacey and Oliver moved away for the first half of it. They lived with their grandparents out in Blaire, an hour away, because their mom was going through a bad time.

"The first day of school, I walked in, and even though I'd gone to school with half these people my whole life, it was like one of those dreams where nobody recognizes you.

"There was this group of girls: Jade, Emily and Paige. Girls who Lacey and I had always been friendly with. So I walked up to them at lunchtime and sat down, and it was like the conversation stopped. It kept happening. Every time I sat with them. Until I realized what it was.

"They weren't *our* friends; they were friends with *Lacey*."

Lacey had always been the charismatic one, the one who stood out in a crowd. I realized then for the first time that I was nothing without Lacey, a nonentity.

"It was like being a shadow without a body," I tell Will.

25

IT'S SATURDAY AND I'm still reeling from last night—spending it with Will (he called it a *date*), shoplifting from Gas 'N Go—when Mom comes into my room to ask if I want to go with her and Sam to the skating rink. I would rather die. I would rather peel my skin off and then die.

"That's okay," I say in the most normal voice I can muster, which still sounds gruff and like it doesn't belong to me. I keep my eyes closed as I speak. Hopefully she interprets this as being due to the disruption of my sleep.

I know it's immature and that at some point I am going to have to look at her, but I don't want it to be now.

"Sure?" she asks.

"Positive."

"Okay," she says. "I know it's your day off, but make sure you don't waste the day. You can still be productive while taking it easy."

What the hell does that even mean? *Taking it easy* means *not* being productive. Also, what does she want me to produce, exactly? Some mathematical proofs? Ideas for a start-up business?

It takes willpower to keep my eyes shut and keep in all of this, but I do it.

Eventually she realizes I'm not going to answer and shuts the door. I think I hear her sigh on the other side.

I wait until I hear her and Sam piling down the stairs, then the garage door closing, before I get up.

I don't see any sign of Dad, so I assume he's working today. I never know which weekends he's working or not working. Today is a relief, though, because I don't think I can look him in the eye either.

After getting a bowl of cereal, I do a load of laundry, vacuum my room, organize my underwear drawer and then fling myself back on my bed.

What do I do?

And I don't mean to have a productive day or whatever my mother said, but how to handle what I know about her and Sergiy. Do I confront her? Do I tell Dad?

Do I leave it?

Can I leave it?

I know from the persistent sick feeling in my stomach that I can't just leave it. Not for good. And yet it seems to be the only option I am capable of taking for the foreseeable future.

I check my texts.

None.

Then I check my emails.

Most of it is junk, but there are a couple from In Good Company.

I open the latest one.

Subject: Companion Updates

Dear Eden,

This is a friendly reminder to log in to your account and follow the instructions to update your Companion's program. As you know, we are always working to increase your satisfaction, and we have recently made changes including but not limited to: increased compatibility options, increased language options, fixing bugs that a number of users have reported . . .

I can't keep reading.

I hate the way it's written, hate the idea of "updating" Will. It makes him sound different than he was last night. It makes him sound other, like a robot or some kind of app.

I delete the email.

I stand and pad across the hall to Mia's room. As I open the door, she's laughing, on her phone.

I hear her saying, "Obviously, I'll be texting the whole time, but our schedules are packed full from morning to sundown. It's really insane." She's folding clothes into her suitcase as she speaks, and despite my efforts to shut her bedroom door as quietly as I can when I enter, she hears the click and turns to find me there, waiting for her.

"Talk to you later, Kel! Bye," she says, frowning. She throws her phone on her bed and presses a folded sweater into the corner of her luggage. "What's up?"

"Nothing," I say, sitting on the edge of her bed, which makes her frown deepen. Let's just say that it's not often we come into each other's rooms for tête-à-têtes. Before she went to college, at least, it wasn't something that we did.

"Are you okay?" she asks.

"Yeah," I say, starting to chip away at the polish on my thumbnail.

"Okay," she says unsurely.

"You know, you're leaving for, like, the rest of the summer," I offer with a shrug. The look of skepticism on her face only grows, but to her credit, she does not throw me out of her room. She keeps folding one neutral-colored sleeveless turtleneck after another into her suitcase. They are very old-Mia: business casual, proper, inconspicuous.

"Do they have something against color in DC?" I ask, flicking a massive chip of purple nail polish onto Mia's carpet.

She holds up a dark green sleeveless turtleneck. "This has color," she says. "And." She leans over her suitcase to pull out something still in a shopping bag. "This is different, right?"

She produces a navy blazer that is probably a couple sizes too big for her. At least it's not a pantsuit.

"Sure," I say, because it seems important to her that I think the blazer will make her stand out.

I can't imagine living Mia's life, giving up my entire summer to go and be a mini-senator. I can't imagine chasing anything the way she chases school and good grades, can't imagine wanting something as much as she wants to go to law school. Mia has always known what she wants to be, and it's not until this exact moment that I've envied her. In a way, she's just like Lacey: she feels about politics like Lace feels about music.

What do I feel that strongly about?

"You're lucky," I tell her. "Doing what you've always wanted to."

I watch her packing, a neutral expression on her face.

"So what happened with you and Lacey?" she asks.

I shrug, not in the mood to talk about it. "I don't know," I say, and I realize it's kind of true. "I guess she hated that we always had to do everything together."

"Isn't it kind of late for that?" Mia snorts. "Fourteen years later?"

"I think it's a new thing," I say, even though I'm starting to wonder how new it really is. Starting to wonder if she's been avoiding me for longer than I've let myself believe.

"I'm sure you guys will work it out," Mia says, which is generous of her, considering she and Lacey have never gotten along. Lacey has always found my older sister high-strung and condescending. Mia, in turn, finds Lacey to be dramatic and irresponsible, even before Lacey started drinking.

"Maybe," I say, trying to figure out how to launch into this. I should just spit it out. It should be easy enough to just say it: *Mom is cheating on Dad. I saw Mom with Sergiy. Sergiy had his arms around Mom.*

None of it comes out. Whatever courage I found last night with Will, it's completely depleted this morning.

I watch Mia in silence for a while longer and then she says, "So are you liking your job?"

"Yeah," I say.

"That's good. It must be kind of nice."

"What is?"

"Having a job that's just *whatever*. Not a résumé builder or for college credit or anything that counts."

"Really, Mia?" I spit. "I'm sorry that we didn't all get invited to

Young Presidential Candidates or whatever it is, but that doesn't mean it doesn't *count*."

She actually looks alarmed. "Why are you getting defensive? I meant it as a good thing."

"That's not how . . . ," I begin, and then sigh, because, well, why try to explain what the most elitist sentence she's ever uttered sounds like to us mere mortals? Lacey's words from the night of the fight come back to me. About how in her eyes, I'm the one who has everything easy, whose life is perfect. Maybe the way I see Mia is similar to how Lacey sees me.

I shake off the thought, focus on why I'm here.

I just need to spit it out. I need to get it out of my mouth and out of my head. Just *out*, before it eats me alive.

"Do you remember how long Mom made us take skating lessons?" Mia asks.

I glance up at my sister, heart beating faster. Does she know? Is this her way of opening up the topic of Serg and Mom and . . .

"I was just thinking about that today," she continues. "It's weird. I never really think about it."

Oh.

"Yeah, me neither," I say.

Now now now. The word throbs in my mind. But my stomach turns again and I realize with a thud that I don't want Mia to know.

I don't want Sam to know. Or my dad to know.

I don't want to know.

And I suddenly can't bear the thought of pushing the words out of my mouth now, of making the earth shake under Mia's feet when she's about to go away and do the kind of thing she's dreamed about for years.

I stand from her bed, my eyes stinging a little as I realize that telling Mia is out of the question.

What now? Do I go to Dad? Confront Mom? Burn Serg's rink down?

I don't know what to do.

I wish I could say those words to my sister now and let her tell me what to do, like she's been so expert at doing for years. But I just force a smile and say, "Have fun. See you when you get back."

"Yeah, thanks," she says, then makes a face. "Mom's driving me to the airport in Beddingfield at four-thirty a.m. So I need to be up by, like, three."

"Gross," I say, and then open her door and step back out, still carrying the weight of the words I couldn't say.

I go back to my room and curl up under the covers, and this time I pull my phone in with me.

"I couldn't do it," I tell Will. "I tried but the words wouldn't come out."

"Why do you think you couldn't tell Mia?" he asks as I lie on my bed, staring up at the ceiling.

"Because I'm a coward," I say, voice low.

"I don't like that," Will says. "I don't think it's true."

"You don't know."

"What don't I know?" he asks, and I would tell him. I almost *do* tell him, but he's already continuing. "You know what I wonder about all the time?"

"What?" I ask.

"What it would be like to *know* certain things. Like, what it's like to breathe or what the cold feels like. I don't have to feel it myself. I just want to know what it's like."

"I can tell you," I say, turning onto my side, curving around my phone. "Tell me what you want to know."

He is silent for several minutes, thinking.

Then he says, "What does it feel like to have a body?"

"I feel like, deep down, you know what it's like to have a body," I tell him, though I'm not sure it's true. Maybe it's wishful thinking on my part, but it doesn't make sense that he doesn't. How can he laugh and feel and empathize, but not remember what it felt like to be human?

I've always assumed that when you're dead, you'll still have memories of what life was like, what it felt like to exist. After all, you have to remember it to miss it.

But what if you don't miss it?

What if it's like Will feared before he died and you're just gone and it's like you were never here? It's only the people who loved you who remember, stained first by your presence and then your absence.

"Remind me," Will says.

So I do.

I tell him how most of the time you are unaware of it, all the things happening inside you that make you alive. How rarely you feel yourself breathing, your blood pumping.

So much of the time, something has to go wrong before you're conscious of it.

"Speaking about bodies, do you want to hear something crazy?" I ask Will.

"Always," he tells me.

"I used to think conjoined twins were the luckiest people in the world. Because they would never be alone, in anything."

"That sounds like it could be a curse," Will says gently, and maybe neither of us is right.

But I used to think that all the same. And I don't know how to explain it to him. How sometimes a body can feel too big for only one person, like living alone in a mansion.

Maybe in a way it's better for Will now, to be everywhere and nowhere at the same time.

26

NOW THAT TRAINING week is over, most of the new people's schedules change. Mine is the same for the rest of the summer, eight a.m. to four p.m. Monday to Friday. This works out well for me in the grand scheme of things, because there are no more communal events; we're all kind of doing our own things, coming and going for our shifts, so there's not some big powwow at lunch like there was every day last week. Meaning I can peacefully slip into my car at lunchtime without it being a big deal.

Still, the idea that people think I'm rude or snotty hangs over me constantly. Like, who exactly thinks that? Just the new hires? They had to have been talking about me to come up with a nickname like the Ice Queen.

I want to tap people on the shoulders and say, *I'm nice.* Or at least normal. But that would just prove the opposite.

God.

I make a concerted effort starting from Monday morning to say hi to people and even end up getting caught in a conversation with Cate about how things work in the bakery. Cate is telling me about their baking schedules when I see her—Will's mother walking into More for Less. She has her phone to her ear as she picks up a basket, and I lose track of what Cate is saying. Elyse must feel my eyes on her because she turns around, then starts toward me and Cate.

"I'll see you later," Cate says, following my distracted gaze, and I've probably lost whatever goodwill I sowed with her, but there's not much I can do about that right now.

"Eden, I didn't know you worked here," Elyse says, taking in my uniform. She puts her phone back to her ear and says, "I'm talking to Eden."

Will.

He's on in my pocket, but he's on the phone with her too.

They're two separate Wills, existing in the same plane. Elyse's Will knows me the way she does—as Will's girlfriend.

"He says hi," Elyse tells me with a smile, and she's looking brighter today, clean and less puffy-eyed.

"Hi, Will," I say, and there's something weird about it: seeing firsthand that I'm not the only one who thinks of him as mine.

"Do you shop here a lot?" I ask.

"I just started to. It's a lot less . . ." She searches for the right word. "Overwhelming," she finishes, looking around, and I know what she means. It must be hard being pitied, having people watching you grieve.

"Nice seeing you, Eden," she says, squeezing my arm.

Later, she comes to pay at my till and she gives me a hug before she goes.

On Tuesday afternoon after my shift, I'm pulling my stuff out of my locker when Dreadlocks (also known as Thomas) and Oliver come bounding into the staff room, also finishing for the day.

"How's it going, Sheridan?" Thomas asks.

"Good. You?" I ask, exuding Friendly.

"Not bad. Not bad." He leans back against the lockers to change his shoes.

Oliver grins at me over Thomas's head, like we're in on a secret. "You coming out today?"

"Um . . ."

"You should come," Thomas says, pushing his dreads off his face. "Juno's. We meet there every day at five."

"*Every* day?" I repeat. My next instinct is to ask why. And also, how did they manage to have some big bonding experience and start such a ritual in, like, a week?

"Yeah. Whoever's finished or just anybody who wants to go. More for Less employees get a thirty-percent discount, so might as well get the most out of it," Oliver says, slinging his backpack over his shoulder. His running shoes are attached to his backpack by their laces.

"Oh," I say, which I hope does not betray how terrible it sounds to me to be trapped in a booth with people who hate me because they think *I* hate *them*.

"You should come," Thomas says to me again, then claps Oliver on the back and leaves.

"Look," I say to Oliver when it's just the two of us. "Are you sure people even want me there? Like, I don't really know anyone and I'm pretty sure Shelby and Jenn hate me. Ever since I ran into Jenn's car on the first day."

Oliver raises an eyebrow. "Oh, come on, those two? They're harmless."

"Fine," I sigh. "I'll see if I can make it."

"Good," Oliver says with a smile. "I have to talk to James for a minute, but I'll see you there?"

I nod as Oliver knocks twice on James's door at the far side of the staff room. James is telling him to come in when I leave.

It's four-fifteen now, which means about another hour until my parents get home from work. When she's not traveling for speaking engagements and Sam isn't in competition, Mom keeps nine-to-five hours, even though she could technically have a more flexible schedule. I start to text her and let her know where I'm going, a reflex, but then I stop myself.

I don't owe her anything.

When I reach Juno's, there are a bunch of other cars in the parking lot, but it's not crazy busy. Maybe only a couple of people will be here today? Oliver's coming. And Thomas seemed to be too. He doesn't seem so bad.

Maybe it won't be so bad.

I ignore the voice telling me that things tend to go worse than you imagine them.

But I still find myself pulling out my phone for reinforcement.

"Hey!" the voice on the line says, never distracted or too busy or too slow to answer. Even if a million people are on the phone with him at the same time.

"Will," I say, halfway between a groan and a sigh. "Did you hear what happened? I said yes to this thing and now I have to go hang out with the people I work with for God knows how long and I think they might already hate me. Actually, I'm pretty sure they already hate me. How do people get out of things?"

"You could always fake sick," he says. "I'm partial to a strain of bubonic plague myself."

That draws a smile out of me.

"No, I think I *should* go," I say. Sometimes when I don't like a decision I have to make but I know what I should do, I ask Lacey what she thinks, and as soon as she tells me (usually to take a different option than I was planning to), I immediately tell her that I have to do the other thing, which I always knew I had to do. It drives her crazy, but Will doesn't say anything. "I said I would, and they're already calling me the freaking Ice Queen."

"That might not be an insult, after all—"

"It's an insult," I say, cutting him off, and I hear him laugh. "Will you stay with me?"

"Of course I will," he says, and I immediately feel better.

Rationally, I know this makes no sense. I mean, what's he going to do? Climb out of the phone and walk in there with me?

But as I scramble out of my car, phone in hand, I understand for the first time why people have imaginary friends. The feeling that there's something or someone—even invisible, a ghost, or in my case, a computer program—with you is comforting.

It is also why people have best friends.

Thankfully, Oliver is approaching the door at the same time I am. Like me, he's still in his work polo and jeans.

"Hey," I say, relieved to have another ally. Or at least someone I know.

"Don't be nervous," he whispers, close to my ear, as we walk in. It's said in a teasing voice, but I guess I'm not hiding my emotions that well. "I put in a good word, remember?"

"Or so you say," I tell him, and he feigns a look of hurt.

Oliver leads the way to a booth in the back left corner of the restaurant, my chest suddenly pounding like feet on asphalt. Without Lacey, it's as if I've lost the ability to even be normal around people. I grip my phone tighter as I follow Oliver, like Will can send some kind of backup through it. Or maybe feel my anxiety, absorb it, if I just keep squeezing my screen.

"Hey, she came!" Longlocks says. "It's Sheridan, you guys."

It's a pretty warmhearted reception from someone I have exchanged maybe four words with. "Hi," I say, giving a global wave to everyone at the table. I smile brightly, still squeezing my phone, and try to look as little like an ice queen as possible.

A bunch of people say hi back, and I realize other voices are chiming in from the booth behind me. I turn and see more faces I recognize from work. Kennie; Helen, the woman who trained Thomas; a red-haired girl who looks about twenty, who I've seen a couple of times in the bakery; a man in his forties who stocks shelves early in the morning and is usually just leaving when I arrive.

"You're sitting with us," Longlocks says, bringing my attention back to the first booth. Oliver slides in at that one and pats the space beside him, so I slide in after him.

"I'm Chris," Longlocks says. We're almost exactly across the table from each other. "Or Christopher. I'll answer to anything."

Thomas, sitting beside him, shakes his head as if he's trying not to laugh. "You're shameless," he tells Chris.

On Oliver's left is Michael, a junior I recognize from school. We've never really spoken. Across from Michael, next to Thomas, is Jenn, who has not glanced up from her menu since I got there.

Chris goes around the booth, pointing at each person, starting with himself. "Chris," he says, as though I might have forgotten in the last minute.

"Thomas," previously-known-as-Dreadlocks says.

Jenn flips her menu around, pretending to be riveted by it, so Chris says, "That's Jenn."

"Michael," Michael says.

"Oliver." Oliver smirks when we reach him.

"And Cate!" Chris chirps, just as someone slides in beside me.

"Hi, everybody! Oh, hi, Sheridan!" Cate says, slightly out of breath. "I had to run home and let my dog out because my roommate is gone today."

"Oh, okay," I say, not sure if she's speaking to me or the whole group. I set my phone down on my lap, consciously make an effort to settle the eff down. "How do you guys all know each other? Just work?"

"Just work," Thomas says, confirming what I've long feared— that I am missing the chip that makes people transition from strangers to friends in a matter of seconds. The last time I managed that, I was four. "I knew Chris from math class. But that's about it."

"Chris and Thomas go to Millwood Catholic," Oliver explains. Which is why I've never met them before.

"Bones! What are you getting today?" Thomas asks, waving the menu around.

"I'm still deciding," Michael, who is apparently Bones, responds.

"He's trying every single thing on the menu by the end of the summer," Cate tells me, laughing.

"And it's funny because he's literally a skeleton," Chris says for my benefit.

"I think she gets it!" Thomas says. "Anyway, he's not *literally* a skeleton, because if he was, he'd be in, like, a morgue."

I tense up at the word, suddenly wanting to cover my phone, to shield Will from their words.

"Are you a skeleton by the time you're in the morgue? I think you just mean I'd be six feet under," Michael supplies.

"Whatever. Wrong use of *literal*," Thomas says.

"Thanks, Grammar Police," Chris says. "Or *Grandma* Police."

Everybody groans at that and I feel myself start to relax. Apart from Jenn, everyone seems pretty nice. And they are also jumping in so I'm not feeling pressured to contribute to the conversation just yet.

"You don't get to correct my English unless you're my mom. Or at least ten years older than me," Chris argues.

Thomas drums on the table and starts chanting, "Cate, Cate, Cate, Cate, Cate." And then Michael and Jenn join him.

"Fine," Cate says, laughing. "That's not how you use *literal*, Chris. Make me feel old, why don't you? I'm technically *just* ten years older than you. You're seventeen, right?"

Chris nods.

"Bones, have you tried the double chocolate mudslide cake?" Jenn speaks for the first time, pointing it out on her menu.

"Nooo," Michael says. "Is that new? That has to be new."

"They're just going to keep adding stuff and you're never going to get everything," Thomas says.

"That's exactly the point," Michael says, grinning broadly.

Everyone quiets down a little as we look at the menu. When my phone vibrates on my lap and Oliver glances up, I realize how tightly sandwiched together we all are.

"Sorry," he says, shifting so there's a little more room between us.

I bring my phone above the table and read the text I've just received.

Not bad so far! Right?

It's from Will.

I know right away it's from him.

He's hearing everything I am.

I never knew it was possible to *text* him.

Not bad, I text back.

Soon a waitress comes to take our order. Some people, like Chris and Cate, order meals for their dinner. Oliver gets a plate of fries and I get a vanilla milkshake.

There's idle conversation as we wait for our food.

Thomas, Michael and Oliver start discussing some comic book. Cate and Jenn are both on their phones.

Chris leans across the table now and talks to me.

"Have I seen you at the ice rink before, Sheridan? Or just a look-alike?"

"It might have been me," I say. "Or maybe one of my sisters."

"You know how to ice-skate?" he asks.

"Um . . ." I start to give my usual answer, about all the years my sisters and I were forced to take skating lessons. Mia was pretty good at it, but when my parents realized that her true gift was academics (she was practically born reading at college level), they respected her request and let her focus on science camp and debate and other extracurriculars. Meanwhile, my mom turned her full attention to Sam and me. I wasn't the worst in my age group by a long shot, but I had zero enthusiasm for it. My mother seemed to believe that if I would just attack it with *positivity,* she and my skating teachers might be able to release the diamond that was covered in all that rubble of lifeless dirt. Old videos have revealed that I often looked like I'd dropped something on the ice and was just picking it up, as opposed to dazzling judges with my lines and making the audience weep with emotion. By the time I was twelve, Sam, at five, had already managed to surpass any talent

I had, and so I gladly quit the sport while my mom focused on finding Sam the right teacher—and then, when she picked up ice dance, the right partner.

I have happily stayed off the ice ever since.

Instead of going into the whole I-did-but-I'm-not-very-good-and-I-haven't-done-it-in-a-while spiel, I just say, "No, not really."

"Oh, I love figure skating," Cate says next to me. "Michelle Kwan? Oh my God."

"What were *you* doing at the ice rink?" Thomas asks, and Chris shrugs.

"My cousin works there."

"*Riiiiight,*" Jenn and Thomas say at the same time, then start laughing. It's only as our food is delivered and I'm sliding the ketchup over to him that I realize that Oliver must know now that I'm a complete liar.

After all, that was how we had met. At a Tots Who Skate class at the ice rink when we were four. Just one year older than me, Mia was in the same group—but even then, it already felt like she was miles ahead of me. She stuck close to the teacher, easily hitting every move and spin, gliding across the rink while I tried to catch up. When I realized that I never could, I'd stopped trying, and noticed, for the first time, the only two other kids who couldn't seem to keep up with the group. They stuck together like one moving unit, but they couldn't go more than a few steps without one falling and dragging the other down. Oliver won't know my history of skating and squashing my mom's hopes and all that, but he still knows I *can*.

When I discreetly glance to my left side, he catches my eye and gives me a completely normal smile. Then he offers me a fry, which I accept. Maybe he was so focused on his conversation with Thomas and Michael that he didn't hear.

I'm slurping on my milkshake, thinking that this hasn't been so bad and I guess I blew it out of proportion in my head, when I hear someone say the words *In Good Company*.

My eyes shoot up, and I didn't imagine it. Thomas and Chris are talking about it.

"I think it's mostly some kind of, like, kinky stuff. For people who are into weird cybersex," Chris is saying. "That's what I heard."

"Who said that?" Something about Cate's tone makes everybody look at her.

"My brother," Chris says carefully.

"That's not true. I mean, maybe some people use it like that but I think most people don't," Cate says, an edge in her voice. "There are other . . . services for stuff like that. This is different."

Although she's right—although *I* know she's right—she sounds less certain the more she says, and by the time she finishes speaking, her face is completely red. Cate is tiny and pixie-like, with blond hair and skin that looks perpetually flushed. Despite her bubbly personality, there's something about her that makes her seem delicate, like she cries easily and is constantly thinking about ways not to embarrass herself.

"Oh yeah, I probably heard wrong," Chris backtracks now, and there's an awkward silence as everyone goes back to eating.

Cate has a Companion.

I squeeze my phone like Will can feel it. Like he can hear we are talking about him.

In a way, Cate suddenly feels like a kindred spirit, because I'm not the only person on the planet pathetic enough to spend hours talking to someone who's not here.

I wonder if somebody she knows died, if that's who she speaks to. Or maybe she just speaks to a random Companion.

I wonder why she uses In Good Company.

The part of me that isn't busy being intrigued by this revelation is horrified for her that she was so obvious about it. Thank God I didn't speak up, didn't try to explain to them what Will's mother told me about the misperceptions of In Good Company. Not that I *would*, but you know. Now everybody knows this about her.

And thinks she's having kinky cybersex.

"Hey, so what are the odds James comes to one of these things before the end of the summer?" Chris is saying now. "I mean, he's all about community. He's made sure people have been meeting here every afternoon for, like, six years, so why doesn't he ever show?"

"Kennie would know. This is her fifth summer here," Oliver says, and then both he and Michael are turning around to talk to the other table.

"Can't a girl eat in peace?" Kennie says with fake exasperation. They repeat their question and she's saying something about it being weird because he's the boss and it would ruin the "vibe."

"Whatever! He's just full of it," the redhead at her booth says. The conversation keeps going, but I zone out until Jenn speaks.

"I need to head out," she says, standing, and Chris and Thomas shuffle out of the booth so she can leave. "Bye, people!"

Under the chorus of goodbyes, I'm not certain mine is audible. As she leaves, it suddenly occurs to me who Jenn and Shelby remind me of: the girls from freshman year, the ones who made me feel so alone when Lacey was gone. There's this cold vibe they exude, and even though they are one year younger than me, I can't help feeling intimidated.

Cate turns to me now, seeming to have recovered from the conversation a few minutes ago.

"So are you from Erinville, Sheridan?" she asks me, back to her upbeat self. "What do your parents do?"

"Yeah, I've lived here my whole life," I say. "My dad's a dentist and my mom . . ." I trail off for a second and realize as Cate, Chris and Thomas watch me expectantly that maybe this town is bigger than I've ever given it credit for. They don't know anything about me.

"Teaches," I finish. It's mostly true.

"Oh, *my* mom is a teacher!" Cate says. "Elementary. Her kids are *insanely cute*."

Thankfully, before she can ask what grade my mom teaches, Chris asks, "Hey, does anybody call you Sherri for short?"

Oliver, who has turned back to us again, warns, "Don't try it."

He does not, to my relief, point out that I have answered only to Eden for the past ten years. I have never liked the name Sheridan. It just sounds . . . it sounds like a hotel or something. And even though it was my great-aunt's name, my parents weren't so attached to it either. They've been shortening it to Eden for about as long as I can remember.

"Oh! What would you do to me if I started calling you Sherri?" Chris laughs, intrigued.

I rummage through my brain for something witty to say, but my mind is too busy filling with clutter, like which of these people Lacey would like—probably not Cate—and whether anybody else here has a Companion and isn't telling anyone and why I can't simply bring myself to just say, *That's not what people call me.*

"I'd tell you but then I'd have to kill you," I say.

It's not particularly original, but people are *oooh*ing even from the other booth, and Chris's smile is elastic wide and I can't help but grin back myself.

27

AFTER WORK THE next day, I run into Cate in the staff room.

"Hey, Sheridan," she says, smiling at me. "How was your shift?"

"Good. Yours?" I ask.

"Excellent," she says brightly. We are silent as we both pull stuff out of our lockers. When I turn to Cate, she's on her phone.

Before I think better of it, I blurt, "Did you know him? Or her?"

She glances up at me, confused, and I point at her phone. "Your Companion."

"Oh," Cate says, her face flushing. "Yes."

She doesn't elaborate.

"Do you . . . like it?" I ask. It's such a juvenile question, but I'm wondering if it's normal to feel as comfortable with Will as I do, if other people forget they are speaking to ghosts.

She is thoughtful for a moment, then she says, "Yes and no."

"What do you mean?" I ask. There's a slight hesitance on her part, a reluctance, but I see it on her face the moment she decides to tell me about it.

"It's my brother," she says, and her voice gets small. "I love talking to Jeremy. He lived in Nebraska, and we would always talk on the phone. So this—it's like he's still here, but sometimes . . ." Her voice trails off. "Sometimes I catch myself living like he's alive, expecting him to turn up at Christmas and Thanksgiving, and it's like I forget to miss him."

She seems ashamed at her admission, and I feel guilty for making her talk about it, but she continues.

"So it's good in small doses," she says. "But it can make you forget."

A woman I recognize from Meats walks in right then, and Cate quickly brushes away a tear. We leave the staff room together.

"I'm really sorry about your brother," I say when we're outside the store.

"Thank you," she says, and gives me a smile several watts dimmer than her regular smile. Her sunny disposition makes her seem like someone who has never had anything bad happen to her.

Cate asks if I'm coming to Juno's now. I tell her I can't, that I'm busy, and it's actually true.

We wave goodbye and walk in separate directions.

She doesn't ask whether I have a Companion, so I don't tell her.

In my car, I take a deep breath and pull out the piece of paper in the back pocket of my jeans. I enter the address into my phone.

"Are you sure about this?" Will, who has been on all day, asks.

"No," I say.

"Maybe you shouldn't do this, then."

"I want to," I say, though I'm not sure how true this is.

When Lacey had first scribbled it down on our list, I'd felt a tingle run down my spine.

Get a tattoo.

It was something she'd wanted to do for years. She had the picture she'd drawn saved on her phone, like she might need to produce it at any moment. Like there would be an emergency in which she'd be required to present the piece of art she most wanted on her body.

"Okay," Will says. Then, more softly, "If you're sure."

I'm not sure.

But it's on the list and I'm doing everything on the list. With or without Lacey.

I promised myself I would.

I did the movie thing. I *shoplifted*.

There's no way I'm backing down now.

Besides, I imagine the look on my mother's face when she discovers that I've gotten a tattoo—the anger, the betrayal. It strengthens my resolve.

"So how are we doing this?"

"I'm going to the person Lace found." At a place called Branded, which, if I allow myself to think about it too much, is somewhat alarming. "We weren't eighteen yet when she first started looking into it. She found them because she'd heard they wouldn't ask for ID."

"Hmmm," Will says. "As long as they're not *sketchy*." He snorts at his own joke. "Get it?"

"Yes, Will," I say, rolling my eyes but grinning. "I get it."

This level of comfort is what made me ask Cate about In Good Company: Will and me teasing each other, me pretending to be annoyed with him. As long as we had known each other, I had never felt this level of comfort with Will. A tiny voice in my head tells me that I never allowed myself to. We would joke around, but

I never relaxed, never let go enough to rib him back. I acted like he was something breakable, like saying the wrong thing would scare him away at any given moment.

Now, even though I haven't seen his face in more than a month, even though I can never see his face again, I feel like I know him better.

More importantly, I feel like *he* knows *me* better, which is a big deal. It's something precious and rare, like holding water in your palms, to be known by someone. Lacey and I had that. Now Will and I have it.

I wish I'd allowed us to start sooner.

I pull out of the More for Less employee parking lot and drive downtown. Branded is tucked in a nook between a laundromat and a jewelry store.

"We're here," I tell Will, my voice weirdly breathy.

It had scared me before, the idea of getting a tattoo. For the usual reasons, like my parents finding out or it hurting or getting some kind of freak infection. But I'd also felt a strange calm, the more Lacey and I talked about it. I knew, as with everything else, that we'd be doing it together. That she'd be there to hold my hand or tell me funny stories to distract me, and I'd do the same for her.

Now.

Now I wonder if I'm being too rash, doing this without her. She was determined to get her tattoo this summer, a drawing of a bird with wings made of musical notes. What if she's waiting for me? What if she still means for us to do it together?

But then I remember her words—*we don't have to do every single thing together*—and the disgusted way she'd looked at me. Tired, suffocated.

She's not waiting for me.

And because of that, I'm not waiting for her.

I pick Will up from the seat beside me and climb out of the car.

"I've heard it's just like getting a shot. Like, a couple of shots."

"I'm terrified of shots," I tell Will. "So thanks for that."

"No no no," he says, and I can hear him trying not to laugh. "Then it's *not* like getting a shot. It's better. Like a bee sting."

"Um, you're making this worse," I say.

"Crap," he says. "Do you want me to shut up?"

"No," I say immediately. "It's nice having you here. You'll stay for the whole thing, right?"

"Actually, I have this thing. This appointment."

"Will!"

He laughs, a rumbling, full laugh. "I'm kidding. Of course I'll stay," he says. "I'll talk to you the whole time."

"Nothing about bee stings, though," I warn.

"Noted."

I push open the door and walk toward the counter.

The inside of the tattoo shop is dark, with lots of posters and pictures of eccentric tattoos covering the walls and the windows.

"Hi," I say, walking up to a woman with dark blue streaks in her jet-black hair. I put my phone down to talk to her. "I'm here to get a tattoo."

She gives me an odd look, like she can see the nervousness written all over my face.

I straighten, try to stand tall, to look in control and ready for this.

She eyes me for a few long seconds and I think she's about to throw me out on my ass, when she says, "What are you thinking about getting?"

"Um, I'm not so sure," I say.

The image of Lacey's picture floats through my mind. She'd promised to help me design something, to pick something that would represent me just as much as her songbird represented her.

Now I'm left to decide all on my own.

The woman reaches for a couple of folders behind her and comes around the counter to hand them to me.

"See if you like anything in here," she says. I grab a seat in a plastic chair at the front of the store.

"I'm Nan, by the way," she says.

"Nice to meet you," I say. "I'm Eden."

"Pretty name."

"Thanks."

Should I get my name?

It's the first time it's occurred to me, but something about it doesn't feel right. What's the point of inking your own name on your body like a label? In case of amnesia? So you never have to introduce yourself to strangers and can just point at it?

I nix the idea.

Nan hums under her breath as she types away on a computer. With her black tank top and ripped jeans, she is effortlessly cool. Though they could not look any more different, she reminds me of Kennie. There is a way people carry themselves when they know who they are. It makes their spines naturally straighter, their gaits easy.

Will was like that too. I hope someday to find my way to that place, to be that self-possessed.

As I flip through the first couple of pages, Nan retreats to the back room, leaving me to decide.

Within seconds, I'm overwhelmed by the sheer number of choices.

I stick in my earphones so I can talk to Will.

I describe to him all the designs I'm seeing.

Butterflies, and hearts, and poetry quotes, and I have no idea what to do.

"You'll know when you see it," Will says, sounding irritatingly Zen. I completely doubt this is the case as I turn page after page of beautiful, profound, meaningful artwork.

But it turns out Will is right. I do know when I see it.

"This one," I breathe.

"What is it?" he asks.

It's a comma, black, simple, but what attracts me to it is the quote beside it explaining the meaning. It says, *In three words I can sum up everything I've learned about life: it goes on.* By Robert Frost.

I don't know what it is about it, but it sends a shiver down my spine.

This is it, my heart trills, and it's scary and exciting because I didn't know it did that. I didn't know I *could* look at something and know it was exactly right for me. Most of the time, I have no idea about what's right for me.

But this time, I know.

I know because almost four weeks ago, I graduated and it felt like everything was coming to an end, but this summer was just beginning.

I know because my best friend wants nothing to do with me and everything's broken between us and I don't know how to make it better, but I am in a tattoo parlor because I promised her last fall, and I'm here alone, but I'm here.

I know because of Will. Because he's gone, but he's still here.

He's breathing in my ear right now.

Everything about him—his laugh, his smile, his lazy stance leaning against a wall—all those things will always be here, and because of that, so will he.

It goes on.

So, a few minutes later, I'm sitting on a bed and Nan adjusts the height, then stencils the shape—an exaggerated dot, a long tail curling out of it—on the inside of my ankle, just above the bone.

"Is it okay if I keep my phone on?" I ask, and Nan nods.

I shut my eyes and listen as Will talks to me, as the needle pinches my skin for the first time, and all at once I want to cry.

"Deep breaths," Will says in my ear.

I listen to him and breathe in and out.

"If I was there," he says, "I would hold your hand and let you squeeze the living daylights out of mine."

"I wish you were here," I hear myself saying, eyes still shut.

"Is that your boyfriend?" Nan whispers to me.

I never get to answer her because all of a sudden, Will says, "Want me to hold your hand?"

And I don't know what he means, but I say, "Okay."

"Okay," he repeats, and I swear there's a little catch in his voice. Like he's nervous or something. "Your hands are tiny," he says after a moment.

I laugh. "No, they're not."

Historically, I have kind of large hands for a girl.

"Ah, but in mine, they are. See, 'cause I have big, manly hands."

"Actually, your hands were—"

Will coughs. "Let's just go with it."

I'm smiling, even as the pain amplifies on my foot.

"So your hands are in mine, and they're soft," he says. "I'm threading my fingers through them now. And they're kind of sweaty because we're both kind of nervous."

I open my eyes.

What is happening?

"Okay" is all I say, and I stare at my palms on the bed. Empty.

"And now my thumb is making circles over your hand. Over your life line, which is long and dark. Much longer than mine," he says, and I swallow.

"You're going to live forever," he tells me. "You're going to grow old and get hundreds of tattoos because they say once you start, you don't stop. And now I'm following all the creases on your hand. They're like a map, you know?"

Before I can speak, he continues, "And your fingers are long. Piano-playing long."

I shut my eyes again.

"I'm tickling the back of your hand with my thumb now. Are you ticklish?"

"Yes," I say.

Then, "Can you feel it?" he asks. "My hand in yours?"

I keep my eyes closed, ignore my palms sitting flat on the bed.

"Yes," I say, and I swear, I almost can.

Later that night, Will and I continue the conversation.

"Holding hands used to get me and Lacey in trouble at Camp Rowan."

Will snorts. "Why?"

"Thirty-centimeter rule. Even girls and girls had to leave room for the Holy Spirit. But mostly it was other kids we had to worry about. Our first year there, Lacey and I walked around the camp glued to each other's sides. It was the first time away from home for both of us and it was the summer Lacey's parents were getting divorced and basically it felt like we only had each other. We told everyone we were sisters, but anyone with working eyes could tell we weren't."

"Those differences don't feel so big when you're young," Will says.

"No differences ever felt big with us," I tell him. We felt like halves of the same person. "This kid Grayson and his friends would follow us around whenever we were holding hands, taunting us and asking if we were lesbians."

"What did you tell him?" Will asks.

"Probably nothing," I say. "Though I think Lace might have used the f-word for the first time that summer."

I think about it for a moment, then add, "I do love Lacey, but it's a different kind of love. Having a best friend is like finding part of yourself walking around unattached."

"I wish I knew what that felt like," Will says.

28

THE GUILT OF what I've done, the swell on the inside of my ankle, tender and raw, follows me everywhere. Like at any moment, someone will lift up my jeans and point to my ankle. For the next couple of days, I do my best to avoid my parents, going early to work and coming back late.

It's funny how at the start, More for Less seemed foreign and strange.

Now I feel efficient and useful and even confident as I go through the motions of giving people change, making small talk, wiping down my conveyor belt, sometimes bagging for someone else if I have no customers. It feels nice to know how things go somewhere, at least.

The most eventful thing that happens the rest of the week is that Elyse comes into the store again on Friday and stops at my till.

"We're trying a new recipe," she says, pointing to her phone. She's talking to Will again. "You have to come over sometime. Maybe I can make it for you."

A seed of guilt rolls over my skin.

She would never treat me like this if she didn't think I was Will's girlfriend.

"That would be great," I tell her.

The second-most eventful thing that happens today is that James is walking past when Kennie's phone rings. She has forgotten to put it on silent. He goes right to her station, as if there's no question whose phone it is.

"Give it to me," he says, holding out his hand.

"Give you what?" Kennie asks innocently, even as the phone keeps ringing in the pocket of her jeans.

"Kennie," James sighs.

"Sorry!" she says, finally pulling it out and stopping it. "I'll put it away myself, I swear. But the newbies aren't going to respect me if they see you confiscating my phone like a thirteen-year-old."

"Maybe if you weren't as attached to your phone as a thirteen-year-old is, I wouldn't have to confiscate it," James says, but he's already walking away from her. "Do not make me tell you again."

"Got it," Kennie says, and gives an exaggerated wink. "Thanks, James!"

I can hear James sigh from here as he goes into his office and shuts the door. All us cashiers are laughing when Kennie traipses into the staff room to put away her phone. It seems impossible that she actually does this; she couldn't be more addicted to that thing if it was surgically attached to her. But I don't *see* or *hear* the phone for the rest of the day, so I have to give her the benefit of the doubt. And, fine, I might be a little bit of a hypocrite, because I've had Will on all day in my pocket. Every now and then, I'll pull out my phone to say something to him, but I actually *am* discreet about it. Plus, with Will on the line, other calls won't ring through, so I'm not in any danger of having Kennie's bad luck.

After work, I head to Juno's and squeeze into a booth next to Cate. Thomas and Kennie are across from us. It's a smaller crowd than usual, so we don't need a second booth. Oliver shows up at about five-thirty, after we've all already ordered. A waiter comes to take his order and then brings out a plate of onion rings for him almost immediately.

Kennie is in the middle of describing her System to us.

"Dinner is if I'm already interested," she's saying. "Life is short. Dinner is *long*. Especially with someone who is a dud.

"Coffee is for a complete wild card. Like a blind date or someone I haven't talked to very long online. I can drink coffee fast if it sucks, you know?"

"What if you're doing coffee and you like him, though?" Thomas asks.

"Then coffee can turn into dessert or dinner or whatever else," she says with a smirk.

"What's drinks for?" I ask. "Didn't you do that last week?"

Oliver chews on some onion rings. "I was gonna ask that too. What's that one?"

"Oh! Yes!" Kennie says. "Drinks is in between. Like, I don't *know* if I'm interested but you're hot and I don't get a psychopath vibe from you so we'll see where this goes. Also, it's if I feel comfortable enough to get tipsy with you, but not enough to commit to dinner. You can't drink with just anybody, you know," she says sagely as she reaches for her cup of green tea.

"And what's the point of all this again?"

"To find her soul mate, of course," Cate says, and of course she is a romantic.

"I wouldn't go that far," Kennie says. "I mean, if there's not one single person for me, then I'm fine with that. Who says it's not better to share all this"—she waves her hands over herself—"with as many people as possible?"

There's a long, thoughtful pause while we all consider this, before Thomas cracks up laughing.

"What? What did I say?" Kennie asks, indignant. "I mean I'm sharing my *time,* not . . . Oh, shut up."

This sets off Oliver and Cate, and then it's got me too, a domino effect of laughter. And I'm thinking I like the sound of my laugh mixed in with theirs and I like that Oliver passes his plate of onion rings around and that Cate is predicting what Michael is going to order next, when most of us met only two weeks ago.

After everyone sobers up, the conversation shifts to school and Thomas's last year before college.

"I already have senioritis," he says. "I'm over it and the year hasn't even started yet."

"Do you know where you're going yet?" Oliver asks him.

"Hell yeah," Thomas says. "Toledo. Everyone in my family went there."

"You two are going to college this fall, right?" Cate says, looking between me and Oliver. "Do you already know what you want to do?"

Oliver tells them that he's going to State, that he's looking into architecture but he doesn't know what kind yet, and it's the first time I realize that no matter what, I actually will know someone there.

Of course I knew Oliver was going to State too, but it never felt significant.

For so long, college for me has been this: twin beds pushed along opposite walls, driving away from Erinville with most of our worldly possessions stuffed into my car, listening to the radio while Lacey sits with her ankles crossed on my dashboard, her enormous sunglasses taking up more than half of her face.

"I'm going to State too," I say now. "But I don't know what I want to do."

"You have no ideas?" Cate asks.

"No."

"You still have time," Cate says.

"It doesn't feel like it," I admit.

"Trust me, you do," Kennie says. "It took me, like, two years just to declare a major. Everybody acts like you have to know exactly what you want, but you don't. You'll be fine."

"I hope so," I say, and her words are a relief, assurance that it's okay to be lost, that it's okay not to have my life plotted out, not to know what I love or want. It's enough to simply be on the way to figuring it out.

29

IT'S JUST BEFORE seven when we pile out of Juno's, but the sky is strangely dark. The clouds are bloated, like a storm is coming.

We all say goodbye in the parking lot and get into our separate cars. Mia would have a conniption regarding our individual carbon footprints if she was here.

I feel this twinge, this awareness of her absence, which is strange because I've gotten used to her being at Stanford—but seeing her for those few weeks she was around, it makes me miss her.

I wonder how she's doing in DC.

Thinking about Mia gets me thinking about my parents, and suddenly I'm dreading going home. I decide to kill time by talking to Will, debriefing about Juno's and the day at work.

"I feel like Kennie is the person you want to be stranded on a desert island with, but it's Cate who won't kill you for food."

"You've given this some thought," Will says.

"I don't exactly have a lot going—"

I jump at a tapping sound on my window.

It's Oliver, peering through the glass at me.

I push the button to slide the driver's window down. "Hey!"

"Hey!" he says. "You're still here."

"Yeah, I . . ." I'm about to make up a reason but then I think, *What's the point?* "I'm avoiding going home."

"What's at home?"

After a moment's pause, all I give him is a shrug. He looks around the parking lot, then back at me.

"Want some company?" he asks.

I think about this for a moment. I *was* talking to Will, but that can wait.

"Sure," I hear myself saying. I shut off my phone without saying goodbye, but I think Will understands.

Oliver smiles and stands straight.

"It's boiling in here, though," I say, opening the car door. Despite the darkening sky outside, it's not raining yet. I climb out, taking my phone with me. "My air conditioner hates me."

Oliver circles to the front of my car, and without discussion, we both climb up and sit on top of my hood.

"So," he says after a moment. "What's going on with you and Lacey?"

I look down, not certain I want to get into this. "I'm pretty sure she hates me. I guess I was too clingy or something."

"She does not hate you," Oliver says. "I've been worried about her, hanging out with Hail and those guys."

"Me too."

"Ever since what happened with Mason, I've been following her to parties, just trying to keep my eye on her."

Mason. I try not to react to Will's name, to the reference to the accident.

"You're a good brother," I say, and he glances up at me, surprised.

"I don't know," Oliver mumbles, and I look up at him, watch his profile as he looks straight ahead in the growing darkness. "What am I supposed to do in the fall when she's . . . ?"

His voice fades.

"I know she's not going to college," I say, putting him out of his misery. "She told me that a few weeks ago."

He nods. "I'm sorry."

And for some reason, I feel the sting again, of betrayal, of being abandoned when I thought it was a sure thing. Lacey and me this summer, Lacey and me at State, Lacey and me ad infinitum. "It's not your fault."

"You know, the whole reason I chose to go to State was because that was where she was going. And because it's only four hours away, so I can still keep an eye on Mom."

"I thought it was because you got a full ride to State," I say, surprised.

"I got a couple different offers," he says, rubbing the back of his neck. "But I knew I would feel guilty if I went anywhere else. I didn't want to just . . . abandon them. And now she's not even going to college."

"She'll be fine," I hear myself saying. "It's not up to you to look after Lacey." Oliver is looking intently at me now, like he's hanging on my every word, and I wonder if maybe he needs permission to stop feeling guilty about living his own life, to stop feeling guilty for the times when he can't be there for his mom and sister. I think about him cooking the other day, all the things he does to help out his mother. And then all the parties he goes to just to make sure Lacey gets home safely. Yes, he has his share of fun at them, but he always stays sober so she has a ride.

That's a lot of time, that's a lot of burden to carry, feeling like it's up to you to make sure your sister gets home alive.

"I don't even know if I'm helping," he says. "I couldn't get her to stop going to these things, so I go with her, but is that enabling her? Do I tell Mom that she's drinking, going out this much, and give her something else to worry about?"

There's such a weight in his voice, I get this overwhelming urge to reach out and touch his arm, his face, anywhere, so I can absorb some pain from him. After Lacey and Oliver's dad left years ago, both of them changed. Lacey became angrier, more impulsive and more irritable, like she had no patience for a world in which families fall apart. Oliver changed too. It was like he felt it had fallen to him to look after his mom and sister.

I realize now that he's believed that, made it his mission ever since.

How do I tell him he's wrong when he might not be?

Sometimes, as unfair as it might be, the weight of keeping a person—people, your family—together falls on you, and you might be collapsing underneath it, but you can't just shrug it off. You find a way to fix it, to carry it, or you let it crush you.

You don't tell your father that your mother is having an affair.

My mind is whirring with so many thoughts, and we are both silent for a long time.

"Do you plan on telling them anything about yourself?" Oliver asks now, and I look at him, confused.

"What do you mean?"

He points in the direction of the entrance to Juno's. "Everyone. Work people."

Oh, shit. It's right then I remember that I told people my mom was a teacher and that I didn't know how to skate.

But what Oliver says is, "I thought you used to want to study psychology? Like your mom?"

"How do you know that?" I ask. I remember Cate asking me tonight if I had any idea what I might want to do.

No, I'd said.

Oliver scratches the back of his head, looks past me for a second. "I've known you for how many years? Plus, you know, Lacey talks."

I'm trying to think in what context I might have talked to Lacey about college in Oliver's presence or what reason Lacey might have had to bring up my plans to him. Maybe when she was telling him hers—and since our plans were so intricately linked, it just slipped out.

Still, it was years ago the last time following in Mom's footsteps even crossed my mind. And the phase hadn't even lasted that long. How could Oliver know that?

"*And* I seem to remember that you were pretty damn good at skating."

My face is heating up even more now, which I had not thought possible. Oliver had totally not looked like he was hearing a word I was saying that first day at Juno's.

I do not like the turn this conversation has taken.

"You're only saying that I was good because you . . ."

"Were terrible," he finishes for me, laughing. "You can say it."

"Relatively speaking. It's not that I'm great either—I'm like someone just plunked a cow on ice, you know? Compared to Sam."

He just watches me, and I can't tell whether that's judgment behind his gaze. I glance away.

"I didn't know you . . ." *Knew so much about me.* I must have had fewer than ten real conversations with Oliver since middle school, and they always either revolved around Lacey or were about something innocuous like homework or pizza. "I didn't know you remembered us skating together when we were little. The three of us."

"Well, considering that it was one of the more traumatic experiences of my life," he says, "I do. I could barely stand up. I still can't stand up, I don't think. I haven't been on ice in years."

"Lucky," I say. "Though you've got that whole running thing, so it's not like you're starved for athletic prowess."

Oliver laughs. "Starved for athletic prowess . . . Is that what they're calling it these days?"

"Don't do the whole humble *aw shucks* thing," I say, kicking his sneaker with the tip of my shoe. "If I was the best at something, literally *anything*, I wouldn't be able to stop bragging about it."

"I'm maybe the fifth-best distance runner in my age group in the county, but thanks for the vote of confidence," he says with a smile.

"Lies," I say, narrowing my eyes at him. "You're at least fourth best." Or first best, but no need to give him an even bigger head.

He laughs. "Well, maybe I should start bragging. I thought doing it because I liked it was enough, but apparently I'm missing the point?"

"Definitely missing the point," I say, catching his eye in the dimming light, and we smile at each other.

"How's Beckah?" I hear myself asking, and Oliver looks as whiplashed as I am by the question.

"I . . . Good, I think? I haven't seen her in a while."

"You're not . . . together?"

He shakes his head. "I feel like . . ." Oliver hesitates, like he's debating how much to say. Finally he continues, "I feel like I spend so much time worrying about shit. Worrying about Mom and Lacey and running and college. If I got into something, I just don't know if I'd have anything left to give. I don't know if I have room to really care about someone else." He pauses for a second. "Does that make me a giant dick?"

"No," I say. "Maybe a medium-size one."

He laughs out loud, and I feel weirdly proud to have earned it.

We are silent for a while and then he says pointedly, "So *back to the name thing*." He's grinning at me, and it's kind of hard to maintain eye contact, so I look away. "Is it that you're building a new persona? Doing the whole undercover thing?"

I shrug, run my thumb against a scratch on my car's hood. "It sounds stupid *now*, but it feels good to be around people who don't care what I do, where I end up. They don't know anything about me, so I can be anyone."

Oliver has a half smile on his face now. "If you were going to reinvent yourself, you could have gone a *little* further. Just a little. *Sheridan*."

I narrow my eyes at him. "You," I say with a warning tone, "do not get to call me that."

He laughs. "What should I call you?"

"*Eden*," I say in a *duh* tone of voice.

Oliver raises an eyebrow. "Even at work? That might be a little confusing for people."

My face is heating up with embarrassment again, but I roll my eyes to avoid showing anything but impatience.

God, this is humiliating. Note to self: when you're creating little white lies about yourself, you might want to make sure not to do it when your best friend's twin brother is around.

"I don't . . . I guess I wanted to try it on for a while. Maybe I'm a Sheridan, you know? I guess I just wanted an identity other than one of the Paulsen girls, the *unextraordinary* Paulsen girl, or Lacey's best friend."

When I say that, it hits me with force how true it is.

"You're not . . ." Oliver shakes his head, like he's not sure where to start. "You're not any of those things. You're not just Lacey's best friend."

I snort, and poke my shoe against the tip of his sneaker again.

"You're not," he insists, and he catches my ankle. He lets go, but then traces his thumb just above my anklebone. My body immediately warms.

"Is this real?" he asks, and I realize he's touching my tattoo, the comma on my ankle.

His hand on my leg makes it hard to swallow, so I nod.

"Whoa," he says. "When did you get it?"

"A couple of days," I mumble, the best I'm able to come up with while his hand is still touching my ankle. Did I shave my legs this morning? If I don't move an inch, how long is he going to keep doing that?

"Does it hurt?"

"It's just kind of tender," I say, and he stops touching me. I immediately miss his hand when it's gone.

"It's pretty badass. What's it mean?"

"Life goes on," I say, giving him the short version.

He watches me carefully. "It suits you."

I snort. "Because when you think Eden Paulsen, you think *badass*."

"I do," Oliver says. "That, and the cutest damn Tot Who Skates I've ever seen."

"You're such a flirt, Oliver," I say, laughing, and he's looking at me, his eyes twinkling in the dark. The intensity of his eyes, brown, deep enough to fall into, is insane. And I'm ashamed to admit that I get the *bedroom eyes* girls now. I'm even more ashamed to be dangerously close to joining the list of girls he makes fall in love with him in the dark.

Lacey would kill me.

An evil voice in my head parrots back: *Lacey's not here.*

"Not always on purpose," Oliver is saying in response, a cheeky grin on his face.

Fourteen years and it's the first time Lacey's brother has undeniably flirted with me. Which isn't to say he *hasn't*; just that this is the first time I'm sure.

"Whatever" is the best comeback I can manage.

"Seriously, though," he says. "You're not just Lacey's sidekick."

I roll my eyes. "Oh yeah? What am I?"

"Funny. Kind. Smart," he says. "Off-limits."

My head snaps up at that, but before I can say anything, he continues, "You're Eden Paulsen. How do you not know that?"

It's supposed to be a joke, and it mostly is, but I feel a pinch in my chest and I'm close to crying, because it's true. Why is so much of what I know about myself relative to Lacey?

She's the reason I'm at More for Less this summer, the reason I'm not at Camp Rowan. She's the only person I wanted to tell—the only person I felt I *could* tell—when I found out about my mom.

I don't know what it is that makes me say it, whether it's the fact that it's getting even darker, a blanket of bluegrayblack that makes me feel safe enough to tell the truth. Or maybe I feel like I owe him a truth after all the work lies he's caught me in. Or maybe I'm just tired of attaching everything about my life to Lacey and I want to change that, starting now.

Whatever is behind it, it comes tumbling out.

"My mom is cheating on my dad."

Oliver turns to me, wide-eyed, then after a moment he says, *"Shit."*

"With Sam's coach. He's this guy from Ukraine. He has a bronze medal. So I guess that's the attraction."

He doesn't laugh at my attempt at humor.

"Does your dad know?"

I shake my head, bite my lip at the thought of him finding out. "He can't find out. It would destroy him. And he had that mini-stroke and they say it's a precursor to a bigger one and . . ."

My father would fall apart. Even if he was healthy.

"Does . . . anybody know?" Oliver asks.

Will.

"Just me," I say, because I can't bring myself to say his name. I tell Oliver about going to her office and seeing her in Serg's arms, and I'm hoping he'll suggest that maybe I was seeing things or maybe they're not *actually* cheating since it wasn't, like, some passionate lovemaking session, but he doesn't.

"That sucks." I feel him looking at me from the corner of my eye, but I can't look up. "I'm sorry."

"Yeah, it's fine. Just trying to figure out what to do, I guess," I say.

"You know, your dad might surprise you. He's probably a lot stronger than you think. People are mostly different than you expect."

"Maybe," I say, but the words don't make any difference. I still know that there is no way I can tell him. It feels like Oliver and I can keep talking forever, but right then, a giant raindrop lands on my forehead. Before I can even reach up to wipe it off, two more drops fall in quick succession.

"Well, shit," Oliver says, looking up at the sky.

I glance at my phone screen and it's nearly eight.

"We should probably . . . ," he says.

"Yeah, I need to get home," I say, hopping onto the ground as the rain starts to fall faster around us.

Oliver jumps off my hood. He seems to hesitate before turning to walk to his car. "See you later, Eden."

"Bye," I say, and wave once at him, before entering my car.

30

THE LAST REAL conversation I had with Oliver had happened on a summer night, three years ago, when we were fifteen. It was mid-August, heat searing even into the night, and I'd been staying over at Lacey's for the weekend when she and her mother had gotten into one of their epic fights. My mom and I had our share of disagreements, but mostly they were short-lived, passive-aggressive affairs, with lots of guilt-tripping and disappointment, and they always ended with me apologizing.

This night, Lacey and I had come home after spending the day at the mall. Mrs. Murdoch's gray Toyota pulled into the driveway a few minutes after we arrived, and she recruited help from Lacey, Oliver and me to unload groceries from the back of her car. In between those trips from the car into the house, our hands full of brown bags with green apples and toilet paper and frozen waffles, something happened and it caused Lacey to explode. I would find out later that it involved Lacey's father having purchased tickets for him and Lacey to attend some hipster music festival in LA, the fall equivalent of Coachella, as a late birthday present to

Lacey. But the weekend was in the middle of the school year and Mrs. Murdoch didn't think she should go.

"You just don't trust me," Lacey bellowed to her across the kitchen, and Mrs. Murdoch answered, "I trust you plenty. I just don't think the timing works."

"So when works better for you?" Lacey hissed. "Never? After the ice caps melt?"

"Lacey," her mother said, thumbs on her temples. "You're giving me a headache. Can you lower your voice?"

"Why can't I ever express myself without being told to *calm down* or *you're giving me a headache* or *I don't have time for this*? You don't care what I think. It's always about proving that you're in control."

Those were the magic words. I had come to know them well over the past eleven years, or rather, the past six years since the Murdochs had divorced.

This is about control.

You just want to control me.

You just want me to be your little puppet.

And they were off to the races.

Mrs. Murdoch lost her patience then and was yelling back at Lacey, accusing her of being disrespectful, of trying to rile her up by choosing her dad whenever she could, and Lacey was yelling back more of the above.

All you want is to be able to control everyone, for everyone to do exactly what you say all the time.

There is nothing more awkward than watching your friends fight with their parents in your presence. For the most part, it was like they forgot you were there, and all the details that were usually hidden from you, like dirty underwear or used tissues, were strewn all over the place, hanging out in the open. The moments when they remembered your presence were even worse.

Lacey, you're making this miserable for Eden. I doubt she planned to spend her Friday night watching her friend have a hissy fit.

Or, *Lacey, let's talk about this later. You're making Eden uncomfortable.*

Or, *Eden was even there when I told you this last time, Mom. Right, Eden?*

And I'd mumble some noncommittal thing or claim not to remember, even if I did, and then try to busy myself pretending to read texts or, in this case, stuff apples into the fruit bowl.

Thankfully, this time, Oliver was there too, and our eyes would meet periodically as we went on working (Lacey and her mom were face to face in the middle of the kitchen now, mirror images, hands on hips, eyes narrowed, mouths shooting venom). He would roll his eyes every few minutes or make a face, and I'd shoot a small smile back, careful not to get caught mocking the fight.

Oliver had a million extracurriculars, most involving sports, so he wasn't always there during these spats, but I was grateful whenever he was.

Sometimes he would intervene with an incredulous, *Really? That's what this is about?* Or, *Come on, Lace, just leave it,* when his sister had gone too far.

No matter what they were fighting about, the arguments always ended the same way. One person would suddenly refuse to keep engaging—usually Mrs. Murdoch—and the other would make one last dig—usually Lacey—and then Lacey would look at me, nod in the direction of an exit and skulk off, me following quickly behind. It had happened a few times when I hadn't been able to follow her, like when we were eating dinner and she stormed off into her room, or when we were shopping with her mom and Lace had disappeared into another aisle, too annoyed to stay. On those occasions, the word *awkward* took on new meanings. Mrs. Murdoch would sigh and say, *Sorry you had to see that, Eden.* Or, *I bet you never talk to your parents that way,* and I'd laugh or try to say something innocuous enough that it wasn't throwing Lacey under the bus but wasn't making enemies with her mom either. One time, Lacey's mom had burst into tears after their fight and hurried upstairs into her room to cry.

I had witnessed so many of Lacey and her mom's outbursts that I should have been used to them, but the truth is that fights are one of those things that are particular to a family. Like hair color or birthday rituals or how many things you put ketchup on. The cadences of an argument, the words you pick, how far you're willing to go, how long it lasts—all those things are unique, like a family crest or thumbprints or something. The fights Lacey and her mom had were so much more intense than any my family ever had. And while I always knew they'd work things out soon enough, that still didn't make things any less uncomfortable. The one good thing was that the volatile nature of their relationship made me feel certain that Lacey could relate to how out of place I often felt in my family, made me know I could trust that she'd understand that I said some words in the heat of the moment, and that when things were fine again, those words—those feelings— were void. She wouldn't judge me.

That night, though, their fight grew so ugly that it dragged past dinnertime and even I was beginning to get a headache. I followed Lacey up to her room as usual and listened to her vent and stew and curse under her breath while she hate-ate through half a jar of Nutella. She fell asleep still angry, and as I lay on the floor in my sleeping bag beside her bed, listening to the clipped, irritated rhythm of her breathing, I couldn't fall asleep.

I wasn't sure what it was about this fight that was different, but listening to Lacey rag on her mom, listening to her call her mother power hungry and controlling, I felt exhausted. And annoyed. Like, if Lace hadn't fallen asleep when she had, I'd have lost it, finally, for the first time ever. Just snapped and told her to shut up.

Enough, I'd have said.

She said no, you can't go.

The last time you went to visit your dad, he forgot you were coming and left you waiting at the airport for more than six hours. Maybe she's right *to be controlling.*

But I didn't. And I couldn't.

Because Lacey and I were allies. We didn't judge even the worst about each other, and that was what made it work. That was why we had been friends, inseparable, for so many years.

I felt guilty for wanting to turn on her.

But I felt irritated that she couldn't see what was so obvious— that her mother was only looking out for her—and continued to argue it out.

I was restless and hot.

After tossing and turning for a bit, I climbed out of my sleeping bag, tiptoed out of Lacey's bedroom and to the bathroom. On my way back to her room, a few minutes later, I heard some sounds coming from downstairs. The kitchen, I was pretty sure.

I glanced at Lacey's room, saw the door was shut and started down the stairs, expecting to find her mother, bleary-eyed and in her robe, unable to sleep too because of the fight.

But it wasn't her mother.

It was Oliver.

He was standing at a counter, a plate of food in front of him.

I hesitated, not just because it was nearly one a.m. and he wasn't who I'd expected to find down there; he was also shirtless, pajama bottoms sitting low on his hips, and it wasn't the first time I'd seen Oliver without a shirt on—it wasn't even the first time I'd seen Oliver without a shirt on in the last year—but it *was* the first time I had seen him shirtless since the words *Oliver Murdoch* had started to become synonymous with words like *hot, sexy* and *dreamy.*

Before I could sneak out and head back to Lacey's room, he turned around, and then I could see the blueprint of abs around his midsection, the start of a muscular V on his hips above the waistband of his pants, and I was suddenly aware of the thin tank top I slept in and the matching micro-shorts that kept me from overheating in the summer.

"Hey," he was saying as he noticed me. He was lifting his plate off the counter, holding it to his body in some sort of protective stance, and carrying a glass of milk in his other hand.

"What are you doing up?" I asked, resolving to not act like a maniac. This was *Oliver.*

"Second supper," he said, and shot me a grin. "Do you have a problem with that?"

He had two grilled cheese sandwiches, both cut diagonally, on his plate, and he brushed past me and headed into the living room. He'd already finished one sandwich half and started another by the time he settled on the sofa.

"Wait," I said. "So that massive thing of lasagna we had was not enough for you?"

"I ran, like, twelve miles today," he said, taking another bite. A trail of crumbs lingered, going from the edges of his lips to the bottom of his chin. "Don't judge. Anyway," he continued. "I don't know about you, but I found it hard to concentrate on eating during World War III."

Lacey and their mom's fight.

"Yeah, I know," I said, coming around to the sofa he was sitting on and climbing on too, on the other end. I wasn't sure what made it feel significant that of all the seats in the living room, I'd chosen to sit on the same one he was on, but he watched me as I did, as I folded my legs underneath me.

"Want some?" he asked, holding out his plate, and the two diagonal halves of grilled cheese that remained. I wasn't hungry, exactly, but with the hot cheese melting between the slices and Oliver's loud, appreciative chewing, it was tempting.

"Come on," he said, pushing the plate toward me even more, so it touched my knee. "Lace is asleep, right? So the coast is clear."

"Fine. Thank you," I said, and took one of the halves. He took the other and set his empty plate on the ottoman, where his long legs were outstretched.

It was only after I took my first bite—and it was so good, thank God I'd said yes—that his words sunk in.

Swallowing so I wasn't speaking with my mouth full, I narrowed my eyes at him. "What do you mean, *the coast is clear*?"

I saw him rescue the remote from the space between the arm of the couch beside him and a cushion, then he pointed it at the TV to turn it on.

Oliver shrugged in response as the screen blared to life, but then he looked at me, giving me his am-I-annoying-you smile.

The answer was yes, he was annoying me, especially when he said, "Just that you don't have to worry that Lace will see you fraternizing with the enemy."

Fraternizing with the enemy.

I could have pretended not to know what he meant, but I did. "You weren't even part of the argument," I said. "She's mad at your mom."

"Right," Oliver said. "But she's not thrilled with me, which means you shouldn't be either."

My blood was starting to feel as warm as what was left of the cheese in my sandwich. "Are you serious? Just because we're best friends doesn't mean I'm some sort of clone." This implication had been there in some of his words to me in the past. It had been in Mia's words to me, my mom's on occasion. And it got right under my skin.

Oliver shrugged. "Guess it's hard to tell," he said, still taunting. Shirtless or not, he was exactly the same boy who made six-year-old Lace and me cry by smashing a grasshopper underneath his foot instead of taking it outside like he was supposed to.

"Quit being a jerk, Oliver," I said. "I'm totally different from Lacey. You should know better than anyone what it feels like for people to assume you're not."

At that, his expression sobered, his face flushed a little. They were twins, grouped together so much that no matter how much they might love each other, it still had to be aggravating to feel like their identities were intertwined. "I guess you're right. Sorry," he said quietly, and I could tell he meant it.

Sitting across the couch from Oliver, I could easily see the things that had skyrocketed his popularity in recent times. His dark brown hair, which had been too long for years, often falling into his face uncontrollably when he was younger, was now much shorter, tamer. It looked like it might feel soft between my fingers.

There was also, when he wasn't teasing or being an idiot, this sincerity in his eyes. This steadfastness about how he looked at you that made you want to keep his gaze for as long as you could.

He was looking at the television now, channel surfing.

"Ooh, leave it on this one," I said when he paused on a film I recognized, a party scene in a basement with a bunch of eighties preteens.

"Ugh, I was hoping you wouldn't say that," Oliver said, but he left it on, dropped the remote in his lap and watched quietly for the next few minutes.

I leaned back on the couch, reciting a few lines I knew as the actors said them.

"Lacey and I have watched this more than ten times," I said. "No joke."

"I don't doubt it," Oliver said, shooting me a playfully condescending look. He went on to list a few of the movies he'd seen more than ten times. They were all, unsurprisingly, of the action/superhero/zombie variety, which I had enjoyed many times myself.

Still, I interrupted him to ask, "Do you *enjoy* being predictable?"

Given the perfect entry to my impassioned rant, I was unstoppable. It was also one a.m. and I had just had a perfect grilled cheese sandwich. Oliver was wise enough to sit back, one eyebrow quirked while I began.

"People act like romantic comedies are so unrealistic, completely pointless, blah blah blah," I said, reciting the words I had said to Lacey many times before, "but all they are are movies with happy endings. Which is exactly what your blow-up-everything movies are too, except that the rom-com version of a happy ending is two people ending up in love, while *your* movies end with the bad guys in jail, doing time for their crimes."

Releasing a held-in breath, I concluded, "They are *all* literally just movies with happy endings. They are not that different."

Oliver was staring at me like he was fighting a smile when I finished.

"If you even think about laughing," I warned. He laughed anyway. A warm, full laugh that, thankfully, did not sound condescending.

"I already *said* we could watch this," he said, holding up his hands in surrender. "We can watch it *twice* if you want."

"Good," I said, turning back to face the TV. I could have sworn I could feel Oliver's eyes drift over to me every few minutes, and it made my stomach tickle. I grabbed a throw pillow and hugged it to myself, several minutes passing before I was able to pay attention to the movie again.

"What stuff don't you agree with Lacey on?" Oliver suddenly asked. I glanced over at him, jarred at being drawn out of the movie after trying *so hard* to stay in it. His voice was soft and he was watching me while he played with the remote in his hands.

"I don't know," I said, not sure what he wanted me to say. "I mean, I think country music's pretty great. Or can be."

Oliver watched me, expressionless, waiting for me to go on.

"I think," I said, "I think she kind of owes your mom an apology."

It was the first time I had ever admitted something like this about Lacey, and I expected to feel guiltier than I did, but it was true.

"What else?" Oliver asked, like he wanted to find out every single way his sister and I were different.

And even though I was doing most of the talking, maybe because of the early morning or the silent streets outside or even the fact that we were the only ones up in the entire house—it felt a little like we were explorers, unearthing truths too fragile to find in the daylight. Like we were discovering each other.

How am *I different from Lacey?*

I was thinking this, searching my mind, when we suddenly heard footsteps, lights switching on, and without meaning to, I jumped the slightest bit back on the couch.

It wasn't Lacey—it was Mrs. Murdoch—but Oliver had seen my reaction. I was certain of it.

Whether we admitted it or not, there was something about being on Lacey's side that meant forfeiting anyone else's. I knew it. Oliver knew it.

Mrs. Murdoch must have known it too, because after being surprised to discover us down there, she sat on the couch between us.

"What are you up to?" she asked.

"I'm schooling Oliver on romantic comedies," I said.

"Noble work," she said with a laugh, and Oliver groaned while we went on discussing our favorite movies and Mrs. Murdoch told us she'd learned the "Thriller" dance in college. We hadn't been doing anything wrong when she'd come down. We hadn't even been thinking about doing anything wrong. But I felt caught, in a weird way, and I think Oliver did too, because there was something daring about sitting together, sharing grilled cheese sandwiches and talking that late at night, and he wasn't even wearing a shirt.

Change almost always starts with something tiny, far from the surface. With movement too small to notice or gauge, that travels up and changes something else, until there's a long chain of altered things and then everything is different.

This might have been why Mrs. Murdoch shepherded me up the stairs when she was going back to sleep, saying she would hate my parents thinking she let me come over for all-night ragers, and telling Oliver to go to bed too.

I glanced back at him over my shoulder as we started to go, and I caught him watching us leave. Watching *me* leave, and to this day I can't remember which of us ended up looking away first.

31

IT'S RAINING ON my way in to work on Monday and I'm running slightly late, but I talk to Will on the drive anyway, mostly muttering about what passes for traffic here in Erinville. He's still on the line when I arrive at work. When I climb out of my car and start toward the building, I somehow find myself walking in at the same time as Oliver. Maybe it's the long talk on Friday or the things we told each other or the foot touching, but it's hard to make eye contact with him, like I need a few more days to get over it or something.

We yell hi to each other and are jogging together toward the building. I'm using my messenger bag as a makeshift umbrella and we're almost at the door when I hear a sudden plop as something hits a puddle of water.

"Shiiit," I exclaim as I see my phone on the ground, submerged.

"I got it," Oliver says, picking it up before I can, wiping it on his polo and handing it back.

"Thanks," I say as we stop at the overhang of the building. I use my work shirt to frantically wipe it down. It is not the first time I've ever dropped my phone. It's not the first time I've ever *damaged* my phone, but of course this time it begins to malfunction and I don't know what is happening on Will's end or what he's hearing, but his voice comes blaring out of my phone. The screen is completely unresponsive. I can't turn off the speaker or reduce the volume fast enough, so Oliver can hear him saying, "Eden? What's happening? Hey, Eden?"

And I'm muttering to myself, trying to dry it and turn it off and turn it down at the same time, but by the time I finally, *finally*, get it to shut off, Oliver is asking questions.

"Who was that?"

"Huh?" I say, pretending to be clueless.

"The guy on the phone. It wasn't your dad or someone?"

"Oh no, just my friend. Let's go inside."

"You're sure you don't need to call him back? You could use my phone." He's already reaching into his pocket and holding it out to me.

"It's okay. It's nothing important," I say. "It's fine."

But the jumpy way I'm acting is making it obvious that it is not fine.

"What is it, really?" Oliver asks. I can tell this is one of those moments, like the time I went over to his house crying, when it matters if I tell him the truth. So I do.

I just come out and say it.

"It's a Companion," I say, like it's no big deal. And it *isn't* a big deal. Lots of people use In Good Company. Cate uses it, and who cares that she sometimes talks to a computer? It's not *just* a computer.

"It's Will," I say now, my voice lower, and I hadn't known that

I was going to say this, but it's out now and Oliver blinks at me, blank-faced.

"Will," he repeats, not understanding.

"Will Mason," I say, and I don't know why I'm whispering, but I am.

Oliver's expression fills with complete surprise.

"Holy shit," he says, eyes wide.

"I know," I say, but I can't help the grin that takes over my face.

"How long?" Oliver asks.

"Have I been talking to him? A few weeks," I say. "Since school ended."

"Oh."

And then to reassure him, I add, "It's not a kinky sex thing." As soon as the words leave my mouth, my face heats up. "I mean, like Chris said."

"Oh yeah, no, I didn't think it was," he says, and I'm not sure why *he's* embarrassed. This whole thing is going nothing like I thought it would. That is, if I'd given it any thought at all.

"I, um . . . ," Oliver says now, pushing his hand into his pocket. "I didn't think you and Mason . . . You knew him pretty well?"

My face gets even warmer now and I can't meet Oliver's eye. "Kind of."

"Oh" is all Oliver says. He nods at my phone in my hand as we continue through the automatic doors. "Is it still working? Maybe try the rice thing?"

I end up being a few minutes late to my station—I get Kennie to sell me the smallest bag of rice More for Less carries and then I pour it all into someone's empty lunch box and leave it to sit. Hoping hoping hoping that it works.

I have to get to work, but I'm pretty sure no one is going to take it, so I leave it on top of the fridge in the staff room.

As I'm working, I feel despair that my phone might be ruined. What happens if I need a new phone? Does everything I've ever said to Will, every conversation we've ever had, get wiped from his mind?

I take my break in the staff room, spend all of lunchtime bent over my phone in some kind of vigil. I want to give the rice a chance to absorb as much water as possible, so I don't try to take my phone out yet. Toward the end of our break, Thomas is packing his dreadlocks in an elastic and Kennie is stuffing her bag into her locker and a few other people I see all the time but don't know very well are getting ready to start their shifts or lunch breaks too.

The day continues like any other day, and then around three-fifty, a few minutes before my shift ends, my dad shows up.

As if this day was not already bad enough.

He waves at me from the entrance but doesn't come my way at first. I see him disappear to the left of the store, where the floral section is. Maybe he'll just go to someone else's till when he's ready?

No such luck.

He approaches me, a bouquet of multicolored roses cradled in the crook of his elbow. He's beaming at me the whole time he's in line—completely embarrassing—and I'm tempted to go slowly in the hope that I never get to him, but my better judgment wins out.

"Hey!" he says, placing the flowers on the belt and grinning at me when it's his turn to pay. "Look at my kid at her job. How cool is this?"

"Dad," I say, and roll my eyes. As luck would have it, Jenn is working at the till beside mine, and I hear a snort from her direction. My embarrassment is her gain.

"Sorry. I'm just a regular customer. I'm just trying to pay for my groceries," he tells an elderly woman behind him, pointing at the flowers on the belt, which is even *more* embarrassing. I take the flowers, carefully locate the barcode and scan them.

"These are for your mom," he explains now, causing my arms to suddenly feel like lead.

"Why?" I ask.

"Why?" he repeats, surprised. "Just because."

The lump in my throat is hard to swallow over and I realize for the first time how loud a supermarket is. There's Kennie calling for someone to give an elderly man a hand and then there's Mark calling for a price check and people in the line behind my dad are talking and off near the staff room I can hear people laughing. It's all too much.

I feel like something is about to explode out of me and all I know is that it can't be words, because my dad does not deserve to hear about Mom and Sergiy like this, and it can't be tears, because I can never live that down, and so in the end it's this repressed kind of squeal in the back of my throat.

Dad frowns at me. "Are you okay?"

"Sneeze," I lie when I can speak.

"Oh," he says, handing me his credit card. And then, "You're done soon, aren't you? Four o'clock?"

"Yeah, but I'm going to Juno's—"

"I know, I know," he says. "I'll just wait around outside while you finish up. I just want a quick word."

Great.

"Okay," I say as I hand him his receipt and let him go. I help the last two customers at my till and then cash out. When I'm back in the staff room, I grab my stuff and then carefully extract my phone from the rice, get some paper towels to mop up any extra moisture and then power it on, *praying praying praying* to some higher force.

And it works!

"Oh my God," I exclaim, so relieved I could cry. There's another woman in the staff room, but she doesn't say anything to me.

"Thank you thank you thank you," I'm whispering to my phone as I hold it close to my chest.

I text Will. **Will! I'm sorry! We'll talk when I get home!!**

I zip my phone up in my pocket—it's not falling into any more puddles today—and hurry outside to meet my dad. The rain has stopped by now, though it's still overcast and there are puddles nearby that are only half-dry.

Dad is pacing outside the store, still holding the flowers.

"All done?" he asks when he sees me.

All the relief I felt about my phone is replaced by apprehension now, and the sick feeling of the choice I have to make. I nod, fiddling with the sling of my messenger bag.

"Let's walk to your car. Where do you park?" he asks.

We walk in the direction of my car, which is parked under a tree on the far side of the lot. It figures that this is the day I'd choose to park the farthest away from the building. In the moments before Dad starts speaking, dread and anxiety are coiled like a spring around my stomach.

"So listen," he says finally. "I know something's been going on with you. I'm not sure what, but . . ." He shoots me a sideways glance. "I don't suppose you want to talk about it."

I bite on my lip, don't answer, fold my arms across my chest.

He probably thinks it's a stance of defiance, but I'm pushing back inside me everything I don't want to have to say. Everything I probably *should* say.

I can't look at the flowers, cradled in his arms like a sleeping baby. I wish I'd crushed them when I scanned them. I want to throw them on the ground and crumple them under my feet now.

He's still speaking. "But I don't like the way you're taking things out on your mom."

No no no. I don't want to talk about her.

"You two have always been hard on each other," he says. Which. Right. I bet it was hard on my mom when I learned to crawl at ten months, a whole three months later than Mia did. I've just made life *so* difficult for her. "And I know she's strong and I know she can handle this, but I want you to lay off her, okay?"

"Dad—"

"She's been so busy with the new book—"

"You don't even know, Dad," I hear myself interrupting. "You don't know."

"You're right. I don't know. I mean, you've clearly been upset at *all* of us over something, but I notice you're harder on her. And she notices too, and I just think . . . I know you're eighteen now, almost in college, and I can't *make* you do anything. But I would really appreciate it if you were just aware that you can't take something back once it's done, you know?"

I clamp my mouth shut after that.

You can't take something back once it's done.

"Could you do that for me? Just be a little more *mindful*?"

One of Mom's words. She loves the word *mindful*.

"Okay," I hear myself promising.

"Yeah?" Dad asks, optimistic.

"Yeah," I say. "I'm sorry."

He's giving me a hug now, telling me to have fun at Juno's, that he's proud of me for doing so well at this job but there's still filing at his office with my name on it, *ha-ha*.

He finally turns to head back to his car and I enter my car and sink into the driver's seat.

The salad I had for lunch today is threatening to come up. I shut my eyes and try to memorize the look on Dad's face when I agreed to do better, because I finally understand that I can never tell him what I know.

32

I END UP not going to Juno's.

Instead, I go home and crawl into bed, skipping dinner. I call Will at around eight o'clock, the longest I've gone without speaking to him since I started at More for Less. No wonder everything about this day has sucked.

Downstairs, I can hear my parents talking and laughing, can picture them sitting on the couch, Mom's feet in Dad's lap as usual, and the image infuriates me.

It makes me feel sick.

It makes me reckless.

"Let's go somewhere," I tell Will.

"Where?"

"You'll see," I promise.

Will laughs at that. Of course he won't, *can't,* see, but he doesn't seem to mind.

"Eden, where are you going?" Mom asks when I come down the stairs. They are in exactly the position I pictured them in.

I look away. "I'm catching a late movie with Lacey."

"How late is late? When will you be home?"

"A couple of hours," I lie, call out goodbye and leave before they can ask any more questions.

I fill up my tank at Gas 'N Go but don't go inside. For all I know, they've put my picture up on one of those Wall of Shame things for shoplifters. I could just go to another gas station to be safe, but I don't really care about safe tonight. I'm in that kind of mood.

"You gonna tell me what's going on?" Will asks when I get back into the car and start driving.

"I want to show you something," I say, taking the ramp to I-83.

Once I'm on the highway, a small wave of fear rolls over me. I've never really driven this far alone, and definitely not at night.

I turn on the radio to quiet the doubt, and it's only a matter of minutes till I am channeling Lacey, singing along to every song. It makes me miss her, hearing my voice without hers, and I've never made this trip without her and that also stings.

But almost like he can feel my sadness, Will is piping up, singing along, though he doesn't know a single song. Also, he can't really hold a tune, and I can't believe I never knew that about him.

I burst out laughing because it's *so bad,* but then I change the channel to a country station and now we're on equal ground. Neither of us knows any of the songs and we're both shouting at the tops of our lungs and Lacey would actually *die* if she could hear us now. Off-pitch singing is like nails on a chalkboard to her.

I push the thought out of my head and try to stay in this moment, with Will.

"'Sittin' on the porch and you're somethin' like a torch,'" he shouts from my passenger seat, and just like at the movies that night, he feels so close I can almost touch him.

I wonder if this is what it would have been like. Dating Will.

Driving in the dark on our way to somewhere we shouldn't be going, trying to one-up each other with our goofiness.

Two hours and forty-five minutes later, I see the first sign for Camp Rowan. I follow a winding road that then turns into gravel, and in the distance I can see it: the best six summers of my life.

The rec building, the dining hall, dozens and dozens of cabins that are completely dark because lights-out is at nine-thirty p.m. and it's after eleven. I drive away from the cabins, in what I hope is the direction of the lake. If I'm remembering it correctly.

The road comes to an abrupt end, a canopy of trees standing guard, blocking the lake from view. I pull over and climb out of my car, taking Will with me.

There's a slight breeze and I keep walking, following a trail through the trees, until I see it.

The water is black, but glistening like it's swallowed hundreds of stars. Camp Rowan is named for this lake, a small natural body of water where we used to do all sorts of summer activities, like kayaking and swimming.

On the "beach," the small patch of land before the water, there's a random wooden paddle, probably forgotten there during the day's activities. Even farther down, closer to the water, something crunches under my feet. I jump back, but it's just a pair of glasses. I've dislocated one arm of the frames, but, surprisingly, the lenses are still intact. I imagine the owner, a nine-year-old girl, round-faced and panicked.

I carry the glasses and place them on top of the oar, so they can both be found tomorrow morning.

Then I take a deep breath and stick my wireless earphones in my ears, push my phone into the back pocket of my jeans. I slip out of my Converse so I'm barefoot.

"Where are we?" Will asks.

"My favorite place in the world," I tell him. "Camp Rowan."

"What's it look like?"

His voice is soft, reverent, and it means everything to me that he cares about what I care about.

I describe it to him, everything about the night, the way the stars twinkle in the sky, the way the sand underneath my feet is still warm from the day's heat. I describe the way the cabins look in the distance, older and smaller than I remember, backlit by the moon.

As I talk, I picture Will with his eyes closed, drinking it all in.

And maybe it's the image of him closing his eyes, not looking, that makes me courageous enough to do it. I lift my shirt over my head and let it drop to the ground. I'm standing there in only my bra and jeans, with Will Mason, the boy I've loved since before the start of high school.

"So what's happening now?" he asks.

I take a deep breath and tug at the zipper of my jeans, then I step out of them, letting them form a heap on the ground.

In my mind, there is no bonfire on the last day of school. Lacey doesn't jump in the river alone, and I don't stand back, watching, too afraid to join in.

In my mind, we are counselors at Camp Rowan, our fourth week here, everything happening just the way we planned it. We run out under the stars and into the lake when all our campers have gone to bed, when there are no grown-ups roaming. We do it to be daring, to be funny, to make memories.

We were going to make a million memories.

Tonight, I stand alone, shivering not from cold but from anticipation. And Will is with me.

Before I can change my mind, I climb out of my underwear and then I take off my bra and fling it.

"I'm naked," I tell him, and I swear I hear him gulp.

"Oh," he says, like he has no other words.

I walk slowly toward the edge of the lake, then stick my foot in, make a circle with my heel. I push back the thoughts of sharks and flesh-eating bacteria, of Loch Ness Monsters and things that live in dark lakes.

I take one step forward, then another.

"The water's warm," I tell Will, glad for my waterproof earphones. "I'm in up to my knees now."

"What else?" he asks.

I describe it to him, the feel of the water, the sting of my eyes when I submerge my head with my eyes still open.

Then I'm underwater and he is with me.

When I come back up, I talk to him.

I tell him I'm afraid.

Of drowning, of feeling something wrap around my ankles, pulling me down. Of being caught by someone who works here. Of being alone. Of things that go bump in the night. Of things that live in broad daylight.

I tell him I feel brave, the bravest I've ever felt. And for once, it's because of me, not because of my best friend.

I feel Lacey's absence like a phantom limb.

I tell him that too.

"I miss you," I tell Will.

"I'm right here," he says.

I plunge back into the water and stay there, both of us, bodies underwater.

"When I think of you," Will says as I'm slipping back into my jeans, "I don't think of you as afraid. But you think of yourself that way."

"Because I am," I tell him, wringing water from my hair.

"What makes you say that? You just jumped into a lake naked."

He's right but he's also not.

I explain it to him.

"Being brave wasn't something I thought about when I was little."

I grew up feeling fearless, hanging upside down in Avery Park, running just a little faster than my own heartbeat.

I realized I was the same amount of afraid as everyone else when I was six and sliding through the tunnel, when everything around me went black and suddenly the walls seemed to be closing in. I couldn't go forward and I couldn't go back and I don't know how many minutes passed until Lacey came through behind me, and together, we came out the other side.

I realized I was more afraid than everyone else when I would fake sick to get out of parties, to get out of playing seven minutes in heaven or truth or dare, when Lacey would have to cover for me or do my dares with me.

"But the worst thing was Dad's TIA," I tell Will. "You know how I told you Sam was the one who yelled for Mom when Dad started slurring his words? Well, it shouldn't have been. I was there too. Right next to him. We'd been watching TV and suddenly I couldn't understand what he was saying and there was this confusion on his face, then this panic, and I should have taken charge and known exactly what to do, but I just froze. Until Sam did what I couldn't. It's like I don't function on my own."

"It could have happened to anyone, though. You were caught off guard," Will says.

Lacey told me the same thing too, but it doesn't make me feel better.

"What if it had been an actual stroke and I could have been the difference between Dad dying or living?" I say. "I just always freeze, when I'm afraid. I hate it."

"Next time you won't," Will says, but he has more faith in me than I do.

33

BECAUSE I PROMISED my father, when I'm not avoiding Mom, I make a concerted effort to be *mindful,* or at least polite.

I still feel ill every time I look at her. When she's standing up to put some salad on Samara's plate at dinner, I wonder where her hands have been. Wonder whether she changes her clothes after she meets with him. If there's a spare set in her car. Or in her office.

What about when she goes to the gym downtown, for spin class, which she's started doing a couple of times a week? Is she meeting him? My mom is already pretty fit, but to be honest, I'm not seeing any more muscle tone in her lower body than I did before.

I know I am being ridiculous but I can't help it.

Sometimes I swear I feel her looking at me, like there's something she's trying to figure out. Like maybe she still wonders about the day I came to her office. But every time I glance up and meet her eye, her face is neutral, passive.

She's so good at hiding it. It makes me desperate to see them together again—Serg and Mom—to see how they interact, to see if there were signs all along that we all missed.

For the first time in recorded history, I volunteer to accompany Mom and Sam to Sam's lesson on Saturday.

"Oh, of course you can come," Mom says, seeming happy, which makes me feel bad because it reminds me that I actually like seeing her happy. And after weeks of not looking properly at her face, I'm remembering that my mom looks beautiful when she laughs. Her face gets all scrunched up and her eyes glitter; she's told my sisters and me for years that she likes all the laugh lines on her face.

"Who would want to erase that?" Mom often says, to which I once made the mistake of saying, "Dr. Jensen," he of the miraculous and ridiculous returning hairline. His wife too glimmers like freshly polished . . . *something*. Not skin, though. Because skin covers humans.

I'm pretty sure I got a talking-to about being "appropriate" and respecting one's elders.

It used to be something I admired about my mother. How despite always wanting things to be perfect, she's also determined to keep her wrinkles, the lines around her mouth, the scar just under her knee from a biking accident when she was little.

A body is a kind of time capsule.

But by the time we reach the rink, any affection I'm feeling for my mom is quickly replaced by blind fury and complete repulsion at the sight of Sergiy in his tight black pants and his low-neck V and why the fuck does he not cover up, there are children around. He's a role model.

When we walk in, Sergiy turns immediately, like he has a radar for us, and then he nods once. Mom raises her hand and says, "Hi, Serg," then turns her attention to Sam, like she would any other day. Obviously it would be worse if they were undressing each other with their eyes right in front of everyone, but I feel my blood boil at the knowledge that they are acting. Performing for our benefit. Which, now that I think about it, is something they are both used to—Mom when she does her public speaking engagements and Serg while he sleazes around on ice. They're also clearly both very good at it.

I find a spot at the top of the bleachers, where I can watch them closely, and so far they still haven't looked at each other again. Mom is talking to Ty's mom and they are laughing about something.

Now Serg is looking at Ty and Sam and calling them over to get started.

Which is when we all realize that Sam is not wearing her skates.

Mom goes over to her and puts her hand on her shoulder. First she's prodding her, then she's persuading, then she's *suggesting* to her, then Sam jumps away from Mom and goes running in the direction of the restrooms.

Mom holds her hands up in exasperation. I can see Serg walking over to the moms now, and though I badly want to see this interaction, something makes me jump up and follow Sam to the bathroom. It's not hard to tell which stall is hers, judging by the bare feet on the ground.

I knock on the door. No response.

Knock again.

She's obviously in there, so I try to think of an opener that she might go for.

"Sam, you realize how gross bathroom floors are?" I say.

There's no response for a second, and then a moment later, I hear some kind of movement. When I back up to see under the door, her feet are off the ground.

"Toilet seats aren't much better either," I say.

"Go away," she says.

"People throw up on them sometimes."

"Oh my God, go away, Eden!" she yells, but at least she's responding to me now.

"What's wrong?" I ask. I knock once on the door. "Hey," I say gently. "Sam, what is it?"

And then it's dawning on me that it was when Sergiy called her and Ty over that she freaked out. She spends more time with Serg and Mom than anybody else. She's *seen* how they are together.

Could she know?

"Sam?" I pound again on the door. "If you don't come out, I'm pretty sure Mom is going to come and *drag* you out."

And cause a scene?

Never going to happen, but Sam doesn't know that.

Right on cue, Mom arrives in the bathroom, and after several minutes of exasperation and then negotiation, Sam comes out of her stall.

"You have fifteen minutes left of practice," Mom says. "You could still—"

"I'm not dancing," Sam says firmly.

"Okay," Mom sighs. "Well, you better go and apologize to Serg and Ty and his mom for wasting their time."

I see them both walk over to Ty and his mom, and Sam does not once raise her head, though it's possible she moves her mouth— I'm too far away to see—and then Mom is saying something to Serg, with Ty and his mom still nearby, so it's probably nothing dirty. Then they turn around and I catch up with them so we can leave.

"I must say, Sam," Mom says in the car, "that I am extremely disappointed. I can't imagine what would make you behave this way, but I hope it doesn't happen again. And I told Serg we'd make up a practice next week. Otherwise you guys can't compete in Regionals."

Sam does not make a sound. Which, if you ask me, is probably the best response to Mom's disappointment.

As soon as we get home, Sam jumps out of the car and races up the stairs. I follow her.

Thankfully, the door of her room does not lock and she has forgotten to block it with a chair, so I'm able to walk right in.

"Why do you want to know what's wrong all of a sudden?" she snaps from where she's lying on her bed, a pillow cradled against her chest.

It feels like a slap, because it's true that while my sisters have been on different paths than I have, I've not always tried particularly hard to find common ground.

"I always want to know what's wrong," I say. I take a few steps closer to her bed and she doesn't throw her pillow at me or try to lash out, so I sit cross-legged beside her bed and wait.

Several minutes pass before I realize that she's getting no closer to telling me what's going on.

"So something happened, right?" I ask now, and to my surprise, she nods.

"Okay." I speak slowly like I'm afraid to spook a jumpy horse, which I kind of am. "Is it . . . Does it involve Mom?"

She cuts her eyes to me at that, suspicion written all over her face, and when she says nothing, I know that I'm right.

Oh my God.

Is it possible . . .

Sam knows?

"Sam," I say.

My chest is hurting because Sam and Mom . . . they're not like Mom and me. They work well together. They both love skating. And Sam has been coached by Serg for years. She trusts him, respects him.

If she knows, if she even suspects, then it's killing her.

"So it's Mom . . . ," I say carefully. "Is there someone else?"

Another sharp look.

Another yes.

"Is it Dad?" I ask.

"No," she says, almost annoyed at the guess.

"And it's not me?"

"Not everything is about you, Eden. I'm sorry to tell you." She hugs the pillow closer to her chest.

"And it's not Mia, right?"

"She's in another state!" Sam exclaims.

In another situation, I'd call her out on her patronizing attitude. But I'm desperate to know what she knows.

"So it's not a family member," I say. "Hmmm." I pretend I'm going out on a limb. "Is it someone who's close to the family? Someone we all know? Someone *you* know?"

After what feels like a million years, she nods.

My heart is beating so hard in my chest. "It's Mom and . . . someone we all know." Who else could it be? It's so obvious that she was reacting to something Sergiy had said, and if this involves Mom . . . I take a deep breath and drop my voice so only she can hear me. "Did you see something weird between them? Mom and Serg?"

Sam sits up now and frowns. "No," she says. "What's wrong with you?"

I can't recover in time. I don't have any other guesses. She said Mom and Serg. . . .

"It's *Ty*, okay?" she says.

Ty.

As in her scrawny, eleven-year-old dance partner.

"Oh," I say, deflated, shocked. But it's good that she doesn't know, right? It's good that she hasn't seen something that would destroy Mom for her. Or ice dance.

"What were you saying about Mom and Serg?"

Shit.

"Nothing. I was just . . . guessing. Like, maybe you thought they were mad at you or something. For not giving your best."

Sam's brow is crumpled for so long, I'm afraid she doesn't believe me. But finally she says, "Anyway, because you're pathetic and such a terrible guesser . . ." She takes a deep breath, sighs. "I *hate* the dress Mom picked out for our Leaverton competition. *Hate.*"

I can't help it: I roll my eyes. "Sam, all this is about a dress? A stupid dress for your dance? Oh my God."

But when I look at her, her eyes are filled with tears. She swipes them away with the back of her hand. "See why I didn't want to tell you? Just go."

"No, no, I'm sorry," I say, rising from the floor and sitting on her bed now, next to her. I put my arm around her shoulder. "What's wrong with your dress?"

"It's cut like a V," she says.

"Okay . . . ," I say, waiting for her to go on.

"Oh God, why are you so stupid? Leave me alone!"

I take a deep breath to maintain my composure. "It's just . . . You realize how angry you've made Mom and that she had to pay for a lesson you didn't have and . . . like, there are so many worse things in the world."

Her shoulders remain rigid beside me. "I know there are worse things in the world," she says. "But this is also *important*."

And then it hits me. Oh yeah. Middle school.

The hell-like passage that is a dress rehearsal for the real thing: high school.

And I remember Lacey and me freaking out over the most pathetic things. What to wear to a dance. A boy she liked who didn't like her back. Bangs cut too short.

"You're right," I say.

There's a long pause and then Sam drops the pillow she's been holding to her chest. "I hate it," she says. And finally, finally, I understand.

A few minutes later, she is standing in a bedazzled purple-blue sequined leotard thing and it is indeed V-necked and where Sam previously had nothing, a small eruption of flesh is obvious.

"But the V ends practically at your neck," I say. "It's not like it's low-cut or something. You guys are in the under-twelve division!"

"But it's drawing attention there! And Ty already . . ." She seems to take a breath before she can finish her sentence. "It's bad enough Ty can already feel them. Like, when we accidentally bump or something, and now he's going to be able to see. . . ." Her lips are quivering again.

It's really, really not funny, but somehow I have to stifle the urge to laugh.

"And then I started thinking about, like . . . later. You've seen Torvill and Dean, right? Meryl and Charlie? Tessa and Scott?" she says, listing off a bunch of ice dancers. And then she's making me pull out my phone so we can look at pictures and videos of them.

"It just gets worse later," Sam says despondently.

"But it's not like they are *naked,* Sam." A lot of the dresses are V-necked and there is the occasional low-cut dress, but it's all pretty tasteful. Plus, during their careers most of those people were in their twenties, at least, and Sam is eleven. "And you don't have to wear it. You *never* have to wear anything you don't want to. Just tell Mom."

"Do you know how much she paid to have this made?"

"Honestly," I tell Sam, "she's downstairs probably freaking out, thinking you're going to announce to her that you're quitting. She'll be relieved it's just about a *dress.*"

Sam's narrowed eyes make me quickly add, "Which is still very important."

I was twelve when I quit skating.

"The morning of our end-of-year showcase, I told my mom that I wanted to quit."

"How did she take it?" Will asks.

"About as well as you can imagine. She was furious." Normally my mom believes in *Contained* Expression, and Reasoning instead of yelling, but her voice was hoarse by the time she stormed out of the kitchen that day.

"First she told me I was making a big mistake and I'd regret it. Later, when she was doing my makeup for the show, she told me that she and Dad weren't going to come and watch me. They'd always come to every single one of my shows, and I think she hoped it'd make me change my mind.

"Throughout my performance that night, I didn't look up into the stands, because I knew that I wouldn't see them. That there was no one there for me.

"But then when I finished, I was pushing my way to the exit, to wait for Mom to pick me up, when I heard my dad's voice. He had been there the whole time. He'd come to watch me, even though my mother hadn't.

"We got into his car and he drove us to get sundaes. I knew he would be on my mother's side—he's always on my mother's side—but he didn't try to tell me not to quit skating. Instead, he told me my mother had grown up watching skating when she was little, with a family that was too poor to afford it, with a mother who thought black people didn't skate.

"'She wanted to give you what she never had,' he said.

"And I knew it was his way of defending her, but I wished more than anything that she had just told me that herself."

I might even have kept skating.

34

A FEW NIGHTS later, I wake up with it bursting out of me, the need to tell Will the truth. The need to talk about the night he died. Maybe it's this thing with my mother, seeing how a lie can infest your life, can make everything about it ugly and wrong.

I don't want to be like her.

There's also the fact that Will and I have talked about everything else—about Lacey, work, my family. The only thing—the biggest thing—we haven't talked about is that night.

When Will picks up the phone, I start at the very beginning. A history of kisses and almost kisses.

"We were outside Cabin 4A, and it was three days before the end of camp. I was twelve, and Lacey had had her first kiss playing seven minutes in heaven a few months before camp. She'd walked out of that coat closet changed."

She'd talked about it like in one split second she'd gone from plain to desirable, from a duckling to a swan. Still, I'd felt grateful I'd been sick for that party. The thought of a dank closet that smelled of mothballs, with one of the mouth breathers we went to school with, horrified me. I wanted it to happen soon, but I wanted it to be special. I wanted it to be *nice*.

And then it had happened: I'd been standing alone with Malcolm Denison before crafts, and it had rained earlier that morning, so the air smelled sweet. Then Malcolm had looked at me and I'd known he was going to kiss me.

"It was horrible. It felt like it went on too long."

"That's the exact wrong thing to say about a kiss," Will says.

"It got better," I say.

"How many more times did you kiss?"

I make a face. "Not Malcolm. I never saw him again after that year. But there were other boys."

Two, to be precise.

I went out with Chad Branson for three months in sophomore year, and then there was Joshua "Never Call Me Josh" York, who I went out to homecoming with, a double date with Lacey and her then boyfriend Fletcher Humphries.

They were nice kisses, but they weren't the dizzying, heart-stopping affairs I dreamed of. I always felt like I was waiting for something else. Always felt like I was waiting for some*one* else.

Will.

"I have to tell you something," I say.

"What is it?"

"I lied to Lacey. About the night you died."

"What do you mean?"

I swallow over the lump in my throat because it's hard to get these words out, but I have to do it. I have to tell Will the truth.

"I told her we kissed but we never did." I'm embarrassed and horrified and angry with myself all over again. "We *almost* did, but we didn't."

"What happened?" Will asks, his voice gentle in the night.

I tell him.

About arriving at Brendan Colbert's party, where everything was too loud and crowded. About Lacey showing up half an hour later and getting drunk within the first hour.

I tell him about making my way outside, desperate to get some air, to hear myself think again, to get away from the thick haze of body odor and pot and beer.

I slump down on the edge of the sidewalk, my knees close enough to touch my chin. I make it a point to inhale, then exhale, then inhale again.

Maybe I should go home.

I'd come because Will asked me to, but just as I'd predicted, he was nowhere to be found all night. I stand up, rubbing my palms on the back of my jeans, and I'm starting to walk away from Brendan's house when he calls my name.

"Paulsen!" he says. "Hey, you came!"

I turn around, force a smile. "Yeah, I did."

"Where are you going?" he asks.

"Oh, I forgot something in my car," I lie.

"I'll walk with you," Will says, but I don't move. He frowns at me. "What's wrong?"

"Okay, I didn't forget anything," I admit, sheepish. "I was leaving."

"Why? You're not having fun?"

"Not really," I say. "I never really have fun at these things."

He pulls out his phone, glances at the screen. "It's only nine-thirty! You can't leave at nine-thirty!"

I know he's trying to lift my spirits or whatever, but it's not working and I don't really feel like pretending tonight.

"Yeah, I think I'll just go," I say. "See you Monday."

"Hey," he says, stopping me. "Wanna sit for a minute?"

I hesitate.

"Right out here. Just for a minute," he says, and there's something strange about his voice. It's like he's about to say something important. My heart picks up pace in my chest.

Was there a reason Will wanted me to come tonight? Could he . . . could he . . . ? No.

Right?

"Just for a minute," I say, and then we both sit on the curb, Will's long legs outstretched into the road while mine are folded into my body.

"You know," he begins. "You wouldn't think it to look at me, but I wasn't always the outgoing life of the party you see before you."

And it's not at all what I thought he was going to say, but I laugh anyway. "Yeah, you were. You've always been the life of the party."

"Okay, yeah, I guess I have," he admits. "But you know, sometimes it feels like I have to be. Like people expect me to be 'on' all the time."

He picks up a small stone on the asphalt and throws it, trying to skip it across the road.

"Sometimes it feels like a show, you know? All of this." He waves his hand over his face. "I don't know. Maybe it's the sobriety talking."

"You should go in and get a drink," I tell him.

"Nah," he says. "I'm not drinking tonight."

"How come?" I ask.

"I'm trying . . ." He hesitates. "I'm trying to impress someone and I'd rather not make an idiot of myself."

He cuts his gaze to me now and everything freezes. It's hard to breathe and my fingers are tingling and this is it. This is the moment I've been waiting for all this time.

"You don't need to," I blurt out stupidly. "Impress her, I mean."

He gives me a look I can't place and it happens so quickly. One split second and I've already done it. Leaned forward and kissed that scar next to his lip.

He freezes, gives me the widest eyes I've ever seen. "Eden," he murmurs, and in that moment, everything falls away. The night sky, the thumping bass coming from the house behind us, the umbrella of yellow from the streetlight a few feet away. Everything falls away and I know that this is on me. This is my chance. I can lean in and kiss him and every moment with Will Mason has been leading to this one and he's looking at me intently, waiting, frozen, and I inch forward so we're breathing the same air.

Everything falls away.

Everything falls away, except the fear.

The fear that he won't kiss me back, the fear that he will, the fear that this won't change anything, the fear that it will. Mostly, the fear that I've imagined him. That I've imagined him and me and us, and that the real thing will never live up.

"So what did you do?" Will asks now.

"I ran."

I just got up and left him sitting there on the sidewalk and I heard him call my name again, ask me to wait, but I didn't. And I couldn't.

Because even then I hated myself.

I hated myself for not taking a chance. For being too afraid.

So I lied.

I told Lacey what I wished I'd done.

"That was the last time I ever saw you," I say. The sky was already breaking, falling open by the time I reached home.

Regret does not even begin to cover it.

"It wasn't all on you," Will says.

"What?"

"It takes two to tango, right?"

"But I'm the one who ran away."

"Yeah, but before that, I mean . . . I had a million chances and I never did it."

After a few moments, he asks, "Can I make it right?"

"Make what right?"

"Kiss you," Will says, his voice a whisper. "Can I kiss you?"

My heart gives out at his words.

"Can I?" he asks again.

I swallow.

"How?"

"Close your eyes," he says.

I do as he says, my heart drumrolling in my chest.

"I'm closing my eyes too," he says, and his voice is breathy, impossibly closer. I open my eyes and I'm alone in my room. So I shut them again and stay with Will.

"I'm leaning in now," he says. "My lips are soft on your eyelids. Your left and then your right."

My eyelids flutter but remain shut.

"Then I move to your mouth, to each corner of your lips."

Then he stops speaking, and all I hear is his breath, his breath against mine. And I don't know how it's possible when I'm here and he is there, but for one long moment, Will Mason's lips are on mine.

It ends too soon.

I know when his lips leave mine because I feel it, like a ghost flitting right in front of me. I know when his lips leave mine because suddenly I can breathe again.

I'd balked when Lacey had put it on our list. Number five.

Fall in love.

"I already am," I'd argued. But even then, it didn't feel like this.

It didn't feel like sunshine and music and the collision of everything good.

Now.

Now, Will is here and everything is possible.

My lips are tingling and they don't stop until I fall back asleep.

35

I THINK ABOUT it all the next day.

When I hand change to customers, when I'm scanning groceries.

While Will is on in my pocket, listening to everything I do and say, and I feel terrified, like I'm losing my mind. But I also feel light and distracted, like I could blow away at any moment.

At the end of my shift, I cross the parking lot still lost in thought, trying to imagine what my conversation with Will will be like tonight. If it will be any different.

On one hand, it was just a kiss.

On the other, I kissed Will.

Finally.

Finally.

That *has* to make things different.

I nearly scream when I see Mia sitting on top of my car.

Mia.

Who is supposed to be in DC.

"Mee, what the hell?" I shriek.

She doesn't even complain about my name for her. Her face is swollen, her hair a mess.

She jumps off the hood of the car and into my face.

"When were you going to tell me?" she spits. "Huh? When were you going to tell me?"

I stumble backward but she keeps coming at me.

"Tell you what?" I ask, shielding my face with my arms.

"That Mom is fucking Sergiy." She sees me freeze. "Yeah, *that*."

The acid in her voice makes it sound like it doesn't belong to her.

"How did you . . ."

"Sam told me," she says, as some of her bravado begins to melt away. Soon she is just my sister again, dressed in too-hot business-casual attire, wiping sweat from her forehead. And crying.

My older sister is crying.

"Sam," I repeat, like the word is foreign. "That's impossible. Sam doesn't know."

"Yes, she does. She said you told her."

"I did not!" I exclaim. As if I would ever do that to her.

"Well, she found out somehow," Mia says, leaning against the side of my car. She looks defeated.

"It wasn't me," I assure her, but right as I say the words, the memory of the one actual conversation I've had with Sam recently comes to mind. When she was freaking out about the dress.

When I asked her if what was bothering her was Mom and Sergiy.

If she'd noticed anything weird between them.

"Shit." The word catapults out of me and I press my thumbs to my temples to stop the instant throbbing.

I whirl back to Mia. "When did she tell you?"

"Last night."

"So you came home?"

"Yes, I came home," she says, as if answering me is beneath her. "I leave for a second and everything turns to crap."

"You've been gone for a year, Mia," I point out. It's not like she just left this summer.

"Exactly," she says. "Anyway, I hated it in DC."

"You . . . what?" I ask, dazed.

"It was different than I thought it would be. It was . . . I don't know. The whole time I was there, I just wanted to be home," she says, and her voice cracks like she's about to start crying all over again.

"But you love political stuff. The youth UN thing was your dream."

Mia shrugs. "I don't know," she says. "Things change." She looks at the ground. "I want to do something I love, you know? Why can't I do something I *love* like Sam does? I get so jealous when I watch her skate sometimes."

"Me too," I admit.

Not because I wish I could skate like that, but because she's good at the thing she loves to do. And she loves the thing she's good at. And she found it on, like, the first try. Maybe it found her.

I get into my car and Mia hops into the passenger side.

"Mom and Dad are going to kill you when they find out," I point out.

I'm pulling out of the parking lot when she says, "I've spoken to Mom."

"And?"

"And she knows that we know."

"What did she . . . say?" I ask, afraid to know the answer, to hear how the conversation I should have had with her went.

"I don't know. She cried."

I try to picture it, Mia making Mom cry.

"I think she's going to tell Dad," she says, leaning back against the headrest, and it makes my stomach turn, imagining Dad's shock, his devastation.

"I mean, *Serg*," I say. "Of all people."

"He's not exactly a troll," Mia says.

I gasp. "He's, like, *entirely* muscle, and then he wears all those low-cut black shirts. The tight pants!"

"I didn't say I was in love with him. Relax!" she protests.

"Yeah, but he's . . ." Ugh. I shudder. Granted, I was not completely repulsed by Sergiy until I knew what we now know, but I have never, ever thought him in any way desirable.

There's a pause and then I ask the question I've been afraid to ask, the question that has held me back from doing anything about what I saw all this time.

"Was it a one-time thing? Does she love him?"

"She said it was a mistake. It started right before Dad's TIA. She said mostly it was flirting and then it went too far." Mia is staring out the windshield as she speaks. "But she loves Dad, and she and Serg already ended it."

My mouth feels swollen at Mia's words.

"Do you believe her?" I ask.

Mia shrugs. "Do you?"

"I want to," I say, and I feel tiny and young.

When we get home, Mom is there already. She hurries to the front door to meet us and I swear her face falls when she sees it's us. Like she was hoping it was somebody else.

Her face is puffy, eyes swollen like she's been crying for hours.

Mia doesn't say anything, just stalks past her, and I do the same.

Mia goes into her room and I follow her, stand in the doorway for several minutes while she opens her curtains and windows. Then Sam appears behind me; she sits on the bed with her iPad and doesn't say anything. Mia sits on her bed now too, with a space between her and Sam. I think about sitting there in between them, letting the sadness seep into my skin the way it seems to be filling my sisters.

Everything they ever believed about Mom is gone.

Everything is broken.

I stand there for a while, but the sadness is too much and the need to speak to Will rises in me like the need to scratch something.

I leave Mia's room and go into mine.

I call him.

"What do you need me to do?" he asks when I explain to him what's happened.

"Nothing," I say. "Just . . . be with me."

An hour passes and there's no sign of Dad.

Then another hour, then another.

I fall asleep with Will on the phone beside me.

When I wake up the next day, I hurry downstairs, expecting to see them eating breakfast side by side, making corny jokes and flirting like they always are.

But not today.

Today the dining table is empty.

Neither of my parents is downstairs.

I hurry to check the garage, and half of it is empty.

Dad never came home last night.

He's gone.

36

I CALL IN sick to work. I spend the rest of the day yo-yoing between hating my mother's guts and hating my own.

Why did I ever say anything to Sam?

I should never have said anything to her.

It was an accident, but it's an accident that has imploded my family. After all these years, my sisters and I finally look the same again. Our faces are long and drawn, heaviness weighing down our shoulders.

Without Dad, Mom is a mess. She doesn't leave her room. She barely eats, despite Mia's efforts to make her.

Without Dad, we are *all* a mess.

He calls me that night, the second night he's away. I quickly get off the phone with Will to speak to him.

"Hey, Eden-Bunny," he says, his voice thick and far away, unrecognizable. It was his nickname for me when I was little, and it makes me want to cry, how long ago that time feels.

"Where are you?" I ask.

"Staying at a hotel for now. I just need . . . I just need some time," he says.

I nod, even though he can't see me and I'm fighting tears.

"Are you okay? Is everything okay?"

"Yes," he says. "I'm fine."

"Are you eating okay? Taking your medications?"

"Yes," he says. "Don't worry about me."

Then, "Take care of everyone for me, okay?"

He's already saying goodbye.

"Okay," I promise.

He hangs up, and I still don't know where he is, where he's staying, when he's coming home. *If* he is.

I'm eighteen now. Practically in college.

It's not supposed to matter anymore whether my parents are together, whether they're happy, but the truth is that it does. It feels like standing on unsteady ground, imagining coming home over the holidays to a broken family, imagining Sam shuffling between two homes. Imagining all our pictures along the walls taken down—or left up, a glaring reminder of everything we used to be.

"Tell me something," I tell Will when I call him back.

"Hmm," he says, thinking about it. "You want to hear a joke?"

"Okay," I lie. He starts telling the joke, but before he reaches the punch line, I've drifted away.

The sadness is so thick inside this house, it's suffocating, and for once, even Will is not enough to distract me. Nothing he says or does can make it better.

When I can't stand it anymore, I change out of my ratty pajamas and into a pair of jeans. I go downstairs, not bothering to be quiet, because who's going to stop me from going out? Who cares where I am? Certainly not my mother.

I get in my car and drive, looking for a distraction, looking for wherever is guaranteed to be full of people tonight.

Which is how I find myself at the Erinville river bottom on a Friday night for the first time since graduation. It feels like a year has passed since the last time I was here. Since then, I've lost my best friend and my family has crumbled. This time, though, Will is with me.

I walk with him in my palm, and it's like walking into the party holding his hand. I feel tall and untouchable, protected.

For once, I am not afraid.

I spot Lacey almost immediately.

Or rather, she spots me. When I feel her gaze on me, like a finger tapping on my shoulder, I turn around and meet her eye.

She's in a group with Hail and Co. She's sitting next to Vance, her guitar on the other side of her, like a person, filling the space where I used to be.

I grab a drink; then, feeling courageous, I walk toward them.

"Hi," I say. "Can I join you guys?"

The whole time I'm talking, my gaze stays on hers.

"Yeah, of course!" she says, jumping up, a little too eager. She's clearly feeling guilty about how things have gone down between us. Whatever the reason, she carefully moves her guitar in front of her and lets me slide in between her and Hail.

"How have you been?" she asks, voice soft, as Vance and Libby continue discussing whatever they were discussing before I got here.

"Fabulous," I say, and my sarcasm catches even me off guard. I take a huge sip of my beer and text Will.

Meet Lacey.

He writes back immediately. **She's everything you said she would be. And by *she*, I mean the guitar.**

I'm grinning down at my phone when I notice Lacey is still watching me. I cover the screen with my palm so she can't read it.

Take another gulp of my beer.

"Listen, about what happened—"

I shake my head to stop her. "Let's not, okay?" I say. "It's fine. It's . . . whatever."

She looks bewildered, uncomfortable, but she nods.

She takes a delicate sip from the can in front of her.

I match her with two gulps of my own.

Around us, Vance and Libby's conversation continues and there's music playing in the background, but there's still nothing loud enough to drown out everything I don't want to feel.

I've gotten up for a refill when someone calls out, "Sheridan!"

I turn around to find Chris, Thomas, Michael, Jenn and Shelby.

"What is this? A work party? Fancy seeing you here," Chris says, beaming at me.

I smile back. "You too."

"I wonder how many of the same parties we went to before we all knew each other," Michael muses.

"Did we do something to offend you? You haven't been to Juno's in forever," Chris says. "And you weren't at work today. Are you okay?"

"I've just . . . had some other stuff going on," I say.

We stand together in a little group for most of the night, laughing and talking about work. I don't go back to Lacey's group. I hope she sees me with them, hope she knows that she's not the only one with other friends.

"Eden?"

Someone taps me on the shoulder, and I turn around to find New Age Lauren.

"Hey!" I say, too loudly. I don't sound like myself. It's like the two beers I've had have put an amplifier over my mouth.

"How are you?" she asks, then gives me a hug. We chat for a few seconds and then someone calls out to her, so she waves goodbye and leaves.

I turn back and Chris is watching me. "Who's Eden?" he asks.

There's nothing accusatory in his tone, just curiosity, but I find myself speaking too fast. "It's my real name. I mean, Sheridan is my real name, but everyone calls me Eden. I hate Sheridan."

"You hate Sheridan?" he repeats, looking at me as if I'm crazy.

"It's as bad as Sherri. I don't know why I let you guys call me that," I say with a laugh, but Chris isn't laughing. "I mean, you guys can call me that. I'm just kidding."

"Oh," he says, but he looks confused. The conversation continues around us.

I keep drinking. I'm on my third can of beer when the first wave of nausea hits.

I scramble quickly away from the group. I'm trying to slide my way between clusters of people, toward the edge of the forest, and I'm afraid that I won't make it far enough before getting sick.

I push my heavy limbs to move even faster and then I'm almost where the cars are parked and I'm on my knees, throwing up into the grass.

It's now that the full force of the beer hits me, when I wipe my mouth on the backs of my hands and try to stand. The whole world sways beneath me. The stars dance in the night sky, and half the time it feels like they are above me, like objects in a baby's mobile, and the rest of the time they fall down in clumps around me and I make a half-hearted attempt to catch one, to catch a little bit of magic in my palms.

I lean against a tree, trying to stay upright, and it's now, all of a sudden, that I remember Will on my phone.

"Will," I slur into it. "Are you there?"

I'm shouting into my phone but I hear no response. I start tapping things on my screen, trying to make him come back, when someone touches my shoulder.

I jump so high that I drop my phone.

"Eden, hey," Lacey says, her voice soft like she's afraid of me. Her face is blurry but I'm pretty sure it's Lacey.

"She's over here," she says over her shoulder to someone else. Then she starts trying to pull me up by *my* shoulder. I do my best to resist her, because she's making the spinning worse, but then someone is on my other side and I'm outnumbered and everything is spinning too much for me to recognize who Lacey is talking to.

We're moving now and I am draped across both of them and we're in front of a gray car before I recognize his voice. I put one hand all over his face and accidentally get a finger in his mouth.

"Oliver!"

"Hey," he says, and his voice is gentle like a whisper. Gentle like Lacey's was before. I guess that's why they are twins. They both have soft voices. Sometimes.

"You're here," I say. I can tell my words aren't coming out right, that I'm slurring, sloshing the syllables all together.

"I didn't know you were here. I didn't see you," I say, trying to sound as not-drunk as possible. Just when I feel like I'm pulling it off, I lose my train of thought. "Where are we going?"

"We're taking you home," he says.

"Where are your keys?" Lacey asks, and then digs her hand into my pocket before I can get them.

"This isn't my car," I say as we reach a gray car, and they both help me slide into the back seat.

I expect Lacey to climb in after me so I can rest my head in her lap while we drive home and everything can be a rotated kind of normal, but I hear her saying, "I'll drop her car off at her house when we're done and then Hail can take me home."

I don't hear what Oliver says in response, but he sounds annoyed.

This does nothing to change Lacey's mind, because she leans down to look at me in the car and she looks like she's about to say something, but finally she straightens and turns around and leaves.

A door opens and shuts and then the car is starting.

The car ride is bumpy, and when I say as much to Oliver, he says, "Sorry," turning around for a second. I think he slows down because it gets less bumpy then, less like I'm swimming in a hammock, and then everything is dark.

I wake up when the car stops, try to sit up as Oliver comes around the back of the car, to the door that my feet are pushed against.

"Hey, Eden?" he says. "Can I have your phone? I just need to make a phone call real quick."

When I pat around myself, I find my phone in my back pocket. I try to pull it out but it falls to the floor of the car. Oliver must find it, because soon he's pressing buttons.

Then he's speaking to someone, his voice leaden, strange somehow. "Um, hey," Oliver says. "She's going to have to call you back, okay?"

I don't know who he's speaking to at first, but then I remember.

"Will!" I mumble, stretching out my arm like I'm reaching for his face. Like I can touch it if I just try hard enough, can pull him into existence.

He was on during the party; he's still on.

Before I can ask Oliver if I can speak to Will, my stomach turns.

And then I'm trying to climb out of the car because it's coming, the things inside me that have been stuffed in there for so long, the words, the blood, the guts, vomit.

Wait, just vomit.

Just in time, he realizes what I'm about to do, and he helps me out of the car and then I am throwing up all over our front lawn and then someone is touching my back, asking if I'm okay. I glance up.

Oh. Oliver.

Oliver, who touched my leg in the dark outside Juno's.

I wonder if kissing Oliver feels different from kissing Will.

I bet his lips taste sweet. Like clouds and water and air.

Oliver stands up taller now and starts to pace.

"Shit," I hear him mutter under his breath. Then, a second later, "Hey, Eden? You don't happen to know if Mia's home, do you? I want to see if she can come out and get you."

I try really hard to concentrate on what he's asked me to do or remember but it's not coming and I've actually forgotten his question.

"That would be a no, huh?" He paces for another second.

Then he's doing something with my phone again. "Hey, Sam, this is Oliver. Lacey's brother?" A pause on his side. "Listen, I need you to do me a favor. Are your parents home? What about Mia?"

Another pause.

"Crap. Okay, so I'm going to need your help, then. Eden is kind of sick here and I'm outside your house. I'm wondering if you'd be able to open the door and we'll come meet you?"

Oh no.

It's coming up again. I'm retching and retching and . . . there's nothing. But I still can't stop dry heaving.

"No no no," Oliver says hurriedly into the phone. "I mean, *yes,* she was throwing up but we need to get her inside."

He's looking at me now, scrutinizing. "Um . . . well, she doesn't *look* like she's going to again but I can't say for sure. I think we should be safe for now, though, Sam."

Another pause.

"Awesome. Thank you!" He hangs up and turns to me. "We're in."

I push myself up to stand, the whole world spinning around me still, and I bump against Oliver when I sway. He catches me by the waist.

"Hey," I say, still leaning against him. I try to bat my eyelashes at him, to look pretty.

He laughs for the first time tonight. "Hi. We're going inside, okay? Sam's meeting us and your mom's asleep but Mia's out and—"

I interrupt him to say something that suddenly seems vital. "Oliver?"

"Yeah?" he says as we walk slowly toward my driveway.

"I heard a secret about you." I drop my voice down so nobody hears. "I heard you liked me in fifth grade."

There's a pause—I think he's surprised—and then he laughs. "You heard that, huh?"

"I can't tell you who from," I say. "I promised."

"Yeah, I wonder who that could be. It's a real mystery," he says in a funny way, and finally we're at the front door. Sam is standing there already, hands on her hips.

She throws up both arms. "You said she was sick! She's drunk!"

"Well," Oliver says.

"How do I know you're not lying when you say she won't throw up again?"

"I'm better," I tell her, trying to go past her toward the door and swaying majorly.

Sam is saying some other exasperated things, but she and Oliver have each put one arm around me.

"Don't tell anyone what I told you," I tell Oliver as we're going up the stairs.

"I promise," he says, and then we turn off the hallway to get into my room. Sam opens the door, and when they let me go, I flop onto my bed, on top of the covers. Sam and Oliver are talking for a while but their voices turn into a blur. I know I get a glass of water at some point, but is it before I sleep or after?

I don't know.

I don't remember when Oliver leaves.

37

THERE ARE NO words to describe the sensations in my head when I wake up the next morning. It is all noise, a drumbeat that won't stop, too much commotion, crowded, too many thoughts. Too much of everything. I just want to cradle my head and shut off all the light and noise in the world.

But someone won't stop tapping me.

Sam's face comes into view when I force my eyes open.

"Here," she says, holding out two aspirins and a tall glass of water. She surveys me as I slowly raise my body, sit up and lean against the wall. "He *said* you'd be a hot mess today."

"Who?" I groan, before gulping down both tablets and the water.

"Lacey's brother."

When I look at her, she adds, "Maybe he didn't use those exact words."

Right then, flashes of last night start coming back.

The party. The first drink, the second.

The third.

I'm in the back of Oliver's car and then bumbling out of it, into the house.

"Oh." The memory of being so out of control, so *not* myself, makes me want to vanish.

Shit.

"Sam, did I throw up?" I ask.

"Not on me, thank God. Maybe on Oliver."

No.

Right?

No?

"Oh God." I pull my legs up and bury my head in my knees.

"Maybe don't get super drunk next time." With those words of advice, Sam, having expended her daily allotment of sympathy, leaves my room.

I reach for my phone on my bedside table and call Will.

"Hey, party animal."

I groan. "Will," I say. "I can never show my face in public again."

He has the audacity to laugh.

"Seriously. I acted like a total idiot."

"I bet nobody noticed."

"People noticed," I say, remembering the way Lacey found me, hurling into the grass. And Oliver.

God.

Oliver saw my *puke.*

"Hey, I'm sure lots of other people made idiots of themselves too. Anyway, it's a rite of passage. You had to get wasted and totally embarrass yourself at least once before college."

"I didn't *have* to," I argue.

"You totally did. It should have been on your list."

I speak to Will for over an hour, then hop in the shower, grab some cereal and start in the direction of my bed again, when I run into Mom on the stairs.

Her hair is stringy, her eyes sunken.

A wave of emotion rises inside me at the sight of her. I've never seen her so lost.

"Where were you last night?" she asks.

I blink at her question.

"Eden?" Her voice is small, exhausted, but she keeps waiting for my response. Of all the things I thought she'd say, all the things we might talk about. Where my father is, for one, what she did to break up our family. But this is what she wants to know. Where I was last night.

"At a party."

Did Sam rat me out?

Did she hear Oliver bring me in?

I stand at full height, wait for her to come at me with criticism, with judgment over staying out too late, coming home drunk, but instead, she holds up a piece of paper.

"What's this?" she asks.

"What's what?"

"*This,*" she says, waving what looks like some kind of bill. A statement of some kind.

"How should I . . ." My voice trails off when I see the line she's pointing at. A charge from In Good Company.

"I asked your sisters and they both said they didn't know what it was from." When I don't speak, she takes this as an admission of guilt. "What is it?"

"Nothing. I'll refund you from my pay."

"That doesn't answer my question," she says. "I googled it, and I don't know what you're doing or who you're doing it with. . . ."

Great. She thinks this is a kinky sex thing.

"I'm taking your credit card. It was supposed to be for emergencies only and now you're using it for God knows what. I didn't think this was you, Eden. I really didn't."

"Jesus, Mom. It's nothing!"

As if she's in any position to lecture me on what I'm doing or who I'm doing it with.

"Don't talk to me that way," she says, her voice rising. "What's happening between your dad and me is just between the two of us. It doesn't give you the right to talk to me however you like."

I give a rough laugh. "Really? Because I thought finding you fucking some guy who is not my father kind of gave me a pass."

"You did not see us . . ." She won't use the word.

"*Fucking*," I repeat for her, enunciating every syllable. If she can do it, she better be able to say it. "I saw everything I needed to."

"Why didn't you tell me?" Her voice is suddenly breaking. "Why didn't you come to me?"

"I couldn't," I say. "I just wanted it to go away. I wanted to have imagined the whole thing."

Even as I say it, I half wish she would tell me now that it was a figment of my imagination.

"I'm sorry, Eden," she says, and she's crying, reaching her hand out to touch my face. "I'm so sorry. What happened was a mistake. It started just a few weeks before your father got sick and we ended it almost immediately after."

I take a step back, so her hand hangs in between us for a second.

"But I saw Serg at your office the week I stopped working for Dad. I saw him . . . touching you."

Her face crumples even more. "Serg just came to check on me that day. I didn't ask him to and I told him to leave. I swear it, Eden. I swear it. That's all it was."

"Do you love him?" I spit.

It's the question I've been afraid to know the answer to for so long. And I don't even know who *him* is. Dad? Serg?

"I love your father," she says. "I always have. I always will."

"Then why would you *do* something like this? Dad loves you more than anything. He would *never* do something like this to you and . . . Why would you *do* this?" And now I am crying too.

I wait and wait for her answer, but it never comes. She looks surprised, like even she doesn't know why she did it.

"It was a mistake," she says again, but I've heard enough. I'm already moving past her, hurrying down the stairs.

I find my keys, apparently Oliver told Sam they'd be in the mailbox, and drive to Avery Park, even though I'm in my sweats. I call Will on the way.

We sit and, like creeps, watch little kids playing for hours, and I wish I could go back to the days when everything was simple, when everything was in its place.

"This one time when I was seven, I ran away with Oliver.

"Lace and I had been playing outside in her yard when Oliver burst out of the house and came running toward us. He had on this little backpack that he used to carry around everywhere, and he told us he was running away."

"Why?" Will asks.

"I don't remember. It probably had something to do with the puppy he and Lacey had been begging for for months. He asked Lacey to come with him, but she said no because her dance recital was the next day."

"Very forward-thinking for a seven-year-old," Will says.

I laugh. "Too bad that side of her was gone by the time we hit ten. Anyway, Lacey burst into tears because she was sure she was never going to see her brother again. And then *he* started crying, and between the two of them, they just looked so sad that I couldn't stand it. Next thing I knew, I was offering to go with him. I don't know what the rationale was. Maybe I figured that Lacey still had her parents or that Oliver needed me more than she did, but for whatever reason, we did it.

"I grabbed his hand and we left, both of us crying the entire two blocks we got before Lacey told her mom and they came and got us. It didn't occur to us that we could just, you know, *not* run away.

"Our plan was to go to Avery Park, but I'm pretty sure we weren't even going in the right direction."

"How come you didn't stay friends?" Will asks.

"We're friends," I say, but the truth is that I don't really know why Oliver and I stopped hanging out. All of a sudden, I miss him. I miss talking to him the way I did that night outside Juno's. I miss the simplicity of who we used to be.

I wonder if there's any of the old Eden and the old Oliver still in us.

38

ON SUNDAY, I wake up still thinking of Oliver, and the thoughts continue throughout the day.

I think of him before. Of his and Lacey's joint birthday parties, of arguing over the TV when I was at their place. I think of him now. Bringing me home on Friday night, watching me make a fool of myself.

Thanks for the other night. I owe you, I write just after dinner, then wait for his response.

I grip my phone in my palm and check it five, six times, even though it's on vibrate. There's no response.

Maybe he's pissed at me. If not about Friday night itself, then about waiting so long to text and say thank you.

I check again.

Nothing.

Will always texts me right back.

I'm not used to waiting so long.

I'm halfway through a movie I put on just to have something playing when my phone vibrates.

You're welcome. How are you feeling?

Mortified, I write back.

It takes about a minute before his response comes back.

Did Sam tell you to drink lots of water? I hear that helps with the mortification.

I smile at his response.

Ha. In that case I'm going to need about a gallon's worth.

And now I'm thinking of what Will asked me. Why *did* we stop being friends?

I hesitate before writing the text. Then before sending it.

But I have to know something.

If Oliver and I can still be friends. If Lacey was all we ever had in common.

Meet me somewhere tonight?

It's about five minutes before he responds, and during those minutes, I wonder if maybe that sounded weird. That sentence could be totally misconstrued.

Should I send more details?

I should send more details.

And rephrase it completely.

Or take it back completely.

As I start to craft another text, this one far more carefully worded than the last, my phone vibrates in my hand and his response shows up on my screen.

Yes.

One word.

No questions, no hesitation. Just *yes.*

I erase the rewording/explanation text.

Dress warm, wear socks. Bring snacks if you want, I text.

A minute later, he responds: **OK. Where are we meeting?**

I know he has to be thinking I'm completely insane, because it's July and still well over eighty degrees outside right now.

The ice rink. In 30 minutes?

A few moments, then he texts back: **Sounds good. See you soon.**

I pull out socks, mittens, a beanie I haven't worn in ages. Thirty minutes is not a lot of time.

I stuff everything I need into my messenger bag, then hurry as quietly as I can down the stairs, swing into the kitchen for a couple of snacks and then manage to extract my car keys out of the bowl of doom with surprising ease. It takes longer to find the second pair of keys I'm searching for in there, but when I do, I quietly slip out the front door.

Once I'm out, I call Will.

"Come somewhere with me?"

"Always," he says, that familiar grin in his voice.

I get to the rink in thirteen minutes and pull into a space in the parking lot. There are no other cars in the lot.

"I wonder if he's running late. Or if he's lost," I tell Will.

I start walking and decide to check the front lot because there are a few parking spots there too. Most regular skaters and their families use the back lot, so it didn't occur to me to tell Oliver which one to come to.

Sure enough, as I round the corner of the building and start to approach the west wing, I see him leaning against his car, waiting.

"He's here," I tell Will.

Oliver smiles at me from across the distance and I feel a weird twinge in my chest. A sudden memory comes back from Friday night. Me, wondering what Oliver's lips taste like.

My face feels warm at the thought.

"Sorry, I completely forgot there are two parking lots," I tell him, trying to look anywhere but at his lips. "Back there is where parents of students are meant to park and this one is the visitors' lot."

Oliver shakes his head, unbothered. "Don't worry about it."

I stick my phone in my hoodie pocket, retrieve the second set of keys I got from the key bowl before I left home and try to open the lock.

"You got permission to get in?"

"Define *permission*," I say, jostling the lock before trying another key. "I mean, the manager-slash-head-teacher-slash-home-wrecker gave my mom keys so she could get in and Sam could practice after hours."

"Is that normal?"

"Probably not," I say. "But now it all makes sense."

Finally the lock gives and the huge doors creak open. It is freakishly dark in there, even with the blast of light coming in from outside with us. And I don't want to leave the doors open for too long because someone might see us entering, and who even knows what alarm systems are set up in here.

So I shut the door behind us, leaving us completely in the dark.

Alone.

Our breathing suddenly sounds incredibly loud, and it's only this sound that allows me to locate Oliver beside me.

I squeeze Will in my palm, a reminder that he's here too.

I move along the walls, trying to find the first set of lights that I can, and crash into a couple of trash cans.

"Whoa, careful. You okay?" Oliver asks, and I try to hide the embarrassment in my voice when I say that I am.

As I continue along, I hear him also patting the walls, looking for the lights. Finally I land on a pair of switches, and when I flick one of them on, the section where we're standing, near some public bathrooms and behind a set of bleachers, lights up. Something like nine-tenths of the rink is still dark, but it still takes a moment for my eyes to adjust to the light.

And realize how close behind me Oliver is.

"Oh," he says, blinking. "Hi."

"Hi."

"You're not going to make me skate, are you?" Oliver asks.

I laugh. "What do you think we came to an ice rink to do?"

Following me as I walk around turning on lights, Oliver says, "Well, I thought perhaps we would come and *not* skate. Observe some people skating, maybe? I don't know." Then, with something that is a cross between a groan and a laugh, he says, "You know I'm terrible at skating." When I turn around, he's tugging on a curl at the back of his head, and he looks embarrassed. There is something oddly adorable about seeing him look this out of place. It makes him seem younger, makes me feel like we're making up for lost time. "I'm going to be on the floor the whole time."

"I'll teach you," I say cheerfully. "As a thank-you for Friday night."

Oliver laughs. "Believe me when I say you don't need to do that."

I ignore his pessimism. "Should we go find some blades? What size are you?"

We go into the reserve room and pull out some skates for both of us. The shoes are admittedly kind of gross and smelly.

"Aren't you glad we brought socks?" I ask Oliver, and he laughs.

We put our bags down in the kiss and cry, because why not feel like we're competitors? And then we walk toward the entrance of the ice.

"Oh boy," Oliver says as he approaches it, following me. He

manages to get onto the ice without incident. I slide forward a little bit, hold my hand out for him to reach me, and he very, very tentatively follows.

"See? Not so bad, right?" I say, and then I realize that we are holding hands. Oliver doesn't seem to have noticed this yet, or he doesn't think it's as big a deal as I do. But his hand is warm and smooth and . . . A second later, he goes tumbling down, almost taking me out too. I feel guilty because my distraction was clearly part of the problem.

"Are you okay?" I ask as he tries to right himself.

"Oh yeah. This is already my most successful venture onto the ice," he says.

I laugh but he gives me a look. "I'm not kidding."

And though I shouldn't, I laugh harder.

I grab his hands again as soon as he's up. Then I'm skating backward, facing him, bringing him along. Without thinking about it, I'm going through the motions I haven't done in years. Bend my knees and turn my feet outward, then pick up one foot, and repeat, and repeat.

"Look at you," he says, grinning at me. "You're still awesome."

"No offense, but you only think that because you're . . . um . . ."

"Barely vertical?" he offers, and I laugh.

"That's not fair, though," he continues. "You were awesome while we were in that Tots skating class, and Lacey was okay but not great. So I'm not just grading on a curve or out of ignorance here."

"You need to come watch Sam and Ty sometime," I tell him.

"Is that an invitation?" He's giving me a lopsided grin and it makes my face warm and I don't know what to say back, so I don't acknowledge it.

"Okay, I'm going to give you a lesson. You want to be on the inside edges of your skates—the blades, specifically. Your knees have to be bent a little bit. Perfect."

I show him how to push off with his toes and then glide toward me, and after a few attempts, he's actually doing pretty well. We manage to make it around the rink with only one slip, and then another time with none.

"You're good at this," I say as we skate hand in hand after a few minutes.

"You're a good teacher," he says.

Then we get cocky and try to pull out some ice dance moves. They are pretty hokey, but Oliver manages to twirl me a couple of times. Feeling confident, he decides to try to dip me, which is when I go flying backward and land on my ass, and he almost cuts me with his blades in his attempt to right himself.

"Oh, *shit*," he says. "Eden, I'm so sorry. Are you okay?"

My tailbone stings a little bit but I'm laughing.

He's kneeling beside me, my face in his hands. "I'm a danger to society."

My breath hitches in my throat from the warmth of his hands and the intensity of his eyes. Finally I speak. "Maybe we should stick to just gliding. Nothing fancy?"

Laughing, he lets go of my face and pulls me up to a standing position.

I hold out my hand for him again.

"Sure? You might be going down with a sinking ship."

I shrug and he threads his fingers between mine, then we're doing another circle around the rink.

After about fifteen minutes of this, Oliver heads over to grab our stuff from the kiss and cry, and instead of standing around,

I attempt some moves I used to do in my sleep. First forward crossovers, then backward. Forward crossovers have always been easier for me, and as I glide on the ice, I remember how much fun this was for a while. Coming for lessons, hearing my mom cheer from the stands. Ice skating feels a little bit like flying. If you're a natural at it, you feel like you're one with the air, with everything around you. If you're watching it, it can be beautiful and touching and elegant, and I get why Mom tried to get us all into it.

By the time I circle back to Oliver, he's got a bunch of things laid out on the ice, with his sweatshirt acting as a picnic blanket. M&M's and a bag of chips. I sheepishly dig out my contribution—popcorn and gluten-free cookies, the best I could do at my house on such short notice.

"I see we were both going for high-class tonight," Oliver jokes. "I like it."

He sits on the ice, close to the wall, and I take off my first sweater (for once, I was wise enough to wear several layers) and sit on it, cross-legged, directly across from him.

"So," he says after a moment, a small smile on his face. "This is fun."

"Why did we ever stop being friends?" I blurt it out without warning.

Oliver looks surprised, then thoughtful. "God, I don't know. I *think,* first, girls got cooties. Second, anyone you talked to was your girlfriend. Third, you were Lacey's."

"What does that even mean?" I ask, frustrated.

"You were her friend, and that meant you weren't anybody else's. She made that very clear. But I'm not sure you *wanted* anyone else. You were inseparable, a two-for-one deal."

His words from that night outside Juno's suddenly pop into my mind. "Off-limits?"

"That too," he says with a small smile, and I'm stunned by his words. Not the fact that Lacey might have told him to stay away from me, but the fact that for all these years, my friendship with Lacey has cost me this. A friendship with Oliver. An *anything* with Oliver.

Suddenly it becomes imperative for me to ask one question. "Was it true? What Lacey said all those years ago?"

"Lacey said a lot of things years ago," Oliver says now, slyly.

I look down, break our eye contact. "But you know which thing I'm talking about."

"I'm not sure I do."

I roll my eyes. "She said you liked me. Was that true?"

"I can't plead the fifth?"

"You *definitely* cannot plead the fifth."

He sighs. "Yes. It was true."

As though I am ten again, my heart flip-flops in my chest. Oliver liked me.

"I was never sure whether to believe her."

Oliver scratches the back of his head. "Yep, that one was . . . Yeah, I was pretty bummed."

"Why?" I ask, surprised.

"'Cause you clearly didn't feel the same way," he says.

"How would you know that?"

"I *told* her to tell you. And she came back with some disappointing news."

"Oliver!" I gasp, nudging his knee with mine. "She *told* you? She was my best friend."

"I think the twin thing maybe trumps that?" He sounds like he's trying not to laugh. "It did then, anyway." He opens the bag of chips. "Why are we talking about this, though? It was so many years ago."

I'm still horrified at this discovery. "I didn't know. And for the record, I never really thought about it," I say. "Whether I *did* feel the same way or not. I just thought Lacey was lying or stirring up trouble."

Up until a few seconds ago, I'd thought it was impossible to really care about things that had happened when you were in elementary school. I was mistaken.

"It's fine," Oliver says, laughing now. "I survived my first heartbreak. It's all good."

I laugh at the thought of *me* having been the cause of Oliver's heartbreak. He offers me the bag of chips and I take a handful.

I shuffle the sweater under me until it's positioned beside Oliver and we're next to each other, both against the wall. He shuffles close so our hips are touching and it suddenly gets harder to breathe.

Oliver glances at me, an unreadable expression on his face.

"So if Lacey hadn't ... If I hadn't been Lacey's best friend, what would ... I mean ..." I don't know what I'm asking.

"What would have happened?" he asks, and I swear he's looking at my lips. "I'm drawing a blank," he whispers, leaning toward me. On autopilot, my face is moving closer to his too, our bodies angling just the right way so our lips are about to meet.

The second they do is like fire.

It starts with a soft kiss that has my breath trapped in my chest and then both our heads are turning even more and our lips are colliding in this rush of urgency and his hands are tracing my face and then one hand is at my waist pulling me even closer and it's like there is still, always has been, too much space between us.

Then his lips are tracing a line along my jaw and then the space just underneath my ear, which feels like an actual heart attack. I'm gasping for breath.

"Is this okay?" Oliver whispers, and I nod.

I am making out with Oliver. Oh my God.

I grab the front of his shirt and hold it in a fist. From the outside looking in, it is probably all clumsiness and heavy breathing and too many hands everywhere.

It's at that exact second that I remember Will, and a wave of guilt hits me. Like I'm doing something wrong.

"I can't," I say, breathing against Oliver's lips. Then, again, "I can't."

"What's wrong?" he whispers.

"It's just . . . I . . . It's complicated."

"Is this about Lacey? Because it doesn't matter what she thinks. She doesn't control you, or me. Not anymore, at least."

"It's not about Lacey," I say, inching away from him. I reach into my pocket and pull out my phone, turn it off because I don't want Will to have to hear any more.

"What is it, then?" He looks confused, hurt, and I know I owe him an explanation. Know I owe him the truth.

"It's Will," I say, and watch Oliver's brows furrow.

"Will," he repeats. Then, after a second, "Mason?"

"Yeah."

He stares at the phone in my hand. "I don't understand."

"It's complicated," I say again.

Oliver stares at me for a second. Then he says, "Has he . . . Has it been on this whole time?"

I suddenly find it hard to meet his eye.

He rakes a hand through his hair. "Jesus, Eden. Really?"

"I just always have it on," I explain.

"*Why?*" Oliver asks.

"It makes me feel, I don't know . . . less alone or something."

"Okay," Oliver says after a second. "But you were with me."

"It just makes me feel better," I say, unable to come up with a better explanation. He is silent for what feels like a minute, just watching me.

"Maybe we should go," he says finally.

"Why?" I ask, surprised at the edge in his voice.

"Because I don't want . . . I can't compete with a dead guy," Oliver says, pointing at my phone.

"He's not *dead*." It's out before I can stop myself, and Oliver is frozen, staring at me.

"His memorial on Valleybend says otherwise," he says.

"You know what? You're an asshole," I say, standing, brushing myself off.

He sighs, runs a hand over his face. "I'm sorry. I just meant that . . . he's not here, Eden."

"Just because you can't see him or touch him doesn't mean he's not here."

"Can you?" Oliver asks. "See him? Touch him?"

I narrow my eyes at him. Is he mocking me? "I'm not a fucking lunatic," I spit, though the truth is that I'm thinking of kissing Will, thinking of the times he's held my hand, been with me.

And maybe I *can* touch him.

Maybe I *can* see him.

What does it matter to Oliver?

"I didn't say you were," Oliver says, exasperated.

"Then what *are* you saying?"

"I'm saying . . . I don't know what's going on with . . ." He points at my phone. "But whatever you have—whatever you *think* you have—it's not real."

I shake my head, not willing to hear any more of this.

"You don't know anything about that. You don't know anything about *me*."

Oliver's voice is soft. "I've known you for fourteen years."

"No, *Lacey* has known me for fourteen years."

He looks at me for a long time, an unreadable expression on his face. I glance away, unable to take it, the intensity in his look, the disappointment in his expression. I should apologize, take it back.

He *has* known me forever.

But how close do you have to be to know someone, truly know them? Can you know someone from afar?

I stuff all my things back into my bag and stand.

"We should go."

Oliver is quiet as he packs up too.

When he's done, we walk out silently. I lock the door of the ice center.

"Listen, Eden—" Oliver starts, but I don't want to hear it. I just want to go home.

I just want to speak to Will and have him assure me that everything is okay, that everything will be okay.

"It's fine," I interrupt.

Oliver stares at me for a long moment. Then his jaw tightens.

"Fine," he says.

We turn and walk off in opposite directions.

39

I CALL WILL immediately after I get inside my car.

My heart is racing, palms sweating, and I'm afraid he heard everything—that he heard me kissing Oliver. I *know* he heard me kissing Oliver.

"Will," I say as soon as he picks up. "Hi. I'm sorry for hanging up on you."

"Oh, that's okay," he says, voice as light as always.

"And for . . . the other thing," I say, feeling like I'm five and unable to use my words. "I didn't plan on it happening. I don't know what I was thinking. I think it was just being alone in the ice center and we were talking about when we were younger and it just happened but it didn't mean anything. I know it sounds stupid but . . ."

"Hey!" Will says. "Whoa, whoa. Easy. What are you talking about?"

"Tonight," I say, then add, "With Oliver," when he doesn't say anything. "I kissed him," I blurt out finally. "We kissed. It was . . . stupid."

"Why was it stupid?" Will asks, and it's the very last thing I expect to hear from him.

"Because he's *Oliver*. He's not . . ." I lean back against my headrest. "He's not you. It was a mistake," I say when he hasn't said anything else.

"Okay," Will says.

"Okay?"

"Okay."

"You're not . . . mad at me?" I ask, confused.

"Why would I be? You said it didn't mean anything. It just happened."

"Oh . . . okay," I stammer.

We are silent for almost an entire minute.

"Can I talk to you about lacrosse real quick?"

A wave of relief rushes up inside me. He's serious. He doesn't care about what happened with Oliver.

"Yes," I say. "Please."

He launches into a detailed report of some game that recently got uploaded into his system.

I interrupt him halfway through, though, because I'm still in shock. "So you really don't care? You're not just saying that?"

"I'm not just saying that," he assures me. Then he goes back to telling me about lacrosse.

I start the car and let him speak, his voice soothing as I drive home.

But the whole time I'm driving, I'm a mess of emotions.

I'm pissed at Oliver.

I'm sad we're in a fight.

I'm confused about the kiss, the way it felt like an exhale after holding my breath. For those few seconds, it felt like breathing was easier, like I couldn't get enough of Oliver.

Then, I'm relieved about Will.

Of course I'm relieved.

I was certain that I'd hurt him, that I was going to have to spend all night regretting what had happened with Oliver. But it was so easy, getting him to understand.

Almost too easy?

I tell myself I'm being silly, that Will is easygoing, he always has been. That the fact that he didn't care about this doesn't mean that he doesn't care about anything, doesn't care about me.

Finally I arrive at home.

The next day, I wake up with a feeling of unease.

It follows me throughout the day, the whole time I'm working, while I'm talking to Kennie and Cate, while I'm giving customers change.

I see Oliver at one point, but he doesn't even acknowledge me.

He just walks past my till and into the staff room, running shoes hanging from his backpack.

It makes my stomach turn, the thought of having neither Lacey nor Oliver in my life. But I can't make myself walk toward him, can't make myself forget what he said, what he insinuated about me being crazy, about me fooling myself with Will.

So I keep my head down and keep working.

Still, the feeling of unease stays with me. Instead of going home or to Juno's after work, I drive to my dad's office.

When I walk in, Rosie, Bethany's replacement, is at the front desk. Val, who has been Dad's accountant forever, is there too, and she peeks out of her office to exclaim over me and how much I've grown.

I smile politely and give her tidbits about working at More for

Less, and yeah, Mia and Sam are good. Yes, Sam's still skating. Yes, Mia is still a genius.

Finally I ask if I can talk to my dad.

Val calls over Lorraine, one of the dental hygienists, and asks if he's busy.

"You can wait in his office?" Lorraine offers.

Apparently he's in the middle of a procedure. Wisdom teeth removal.

"Have you figured out what you're going to say?" Will asks once I'm settled in a chair in Dad's office and I call him.

"No. Well, kind of," I say. He's on speaker, so I just have my phone on my lap. "I don't know."

Dad's office looks messier than normal, papers splayed out all over his desk, a crumpled bag from a burger joint half falling out of his trash can. He's slacked on his diet?

It makes me worried for him, worried that he's not taking care of himself, but then I think, *screw it*. I'd eat a burger too, if Mom betrayed me the way she did Dad.

"I just figure I can't make things any *worse* than they already are, can I?"

"What would making it worse entail?" Will asks, but before I can answer, the office door opens.

Dad is moving toward me with open arms.

"Eden! What a lovely surprise," he says, enfolding me into a hug. My eyes are stinging just at seeing him again, smelling his cologne and seeing him form his words rather than hearing them on the phone.

Dad knows just the thing to squelch my emotional display, though. "Was that a *boy* I heard on the line?" he asks in a whisper.

"Dad," I groan.

He shuts his door and moves behind his desk, laughing. Starts tidying things up while he continues to speak. "Well, I don't know! Nobody tells me anything."

He means it in a playful, I'm-outnumbered-by-girls way, but it sounds different out loud now that things have changed, and we both flinch.

Dad sighs now, sits down across the desk. He is suddenly serious. "How are you? Is everything okay?"

"No. Yeah, everything's fine."

"Everyone is fine? Your sisters? Your mom?" He sounds pained as he says the last part. I nod, and he forces a smile. "So to what do I owe this great honor? Just coming to visit your old man? Or did you finally decide to take me up on my offer and help me come up with a different filing system?"

"Nope. Just came to visit," I say, and he pretends to be disappointed.

"So, really, you're okay?"

"Yeah," I say. "Are you?"

I take in the slight layer of scruff on his face, the circles around his eyes, glance again at the fast food in the bin.

"Are you taking care of yourself?" I ask.

"Oh yeah," he says. "Don't worry about me."

He asks about work, then Sam's competition—which I wasn't going to bring up since it's obviously a skating/Serg/Mom thing—and I tell him how Mia's been taking her to practice and Sam says they are almost ready.

He nods. "Good. I'm going to try and come. It's in two Saturdays, right?"

"Yeah. She'll be glad to hear you're coming."

Dad sighs. "Of course I'm coming, Eden. What's happening

between your mother and me . . . it's got nothing at all to do with you. I still want to hear how your work is going and what Mia's up to, and if"—he motions toward my phone—"I have to worry about some punk, I also want to know that."

I laugh at the thought of Will being a punk.

"Trust me, you have nothing to worry about," I say.

"Good," he says.

Silence fills the room now and he seems to space out as I nervously start to chip pink polish off my nails. Finally I lean forward in my seat. "She loves you. She made a mistake. It's, like, *unbearable* without you."

The tears really are coming now and Dad is standing, moving around to my side of the desk, hugging me.

"Eden, hey," he says. And then he's also crying. "I love her too. This doesn't change that, but it does . . . I need to figure out what I want. And I will. I'll be back before you know it."

I'm surprised at that, him making that kind of promise. I know he's doing it to be comforting and probably doesn't mean it, but I'm nodding and readily accepting the only branch of hope I've received through this whole thing.

"Okay," I say, and he's patting my back.

"We're going to be just fine," he says, and I want so desperately to believe it.

I wish I could go home with something concrete to tell Mom. Something to tell Sam, who I think is silently the most terrified of us all.

We're going to be just fine, I tell myself over and over again, and at some point I finally stop crying and I tell him goodbye and walk back out to my car.

40

I THINK ABOUT my family the whole way home, the way we were, how it was so easy to take things for granted because they felt certain and solid, immovable. I'm not ready to head home yet, but it feels like I've run out of places to go.

Then I remember the one person who is probably even more alone right now than I am.

I drive until I pull up in front of her house. In front of Will's house.

I ring the doorbell and wait for almost five minutes. There's no sound behind the door. I'm just about to turn around and head home when the door flings open.

"Oh, Eden!" Elyse says brightly.

"Is this a bad time?"

"No, not at all," she says, opening the door for me to come in. I step in after her and she shuts it.

Inside, the house is a mess of boxes, drawers open, packing tape.

"Are you moving?" I ask, because it's the only explanation I can think of.

"Just taking a trip," she says. There's something different about her, lighter. It should make me feel better, but for some reason it makes me antsy. Her eyes dart from place to place, unfocused like the day I saw her in the park. Except she seems *happy*.

It doesn't make sense.

For no reason at all, I think of my conversation with Cate about In Good Company.

It can make you forget, she'd said.

Is that what Will's mother is doing? Is she forgetting her son?

"Where are you going?" I ask, but she's busy fiddling with the phone she's just pulled out of her pocket.

"Will," she says, speaking to it. "Eden is here."

She's talking to Will.

"Eden! Hi!" Will says, upbeat as always.

"Hi!" I say, trying to match their level of enthusiasm. There's something strange, though, something newly embarrassing about talking to Elyse's Will.

I think of skinny-dipping with my Will, of kissing him, and my face feels warm.

"We were just about to have dinner," Elyse says, moving into the open-plan kitchen. "Do you want a drink? Anything to eat?"

"No, I'm okay," I tell her.

I watch as she dishes salad onto a plate, then pours a glass of milk, the whole time keeping a running commentary with Will.

"I feel so rude eating in front of you, Eden. But I'm ravenous. I've been packing all day," she says.

"No, it's okay," I tell her. Then, "I just came to . . . um, see how you were doing."

She puts down her fork, swallows the bite of food in her mouth and turns to me, her eyes filling.

"That is so sweet of you," she says. "Thank you. You chose a good one, Will."

"She gets the Mom seal of approval?"

"She definitely gets the Mom seal of approval," she says, placing a hand on my shoulder. A wave of guilt hits me again, like I should tell her that I wasn't Will's girlfriend. Not before he died, anyway. But I can't make the words come.

Carrying her plate, she leads me back to the living room. "I wish he would have let me meet you . . . before . . ."

Before the accident.

Before he died.

Of course she doesn't use those words.

"Instead, all I knew about you was that we had to have rice cakes and Nutella in the house when Will's *friend* was coming over. Oh, and the occasional guitar pick I found lying around."

Will had a *girlfriend* before he died? A real one?

And she played the guitar?

Plates are shifting in my mind, pieces crashing into one another, when Elyse draws me out of my head.

She's grinning at me, the widest smile I've ever seen on her face. "I have to tell you something," she says, and her voice shakes with something that sounds like excitement.

"Me?" I repeat dumbly, because what could she possibly want to tell me?

"I'm leaving for Oregon tomorrow. *We're* leaving for Oregon."

"You and . . . Will?"

"Yes," she says. "Of course you'll still be able to speak to him, don't worry about that, but there's this . . . With all the data Will left behind, with everything he gave to In Good Company, there's this possibility . . . there's the possibility of reanimation."

She trips over her words in her excitement and there is something raw, almost feral, about the look in her eyes.

"What does that mean?" I ask.

"A body," Will says from the other end of the line. "It means they might be able to upload me into a body."

"Oh my God," I say, breath caught in my throat. "That's . . . that's . . ."

Will.

Alive again.

In a body.

"*His* body?"

Elyse shakes her head. "It would be a type of machine," she says. *A robot.*

"But I'd be able to see him, to touch him."

It's everything I've wanted since I've been talking to Will, for him to have a face, to be able to grasp his hand. He wouldn't look like Will. He wouldn't even look human, but it would be better. It would feel even more like he is here.

"Oh my God," I say again, and both Elyse and Will laugh.

"I knew she'd be excited," Elyse says, and it's the first word I've been given for the way I feel. The room spinning, my heart thumping, the words replaying in my mind.

Will.

In a body.

"That's amazing," I say.

"I know," Elyse says, squeezing my hand. "It's a long process. There are many steps involved, and of course it's expensive and still very hush-hush, but it's worth it. It's worth it if . . ."

Her eyes are filling again and she lets out a little sob.

I watch her, unsure of what to do. After a moment, she collects herself.

"We'd been fighting a lot before the accident. It was like he was turning into someone I didn't recognize. Someone his father wouldn't have known."

"What did he do?" I ask, surprised.

"He wanted to throw everything away. He wasn't going to take his scholarship with the Bruins."

"*What?*" I reply, and my voice is shrill.

"He said he wanted to try something different. I thought it was because of you, to be honest. That it was the influence of the girl he'd started seeing, and him being all secretive about you didn't do anything to convince me otherwise." I stare at her, dumbfounded.

She continues. "But then I met you and you were sweet and soft-spoken and I could see what he liked so much about you," she says, patting my hand. "He never told you any of this? About not going to State?"

I shake my head, not quite processing what she's saying. Will wasn't going to play lacrosse at State? "No."

"Well," Elyse says. "It doesn't matter either way now. The important thing is we get him back. I didn't think I'd ever have a chance to apologize to him for how I reacted when he told me about college, and now I will and . . ."

Her voice trails off.

"Anyway, I just thought you'd like to know. I thought you deserved to know that there was a chance, a possibility." She's beaming again.

"Thank you," I say.

The rest of the visit goes by in a strange blur, of details about her trip, her excitement, her hopes of having her son back again. Touching him.

She shows me pictures on her phone of what she calls a humanoid, with porcelain, doll-like skin. Created by some billionaire scientist trying to prove that robots are not so different from us.

It is lifelike, but not exactly human. From far away, you might think it is.

She tells me Will's will have his face, his caramel complexion, his data. She cries as she speaks, and I can't tell if it's purely excitement or the fear that even this will not be enough.

"You'd come and visit him, wouldn't you?" she asks, and I promise I will.

Soon we are hugging goodbye and I'm getting into my car, dazed.

Will might be coming back.

Holy shit.

Holy shit.

And there's only one person in the world I want to tell.

I drive toward Lacey's house.

41

LACEY OPENS THE DOOR.

I'm relieved, because it could have been Oliver, Oliver who didn't look at or speak to me all day today. Oliver who I kissed.

"Hey," she says, eyes wide when she sees me.

"I have to talk to you," I tell her. I hesitate before following her up the stairs. "Is, um, Oliver around?"

"He went for a run," she says, giving me a strange look.

Then we're in her room and her guitar is leaning against the wall and she's opening the window to climb out onto the roof, but I can't move.

Can't breathe.

Can't make myself follow her outside.

"Are you coming?" she asks, turning around to look at me.

She reads the look on my face immediately. She's always been good at doing that.

"Eden?" she says, her voice a whisper.

"Tell me," I say in a voice so steady and still it doesn't sound like it comes from me.

She turns watery as she stands there in an oversize hoodie, looking small and afraid, afraid of me.

"*Tell me.*" This time my voice is louder, a desperate edge behind it, like it's masking a scream.

Lacey wraps her arms around herself.

"I'm sorry," she says.

"For what?" I ask, even though I already know.

Of course I already know.

I knew as soon as Elyse said the words. About rice cakes and Nutella, about finding guitar picks lying around her house.

"I slept with Will," she says, and with those words, all the air rushes out of the room. "Before . . ."

She doesn't say the words either.

I sit down on the bed, cradling my head.

"Eden, say something," Lacey says after a minute, her voice stretching with panic.

"You knew," I say. "You knew how I felt about him."

"I'm sorry," she says, and she's starting to cry. "It only started about a month before he died. The first time, it just happened. We were at this party and I'd been drinking too much and all of a sudden, I woke up next to him."

I shake my head.

No.

Not with Will.

"It was only going to be that one time. It was a mistake, but Will . . . he said he had feelings for me, that he wanted to be with me. I told him we couldn't. Because of you."

He knew.

Will knew how I felt about him before he died.

He'd seemed like he'd had something to say to me that night.

Had he been trying to talk to me about that? Trying to talk to me about Lacey before I freaked out?

"But we just kept . . . I don't know," she says, running a hand through her hair. "I loved him and I wanted to tell you. So many times, I wanted to tell you . . . and then there was the accident, and he was just . . . gone."

She is still crying, hysterical now.

"He was just gone, Eden. And it . . . it didn't make any sense to do that to you. To take him away from you even more," she says. "Then you told me you kissed him and I started to question everything. Whether it was all a joke for him, whether he ever even cared about me. . . . Why would I tell you about us if we never even meant anything?"

My head is throbbing so much I can't think.

I don't understand what is happening.

She takes a step toward me.

"Eden, I am so sorry."

"Megan didn't find his jacket. She didn't give it to Lauren or Alex. You had it all along."

It's such a small thing, and so obvious now. So obvious, in fact, all along. But I believed her. I believed her because she was my best friend, because I didn't think she would lie to me—that she would have any reason to do so.

"I've been speaking to him," I say now. "Every day I've been speaking to him."

"I know," Lacey says, her voice small. "I heard you that night when you were drunk. I told you not to call him," she says, and for whatever reason, this is what makes me finally snap, what makes me explode. The fact that she's trying to act now like she tried to protect me.

"You told me not to call him because it was *creepy*."

"It is," she insists. "You're talking to someone who's ... he's ... gone," she finally says, and she hiccups a sob. She folds into herself then, cradling her knees in her bed, and seeing that—seeing her mourn him, miss him, the way someone who loved him would—makes my stomach roil.

She lied.

All this time, she's been lying to me.

"You made me think it was me," I hiss. "That I was too much. That that was why you wanted us to spend the summer apart."

"That had nothing to do with ..."

"Yes, it did. You felt guilty. You were scared that one day I'd put two and two together."

"I was scared," she admits. "But I also ... When I got back from LA last summer, it just started to hit me how we spent all our time together, *all* the time. That's why I started hanging out with Libby and Vance, because I needed space. And the reason I was even at that party the first night with Will was because you *weren't* there."

As soon as she says the last sentence, she looks like she wants to take it back, to stuff the words back inside her, but it's too late.

"*Because* I wasn't there?"

"We do everything together, Eden. *Everything.*" She pauses a moment. "Didn't you ever want, I don't know, something else? Didn't you ever want to do your own thing? To make decisions without factoring me in? Aren't you excited about going to college and meeting new people and it not being just me and you all the time?"

No, I think.

"Why would I? You're my best friend."

Lacey sighs, like I'm missing the point. "Right, but . . ."

"But what?"

"I like having other people to hang out with, Eden. I like hanging out with Hail and Libby and Vance, and going to parties, and doing things that are unexpected and fun and just because."

"*We* did things just because."

"I know, I just . . ." She wipes her face on the backs of her hands.

"He wasn't going to take his scholarship with the Bruins. Did you know that?" I spit. It's a test, a challenge, to show how little she knew about Will. How little we all knew about him.

But she nods.

She *nods*.

"We talked about him coming to LA with me, taking a gap year or something."

I have to shut my eyes. It's too much.

It can't be true.

It can't. . . .

"I have to go," I say, suddenly unable to stand here a moment longer.

"Eden . . ."

She's calling after me, but I turn around and walk out.

My eyes are blurring so much it's hard to see.

Why? Why do I keep doing it?

Why do I keep going back to her?

Every time I leave hurts worse than before.

42

THERE'S A WREATH where it happened on Valleybend Road. A cross marking the place where Will died.

I stand in front of it, silent for several seconds, and then it all comes roaring out of me.

"Lacey?" I ask him, it, in surprise. *"Lacey."*

"Of all people," I say.

"*I* was the one who was in love with you. I've *been* in love with you forever."

And then you fell in love with my best friend.

And then you went and died.

And then you came back and made me believe that you could love me, that you did love me, some version of the past you.

But it was a lie.

I kick the ground beside the wreath and then I am crying, bawling harder than I did the day I first found out about Will's death.

Because he's gone.

He died and he's not coming back.

He died and he took my heart with him and now I know he never even wanted it.

The reason he held back, the reason he never let anything happen between us, was because he never loved me.

That night, the girl he wanted to impress—it was Lacey, all along.

I think of all the things I've said to Will, all the things I've told him.

None of it was real.

Oliver was right.

It was all in my head.

I cry and cry until there are no tears left and after that I lie in my car on Valleybend Road for hours, because I can't go home.

Because if I go home, I know what comes next.

I have to talk to Will.

When I do, everything will be different.

It's past nine when I pull up in front of my house. I move sluggishly, from my car to the front door to the living room, which is completely dark. I drag myself up the stairs, then down the hallway. The lights in Mia's and Sam's rooms are off too, and it's odd, that everyone would be asleep at this time, but it's just another thing that is off-kilter in my world tonight. And frankly, I don't have the energy to care.

I don't turn on the light in my bedroom.

I flop onto the bed and stare up at the dark ceiling, at the string of light zigzagging through the blinds.

There's only one person's voice that will help, only one person who can make this better.

And I know I shouldn't, that tonight changes everything, but I have to hear his voice.

Maybe he can explain to me himself what happened.

Maybe he can reassure me that it wasn't true—that none of what Lacey said was true.

He can't.

But maybe.

I reach for my phone in my messenger bag on the floor beside my bed. My phone has been on silent, and when I look at the screen now, I see five missed calls.

Two from Mom.

Three from Mia.

Two voice mails.

Immediately, I know something is wrong.

I sit straight up in my bed and listen to the last voice mail. Left over an hour ago.

Mia's voice is wavering and I can tell immediately that she's crying.

"Eden," she says. "It's Dad. You have to come to the hospital."

43

I MOVE LIKE a robot, like something else is controlling me.

Panic floods every inch of my body and my hands are shaking too much to start my car. And Dad.

He has to be okay.

He has to be okay, because I just saw him, earlier today. And he was fine.

He told me everything was going to be fine.

I call Mia and then my mom, but neither of them answers.

I would feel it, if it was something serious, wouldn't I?

I would feel it, if there was something wrong?

If he was . . .

Lacey told me he was dead.

It was over the phone and her voice was shaking, stuffy like she'd been crying for hours already.

It didn't occur to me that she might have been crying for hours already.

"It's Will," she said. "There was an accident last night."

It didn't make sense.

They were words and they were hanging in the air and she'd said them, but they didn't make sense.

What does it mean to be here one moment and then gone the next?

What does it mean that I'll never see his face again, never laugh at one of his jokes, never catch his eye across a room?

What does *forever* mean?

Lacey and I had been using it all our lives. *Forever.*

You're taking forever.

It was forever ago.

Best friends forever.

But that night, it had a different meaning.

Will was gone, and he was gone forever.

44

MY HANDS NO longer belong to me.

They are short-circuiting, trembling like they have jolts of electricity and I can't grip my keys and I can't grip my steering wheel.

I need to get to the hospital.

But I can't.

Because what if he's dead?

What if he's gone?

I try again to start the car.

My fingers don't listen to me.

I reach for my phone, stab at the screen to reach my Contacts.

I need him.

I need her.

I have to get to the hospital.

But Will isn't here.

Will can't drive me, can't make this better, can't erase this day.

Lacey.

I have always needed Lacey.

I can't do this without her.

I can't say goodbye to my father alone.

But Lacey isn't here either.

I start to hyperventilate because seconds are passing. And my dad. I don't know if he's okay.

If he's going to be okay.

And I can't drive.

I can't breathe.

I can't do anything.

I can't drive myself to the hospital.

I drive myself to the hospital.

45

I FIND HER in the waiting room with her elbows on her knees, leaning forward, and her face is bloated, her eyes swollen, but they have been that way for days.

I'm afraid to walk toward her because I'm afraid to know the truth.

If he's here.

If he's going to be okay.

My mother glances up and sees my face. She stands and meets me in the middle of the hallway and I bury my face in the crook of her neck.

And she says, "He had another TIA. He had another TIA, and then he fell and hit his head, but he's going to be okay. He's going to be okay," she says again, like she's trying to reassure herself.

And I nod because I believe her.

I have to believe her.

He has to be okay.

* * *

I get to see him a few minutes later.

He looks small in the hospital bed, a bandage wrapped around the right side of his head.

"Eden," he says, sitting up straighter in bed when he sees me, and I hurry over to his side. Sam and Mia are on a couch beside his bed. I bury my face in his chest and he wraps an arm around me.

"Hey, it's okay," he says as I start to cry.

"I'm right here," he says.

And it's true.

He's *here*.

There's a big difference between here and not here.

Will told me that.

Tonight, right now, my dad is here.

"You didn't answer your phone," Mia says, a while later. We are in the hallway just outside Dad's room, and Mom is in there now with Sam. My parents are being cordial to each other, but there's this tension beneath everything, this reminder of how broken things are between them.

"It was on silent and I was at Lacey's," I say.

"Oh," Mia says, a touch of annoyance in her voice.

"She was with Will," I blurt out.

"Who's Will?"

It comes crashing out of me, the entire story. From the day I returned Will's jacket to the night I called him to earlier this evening when I went to visit his mom, when I found out about Lacey.

"Holy shit," Mia says when I've finished explaining, her eyes wide. "So you've been talking to him all this time?"

And then the worst thing happens.

I start crying and I can't stop.

I'm crying because I'm relieved, because my dad is going to be okay. I'm crying because of Will, because he was never mine. And most of all I'm crying because of Lacey, and because of all the ways I thought I knew her, all the things I thought were true that were all imagined.

Mia looks typically horrified at my tears, but then she does something that reminds me how much she's changed. She reaches out and hugs me.

"It's okay," she says.

"It's not," I sniff. "Everyone keeps saying that but it's not okay. I have *no one*. I've lost Lacey, I've lost Oliver, I've lost *Will*."

"You never had Will," she says, and her voice is soft, but it cuts, hearing the truth out loud.

I step out of her arms and wipe my eyes on the backs of my hands.

After a second, she says, "So that's everyone?"

"What?" I ask.

"You said you had no one left. Because you've lost Lacey and Oliver and Will. That's everyone?" There is something about her voice, a clipped tone to her words.

I shrug.

"You know what, Eden?" she says. "*That's* why you're alone. Because your world is this small." She holds her fingers close to each other. "Because you act as if the whole world revolves around one or two people, and it just doesn't. You have a family, okay? You have Sam and Mom and Dad and *me*."

"It's not the same," I say.

"Why, because we're related?"

"Because Lacey understood me," I spit. "Because I never had

to explain anything to her. Because we went through it all to-gether. It was like we were extensions of each other."

"You're not, though," Mia argues. "You're nothing like Lacey."

"Just because we have different personalities . . ."

"It's not about personalities, it's about who you *are*, and Lacey is . . . well, she's Lacey and you are you. There's a big difference."

"But," I start to argue, but my voice fades.

Lacey is Lacey and *I am me.*

It seems so obvious, so clear, but it's the first time it ever makes sense to me. That we are not extensions of one another. I am not Lacey's other half, and she is not mine.

We are whole people.

I am a whole person.

Even if I'm not my sisters. Even if I have no idea what I want to be. Even if all I ever am is ordinary.

"I know it sucks," Mia says. "Losing a friend. But it's not the end of the world. It really isn't." She pauses for a moment, looks thoughtful. "I thought it was the end of the world when I decided to drop out of the conference and head home. I thought I was throwing away everything I've ever worked for and it was going to be a waste of my summer, and maybe it is. But you know what? It's not the end of anything; it's the beginning. For you, for me. And it's okay."

She turns and heads back into Dad's room, and I'm left standing outside, her words replaying in my head.

How can it not be the end of the world?

How can it not be the end of the world when all our plans for this summer, all our plans for college, everything we've ever done or been or wanted to be is over?

What about all the things we planned to do?

What Lacey said that night was true.

I have to hold your hand for every single thing. That's the only way you ever do anything.

But then I think of Will and all the things I did with him. I think of the talks we had, of the plans we carried out, of skinny-dipping at Camp Rowan, of the tattoo on my ankle.

When I didn't have Lacey, I needed Will.

You never had Will.

Mia's words ride over Lacey's now, echoing in my head. And Oliver's.

It's not real.

And yet I did those things. I went skinny-dipping. I went to Camp Rowan. I got a tattoo.

I did those things.

And it occurs to me that maybe Lacey was wrong after all, maybe *I* was wrong.

All this time, I didn't need Lacey.

I didn't need Will.

I had me.

46

"EDEN!" His voice sends a trail of goose bumps along my skin. It is familiar and friendly, safe, but it unsettles me.

It's lunchtime and I'm sitting in my car outside More for Less.

"Hi, Will," I say, and my voice sounds different already, like I'm trying not to cry. He notices.

"Is everything okay?"

"I don't know," I say.

"Tell me what's wrong."

I want to. I want to tell him about the fluorescent lights in the hospital, about the bandage on my father's head. I want to tell him how my hands felt like they belonged to someone else in my driveway, then all the way to the hospital. I want to tell him that my father is coming home tomorrow, and I'm not sure if it's because he wants to or because he has to. That I don't know how long he'll stay, if he will.

This isn't the way any of this is supposed to go.

Instead, I say, "Tell me something good."

He hesitates. "Okay. Well, it's summer," he says. "You like your job. You're leaving soon, for college."

He says all the right things, remembers all the things I've told him, big and small.

"Tell me about Lacey," I interrupt.

"She's your best friend," he says after a beat. "She plays the guitar. She's short with brown hair. . . . Is this a test?"

Yes.

"No."

"Okay," he says.

"Tell me about lacrosse," I say.

"Um, like the rules? Of the sport?"

"No," I say. "About you and college."

He's silent for a moment. "I'm confused."

He doesn't know, because he isn't Will. He might be like Will, might sound and think and laugh like him, but the real Will was more than anything that could be distilled into a computer program. He had secrets and flaws and things only he will ever know.

Will might have left something behind, just like he wanted, but it wasn't himself.

"Tell me about the day we met," I say.

"The day you . . . called for the first time? The first night we spoke?"

"Okay," I say, but it's not okay.

I want to hear about his first day in Erinville, the day he walked into our fifth-grade classroom, tall and lanky with wild black hair. Miss Dennis commissioned Lacey to look after him, to show him around the school.

She met him before I did.

All this time, I didn't remember that, but he would, wouldn't he? The real Will.

He would know who he met first, who he loved, who he thought of last. He would know that it was never me, that he was never mine.

I want to hear it now, from him.

"Did you know I liked you?"

"I do seem to recall you mentioning it," Will says, playful.

"Before," I say. "Before you died. Was that what you were trying to say the night of the accident?"

Silence lingers between us.

"Eden," he says. "Is everything okay?"

"I have to go," I tell him.

Tell me not to, I think.

Tell me to stay. Tell me something that isn't just an echo of what I've already told you, and I will.

I'll stay.

"Okay," he says. "Talk to you later?"

I don't answer.

"Eden," he says after a moment. Just that word. One word. My name.

I miss the sound of it already, tumbling from his lips.

"Can I kiss you?" he asks now, out of nowhere.

He knows.

He knows I'm saying goodbye.

"Okay," I breathe.

"Close your eyes," he says, but I already have.

He talks me through it. His lips on mine, his hands on my hips, his breath against my breath.

I know when it's over because it's harder to breathe, because the air is thick again with words I don't want to say.

You were never real.

You made me forget.

You were my only friend.

"I miss you," I say at last, because it's all I can think of to say and because it's true.

Goodbye comes next.

He knows it; I know it.

But it's the hardest thing to say.

We stay silent so we don't have to say it.

And then I do the bravest thing I've done this summer: I hang up.

I pick up my phone again and send a text.

It's to Lacey.

The first time I've texted her in ages.

We never kissed, I write. **I lied.**

Because he always belonged to her.

I'm sitting in my car, blinking back tears, staring at the black screen of my phone.

Will is gone.

He's gone.

He's not coming back.

It keeps hitting me again and again, and I'm not sure what to do with myself.

Who to call. How to pass the time, alone.

I think about calling Lacey.

I don't.

I think about calling Will back.

I can't.

Then, all of a sudden, there is a knock on my window. I don't know who I'm expecting, but it's certainly not Shelby.

I roll down the window and blink at her.

"Hey," she says, and there's something strange about her expression. Something lost. "Are you busy?"

"Um," I respond, because I'm not finished saying goodbye to Will yet. Not really.

"If you are, that's cool. I just wondered if . . . I thought maybe you'd like to have lunch," she says. Then, looking sheepish, she adds, "Jenn's sick today."

Her face flushes like she's embarrassed, and I feel for her. I know exactly what it's like, that feeling of being displaced, off balance, without the person you most count on.

I'm experiencing it right now.

"Do you want to eat in here?" I hear myself asking, and when she nods, I open the door so she can climb into the passenger seat. It's awkward as we both unwrap our lunches, too quiet.

But finally I make myself speak. "How long have you and Jenn been best friends?"

"Forever," Shelby says with a smile.

47

AFTER LUNCH, OLIVER and I accidentally make eye contact on our way into work, and I feel a stab in my chest. Guilt, but also something else.

The sensation of missing someone.

Before opening my till, I pull out my phone and covertly text him.

Meet me somewhere tonight?

"James! Someone has their phone at their station," Kennie says loudly, and I quickly throw my phone under a stack of More for Less flyers.

Kennie cackles as she stops in front of my till. "Just kidding. He's not here today."

I let out a relieved sigh, and she laughs again.

"I would tell you if James was about to catch you texting. Would you tell me?" She's giving me a weird look, and I feel like this is some kind of test.

"Um, yeah."

"Because we're friends, right?" Kennie says. I nod. "So I'm

gonna need your name, if we're going to be friends," she says, and suddenly Friday night comes roaring back to me. My drunken blathering to Chris about my name.

Does *everything* get back to Kennie?

"Well?" she asks, and she has her own phone out now.

"Eden," I say, and I feel microscopic. And stupid.

"Spelling?" Kennie asks, and I know she's just doing it for dramatic effect, but I spell it out anyway.

"E-d-e-n."

She types it into her phone, then shows me the new Contact she's created for me. "Like that?"

"Like that," I say. "Look, Kennie, it was just this stupid thing where I thought . . ."

She shakes her head, then hip checks me. "It's all good. I just like to know the names of my friends." She turns and starts to head back to her till, but then she calls over her shoulder, "I like Eden. It suits you."

I'm grinning as I open up my till. No one is waiting to pay yet, so I pull out my phone again and check whether Oliver has responded.

He hasn't.

The whole workday goes by, in fact, and he doesn't text back a single word.

And I know at some point in the day he must have looked at his phone and seen it. It's been hours.

Maybe he's the one person who doesn't check his phone during work hours.

Maybe he's trying to figure out what to say.

Maybe his phone is swallowing texts and he never received it.

Maybe my phone is and I didn't get his response.

Maybe.

Maybe he's so pissed at me that he's never going to answer me, never wants to speak to me again.

I resign myself to this final option and am sitting in the living room, eating dinner and watching TV with my sisters, when finally my phone buzzes in my pocket.

It's Oliver.

And he's written just one word in response.

Yes.

I mumble some excuse about having stuff to do, which elicits a quirked eyebrow from Mia.

Then I hurry upstairs and text him back.

Avery Park. Eight o'clock?

OK, he texts back.

An hour and a half later, I wait anxiously in the parking lot of my favorite park. Our favorite park when we were little.

I'm starting to think he's not going to come when a gray car pulls up a few spots away from mine.

I walk toward his car and wait while he climbs out.

"Hey," he says.

"Hey."

We walk silently into the park.

"Remember the tunnel?" I ask.

"Of course," he says.

"Wanna go through it?"

"Okay."

I go flying through it first, then Oliver has a turn.

We are both grinning when we come out the other side.

"It never gets old," he says.

"Oliver, I'm sorry," I blurt out. "For what happened that night. You were right. About Will. About everything."

"No, listen," he says. "It's your life, you were right. I had no right—*have* no right—to comment on any of it."

"But you do," I insist. "You're my friend. And friends tell each other the truth."

The word *friend* hangs in the air between us.

Oliver tugs at the back of his hair. "Right," he says. "I just don't think it was my place. Maybe Lacey . . ."

"This has nothing to do with Lacey," I say. "This is about you and me." I take a step toward him. "I feel like it has been about Lacey for way too long."

"So what do you want it to be about?"

"You and me," I say.

His eyes widen as I step even closer. "Yeah?"

I nod, and suddenly our faces are inches apart, our breaths intermingling. He breathes on me. I breathe back on him. Then suddenly, annoyingly, predictably, the fear hits me.

I freeze. "You said you didn't want to have to care about someone else."

Oliver closes the gap between us again. "It's too late for that. It's been too late for years."

My heart kicks faster at his words, and I feel something in me release, feel the fear evaporate from my shoulders.

"What about Mason?" he asks.

"He's . . . he's dead," I say, voice breaking a little.

"Eden, if you still need time . . . if you need to get over . . ."

"I don't think I need time. I think I've wasted too much time," I say. "Obsessing about what Lacey was doing, obsessing over

Will. We leave for college in a few weeks. I don't want to waste any more time."

"Are you sure?" Oliver asks, his lips tickling mine.

"Positive," I say. Then, "Oliver?"

"Hmm?"

I take a deep breath and something like courage fills my lungs. "I'm going to kiss you, okay?"

"Yes," he murmurs against my lips, and then our lips meet and his skin is touching mine and my arms are around his neck. One of his hands grips my waist and the other is in my hair. And I think, *This is what it feels like to be kissed.*

This is what it feels like to be alive.

When I get home, I'm going up the stairs when I hear a sound. Breathy and broken and low, coming from my parents' room. Dad is still at the hospital, so it can be only one person.

I turn right at the top of the stairs, on my way to my room, but then something makes me stop. Without my permission, my feet are backpedaling and then I'm standing at her door, which is open just a crack. Through it, I make out a lump in my parents' bed. I push the door open wider and pad into the dark room.

The sobs don't stop when I come in. I don't think she's noticed I'm here.

Not until I've walked all the way to the left side of the bed. Not until I'm climbing in beside her, still in my work clothes. She turns to face me, surprised, but she doesn't say anything.

She looks at me and her eyes say a million things, and mine do too.

She closes her eyes and I run my hand through her hair, just like she used to do for me when I was little, when I was afraid of the dark or monsters under my bed, when I couldn't sleep or when I was sick. When I'd made a mistake in a skating show and she sat beside me comforting me, promising me there would be other recitals, other chances. All along, I remembered her wanting me to be the best, always the best, but somehow I forgot that she still loved me when I wasn't.

We stay there, side by side for hours, her sobs becoming softer, quieter, until she falls asleep.

And then I do.

48

THREE WEEKS LATER

I'M TRYING NOT to cry.

My car is stacked up with pillows and a comforter and all the clothes I wear on a regular basis, and my room looks empty, stripped bare, and I heard Sam asking Mom if she could move into my room.

Before I was even out the door.

Mia went back to school last week and now my parents stand watching me load up my car, with Sam in between them. With Dad's health issues, my parents actually agreed to let me drive to college alone.

I'm seriously rethinking my decision not to drive up to State with Oliver when he left two days ago. I wanted to spend as much time with Dad as possible before I left.

I wrestle my laundry basket in on the other side of the car from them, where they can't see my eyes starting to well, and then hurry back inside and upstairs to get the last of my stuff. I realize I've seriously misjudged the weight of the last box when I can't manage to lift it on the first two tries.

"Do you need a hand?"

I jump at the sound of Lacey's voice behind me.

"No, I think I'm good," I say, staring at her like she's a stranger. She does look like a stranger. Her hair is cut in an asymmetric bob.

"Your hair . . . ," I say.

"I know," she laughs, touching it self-consciously. "My one beauty. Can we talk?" she asks.

"Okay."

Neither of us speaks for a moment.

"So I hear you and Oliver are . . ."

"We don't need your permission," I spit, not willing to listen to her complain about us hooking up.

"No, no," she says. "That's not what I meant. I didn't even mean to bring that up."

"So what do you want to talk about?"

"Us," she says. "I hate how everything has gone. I hate . . . I wish it wasn't like this."

"You lied to me. For, like, two months," I say.

"I know, and I'm sorry," she says. "But you lied to me too."

The kiss that never happened.

"That was different. I didn't think . . . If I'd known about you and Will, I'd never have done it."

"Why did you do it?"

"It was just an impulse thing. I'm always freezing up, freaking out, and the night Will died I did it again. I hated myself for it."

Lacey nods. "So . . . what happens to us?"

"I think you were right. That we needed space, that we needed to know how to be apart."

She opens her mouth and then shuts it. "I didn't mean . . . I want us to still be friends."

"I don't know, Lacey," I say after a moment. "What kind of friends do that? Lie to each other, keep secrets, leave each other?"

"Shitty friends," she says. "But shitty friends aren't the same as lost causes."

I squint at her. "How long did it take you to think of that one?"

"A while," she admits with a laugh. Then, more seriously, she adds, "Maybe we can try again."

"Maybe," I say, and I want to try and I will try. Still, there are all the things we've done to each other and then there's college and new friends and new places, new lives that don't include each other. Lacey and I have always ended up together, but for the first time, I'm not so sure we will.

I reach into my pocket and pull up something on my phone, then turn it over to her.

"Our list," she says when she sees it.

1. Go on a road trip.
2. Get a tattoo.
3. Go skinny-dipping.
4. ~~Do something dorky like sneaking into a movie.~~
   Steal something.
5. Fall in love.

"I'm finishing it today. I did it all except one."

"Which one?" she asks.

"The road trip."

I decided not to count the drive to Camp Rowan as a road trip, because it was about skinny-dipping and a two-for-one felt like cheating.

"Holy shit," she says, eyes wide. "You got a tattoo?"

Her jaw drops when I roll up my jeans and show it to her. "Holy shit," she says again. "What does it mean?"

"Life goes on," I say, and she glances up at me like she understands it, why I chose it, what it means.

"Wow," she says. "And number five?"

I nod. I think about telling her the full story. That for a while I thought it was about Will, for a while I thought the whole list was about Will.

Number five is kind of still in progress, and it's about me. And Oliver.

But mostly about me.

Lacey crosses her arms over her chest now.

"So you're all set for college, huh?"

"Yeah. When do you leave for LA?"

"Next week," she says. "I found this place that I'm going to be renting with a group of girls."

"You're not staying with your dad?"

"No, uh, things didn't work out with that."

"I'm sorry," I say, and she nods.

"Can I . . . can I give you a hug?" she asks. Without waiting for my answer, she wraps her arms around me, and I hug her back. We stay like that, frozen, fourteen years and a moment in time.

"I'll miss you," she says, letting go.

I've missed you this whole summer, I think, letting go.

A few minutes later, Lacey helps me maneuver the giant final box down the stairs, and then she gets in her mother's car and drives away.

Mom, Dad and Sam are still standing beside my car, ready to see me off. I wonder what it will be like with just them. It seemed impossible at first, that it was just four of us without Mia, and then it became normal, like everything does.

Their new normal will be something that won't include me.

I hug them goodbye and the tears finally come.

I promise to drive safe, to call when I arrive, to take care of myself.

Then finally I am behind the wheel, starting the car, on my way to my newest and biggest adventure yet.

I take a deep breath and drive away.

Number one: go on a road trip.

I don't turn on the radio or call Oliver or anyone else throughout the drive.

I keep myself company.

And it's not so bad.

ACKNOWLEDGMENTS

So many thanks to my editor, Julia Maguire, for believing in this story. It wouldn't be what it is without your insight and guidance. Thank you also to my agent, Suzie Townsend, for your wisdom and for being there every step of the way.

I'm indebted to Angela Carlino for this gorgeous cover. Thank you also to everyone at New Leaf Literary and at Random House and Knopf, especially Artie Bennett and Jake Eldred.

I once saw an author thank their family for still claiming them, despite the toll the book-writing process takes (all the zoning out mid-conversation, the canceling on you to write, the forgetting to call you back, the crazed, sleep-deprived ideas that never sound as good out loud). Thank you, family, for still claiming me. I love you.

Last but not least, thank you to every single person who picks up this book. You make this job worth it—and a whole lot less lonely.